# WHEEL AND STEAL

# WHEEL AND STEAL

## PAUL PAXTON

Matador
Unit E2 Airfield Business Park,
Harrison Road, Market Harborough,
Leicestershire. LE16 7UL
Tel: 0116 2792299
Email: books@troubador.co.uk
Web: www.troubador.co.uk/matador
Twitter: @matadorbooks

ISBN 978 1803136 141

British Library Cataloguing in Publication Data.
A catalogue record for this book is available from the British Library.

Printed and bound in Great Britain by CMP UK
Typeset in 11pt Minion Pro by Troubador Publishing Ltd, Leicester, UK

Matador is an imprint of Troubador Publishing Ltd

*This book is dedicated to the memory of Tracey Geddis, whose legendary smile and accompanying hug are missed by so many.*

# PART ONE

VIENNA IN THE SPRING OF 1938

# CHAPTER ONE

Isaac Cohen had been expecting this visit. It was inevitable. He was a wealthy Jewish businessman in a country just annexed by the Germans. He just knew that he was going to be coerced to support the new regime financially, perhaps with punitive taxes, more likely direct payments. He didn't doubt that he would also be asked to subdue voices of opposition in the Jewish community.

He had wrongly anticipated that the meeting would take place at his factory, not his home. That already felt like an invasion of privacy.

The visitor was shown into the drawing room by the family butler, Henry, and formally announced.

"Major Heinz Muller, sir."

Cohen was leaning against the marble fire place and didn't move to greet the soldier. He pulled down his small ivory rimmed glasses from the top of his head. He readjusted his greased, wavy grey hair and inspected Muller; his face, demeanour and manner. Isaac moved only his eyes, otherwise motionless. Muller was immaculately turned out, an intimidating look. Isaac so wished that he had changed out of his sheepskin slippers. Dressed in black and grey, the captain looked like a wolf eying his prey. Captain Muller had removed his cap and placed his black leather gloves inside. His high-necked jacket was fully buttoned up. It was finished off with a black metallic cross. The SS captain's dark pantaloon trousers retained a crisp starched crease. His red cotton armband complete with swastika was gratuitously offensive to Isaac. His face reflected that repulsion. Muller was not perturbed; he had not been expecting a warm reception. He cared not. He did though offer a hand to Isaac.

"Herr Cohen, thank you for meeting with me at such short notice. I appreciate that your time is precious."

Isaac was wary, more angry than fearful, but not rude, and he shook the outstretched hand, albeit with little warmth. He nodded; his civility did not run to words. The SS captain surveyed the room. "You have a fine home, Herr Cohen, and business is good, I hear."

Business was indeed good. Isaac owned the largest clothing manufacturer in Austria. His company, ACC, was one of the largest of its kind in Europe. He owned five factories producing everything from fur coats to ward off the bitter Austrian winter to summer cocktail dresses for the seasonal ensembles that graced Vienna. Isaac was, outside of the Austrian aristocracy, one the richest men in Austria. As for the wealth, if not discrete with it, he was at least discerning.

Isaac said nothing. Muller's attention switched to a painting that took centre stage above an antique mahogany drinks cabinet.

"A Pissarro, if I'm not mistaken, Herr Cohen. *Winter on the Seine*?"

Cohen loved his art. It was a passion and one that his wealth had enabled him to indulge. His country may have been invaded by his house guest's army but his attitude softened briefly towards the captain. He clearly shared his interests.

"Very impressive, Captain Muller. *Winter on the Seine* it is, painted in 1856, when Pissarro was only twenty years of age."

"Not as impressive as you might think, Herr Cohen. I have seen the inventory of artwork you prepared when you insured the paintings and other fine pieces in the house. A fine collection but with only one Pissarro I had noted."

Isaac felt duped. Be it only for an instant, he shown the enemy respect. Muller was right. There was only one Pissarro in Isaac's art portfolio, a collection that included Monets, Cézannes, a Manet, Rubins, and two Rembrandt self-portraits.

"The Fuhrer is himself a connoisseur of fine art. Did you know, Herr Cohen?" Muller was not expecting a reply. "In fact, he wants to put on an exhibition in Berlin. An unrivalled exhibition of Post Impressionistic art. You have one of the finest collections in private hands, Herr Cohen. The Fuhrer felt sure that you would want to share your art with the people, especially now that we are one nation, yes?" Muller turned defiantly to face Cohen.

This was no invitation – it was an ultimatum. Both Cohen and Muller knew it.

"You will be rewarded for the inconvenience, Herr Cohen, of course."

"Rewarded?" enquired Isaac rhetorically.

"Have you and your family been to the Swiss Alps in the spring, Herr Cohen? I am told that they are beautiful at this time of year." Isaac tensed. His right eye twitched. He was being offered an escape route. His paintings in return for a safe passage. For the first time, he did feel fear. He had misjudged the position. Isaac had presumed that his wealth and wide network of connections would protect him. He had never thought that being Jewish defined him. Yet, in his own home, an SS officer felt able to threaten his family in a brazen manner just because he *was* Jewish. It was arrogant but also reflected the shift in Austrian politics. Isaac concluded that he had underestimated the pace of change. The reward for handing over his lifetime collection? An escape route. It was a journey, he thought, that might not be available to all.

"And what if I decline the invitation, Major?"

Major Muller laughed and did not even think that the question was worthy of an answer.

"I have already taken up too much of your time, Herr Cohen. The Fuhrer will be grateful. We will be in touch again when we have drawn up the paper work."

"Paperwork?"

"How you say, Herr Cohen? Everything above board, no?" There was not a hint of irony in his voice.

"You will get your travel visas too when the art is collected."

It was officially described as "Anschluss" or Union but this was not a consensual merger. The annexation of Austria was Hitler's first incursion in Europe. It was expected that there would be more to follow. Czechoslovakia looked to be next in line. Being Austrian himself, Hitler felt a natural affinity with the country. In his mind, Germany and Austria *were* one nation. The lack of resistance to the *invasion* had appalled Isaac. The move had perhaps not come as a major surprise as Hitler had identified it as one of his key goals over the last year. *Why would we be so weak? Why so little pride?*

Isaac was educated and well read. He had observed, with increasing concern, the growth of the Third Reich. This had mirrored the rising discontentment of the working classes. Depression heaped on repression was a dangerous combination. History had taught this lesson too often. The Austrian press had shown little editorial criticism of these political developments for months. Cohen relied more on reports from outside of Austria for objective analysis and fact gathering. The London and New York Times in particular: journals carried by his gentlemen's club in the centre of Vienna.

For Cohen, even the term *annexation* sounded deliberately softer than the reality: *A betrayal, an invasion, the raping of his nation.* Even before the annexation became official three days earlier, attacks on the Jewish community had escalated exponentially. Visits to the architecturally stunning synagogue in the centre of Vienna had become fraught with danger. Anti-Semitic sentiment gathered at a pace, orchestrated and agitated by the Austrian Nazi movement. The group, though increasing in number, was not a large political party. Though, they were very active and violent both at public demonstrations and covertly. This was much to the detriment of the thousands of Viennese Jews. Cohen was part of the Austrian Jewish elite; he was proud of that achievement. He was wealthy and influential, someone employing over a thousand Austrian men and women of all faiths. He had not foreseen this diminution of power with the evolution of the Third Reich. He knew rumours of extortion, violence, and arrest for subversion of the State had spread within the Jewish community. He had been unable to verify the more extreme conduct though one Jewish family after another could tell their individual tales of intimidation. As for Cohen, he had thus far been untouched. This visit had changed all that.

# CHAPTER TWO

As Isaac made his way back to the lounge, he wrestled with what to tell his wife and daughter of the Nazi's visit and the demands made. He paused and entered through the open study door. He put his hands on to his head and gripped his hair tight. *Isaac, how could you have so misjudged the position? You assured them that we would be fine – that money and power would talk. Do I need to tell them?* It was not so much the request itself but the implied consequences that troubled him. Was the threat to his family so great that a safe passage to Switzerland represented a trade to be valued? *Really? Things cannot be* this *bad, can they?*

Upon reflection, Isaac decided that he needed to be candid. Both Eva and Anna were aware that Isaac had a visitor but unaware of their identity. They had all been sitting together in the main drawing room of the house when their butler, Henry, informed Isaac of the SS officer's arrival. Henry was professional and circumspect in ensuring that only Isaac was aware of the true position. He had been a member of their household for nearly fifteen years. His loyalty and discretion were assured. He had lowered his tall and slim frame to whisper in Isaac's ear, appearing to do so for the purpose of not interrupting the flow of conversation rather than imparting unsavoury information.

Eva Cohen, Isaac's wife, wept uncontrollably at the news. Anna, their daughter, had been upset but more so at her parent's distress than the Nazis proposition itself. She was always full of optimism. It was a charming trait, mostly a strength, but, on occasions such as this, it exposed her vulnerability.

Anna was twenty. By her own analysis, she was *handsome more than beautiful.* With shoulder length straight dark hair, pale skin, and distinct cheek bones, her self-assessment was harsh. She had disappointed her father by refusing to take an undergraduate course in Law at Vienna University. She had preferred to continue her more vocational studies at the Viennese College of Music. The institution was not as prestigious as the University but Anna thought it to be socially more energetic. Anna also thought that Vienna had, for too long, relied on Mozart for its notoriety and she wanted to modernise the scene. In reality, her enthusiasm far outstripped her musical ability.

This naïve enthusiasm, which pervaded much of Anna's activities, was tolerated by Isaac for the sake of family harmony, given that she was their much loved and only child.

No one spoke for a minute whilst the impact of the Nazi proposition was absorbed. Of course they knew that anti-Semitism was a part of life. They didn't need to read the history books again to understand that the Jews had for centuries been subject to persecution. The Cohens had though been cocooned from overt discrimination by their wealth. Money had bought privilege and protection. For that reason it was difficult for Isaac to comprehend that a life time of hard work and reward could be at risk. He desperately wanted to believe his daughter's analysis of the position. She had listened to her fellow students. This was but a temporary, turbulent period of politics and the annexation would be, at worst, short lived and not effect day to day living. It was bureaucratic in nature. But Isaac's commercial success had not been achieved without a steely sense of realism. He was less assured. Having followed the wave of support for an uprising, he feared long lasting and damaging change. It was the speed of change that unsettled and surprised him.

He was less sure now of his bargaining position than he had been an hour earlier.

"*Harah*, Daddy, just say no! They are our paintings not Hitler's, after all." Anna banged her desert spoon on the table.

"Language, Anna, please,"

"Sorry, Mummy, but surely we can't be bossed about like this."

Isaac pushed away his untouched apple strudel bowl and stood up. He placed his hands on Anna's shoulders and massaged them gently.

"Anna, my sweet, this is serious. Really serious. My gut reaction is the same as yours but this is not about the paintings; I genuinely think that our lives could be in danger. If we do not cooperate..." his voice tailed off. He couldn't bear to contemplate the position further.

Eva dabbed her lips and out of habit folded the linen napkin.

"But Isaac, are you saying that we may need to leave Vienna? If we flee, how will we cope? Maybe, Anna is right. Should we not stay; be defiant? You are a man of standing, Isaac. Surely, you will be listened to. Don't we know people in Government? Won't they protect us?" Eva's enquiry was more out of pleading than hope.

She too had read that morning of the resignation of the Austrian Chancellor Kurt Von Schuschnigg who was to be replaced by a German counterpart. *A German Chancellor!* Eva began to shed more tears. Isaac patted her hand in an attempt to offer comfort her. Affectionately, he squeezed her six-carat engagement ring of forty years. He then stood up from the sofa where they were sitting and turned away, fighting to hold back the tears of anger and shame that welled up within him. The anger was easy to understand. The shame reflected the helplessness he felt in not being able to protect his family. How could he have not have foreseen the danger earlier? Perhaps, he was as guilty of arrogance as the Germans.

It was to be a restless night for the Cohens.

The following morning, Isaac immediately contacted his bank. He wanted to transfer more funds into an account he had set up in Switzerland several years before. As the political uncertainty had increased over the last six months, he had drip fed funds to Switzerland. He had opened the account originally as an insurance policy against the increasing taxation of the rich. He had not foreseen this current turmoil, certainly not the extent of it. He thought that the account could now serve the Cohens well. The Austrian Bank had been familiar and comfortable with the arrangement. Their fees were high as were those of the receiving bank but it satisfied all parties. Financial diversification was simply sound money management. Isaac had also converted some his savings from cash deposits to gold bullion. A nation's currency was always susceptible during periods of conflict whereas gold had survived generations of dispute. It was a financial refuge. He never took possession of the precious metal bars which were held for him on deposit in Zurich, Vienna, and London.

Isaac was dismayed to be told on the telephone that *for the foreseeable future* restrictions had been placed on his account. Isaac was furious and demanded to speak with the manager, Herr Marc Harnik, a man with whom he had done business for nearly a decade.

"Isaac, I am sorry but it I've had official papers through from the Revenue Office. An order that your account must be restricted."

"On what grounds, Marc? You cannot restrict me. It is my money!"

"I have the paperwork here. It says a pending investigation of irregular tax affairs…" Isaac felt desperate.

"Do they know about the Swiss account?" There was a pause before the reply came in a quieter voice, not quite a whisper, but it was clear that Harnik was ensuring that he was not being overheard.

"That is safe."

"And the gold?"

"Safe too. Isaac, I am sorry. You must take care…"

Isaac's personal account was limited to a daily allowance of 200 Schillings barely enough to cover the running costs of the household, let alone finance a new life across the border. His current corporate account was thus far unfettered presumably so that wages could be met. However, the amounts within that account were relatively modest and he would never deprive his workforce of their hard-earned wages.

Isaac had been relying on his cash to deal with any problems that might arise under the new regime. In order to keep the factory open, he had expected to have to pay extortion money: payments to keep the wheels rolling. As for any tax irregularities, it was true to say that the Swiss account had not attracted tax and that was why Herr Henrik's affirmation was so important. The restriction and possible sequestration of funds was therefore nothing but a sham.

Isaac's conclusions were affirmed when another Jewish businessman had called him within the hour to say that the same restrictions had been imposed on him. The same justification was given – tax irregularity. The situation was poisonous.

Isaac would not tell Eva of the problem just yet. She was already unsettled and worried. He had sufficient cash in the home safe for the time being along with a decent number of gold Austrian schilling he had acquired. These were beautiful coins direct from the Austrian Mint, sealed and untouched by human hand. Rather sentimentally, Isaac had hoped one day to give them to his grandchildren. He imagined having to sell his gold below market value. The thought of *him* having to use a pawn broker sickened him.

# CHAPTER THREE

It was Anna that came up with a solution to their financial crisis. It was a crazy idea, even she accepted that; one dismissed out of hand by her father. She had waited till after supper before broaching the subject, hoping that he might then be more receptive. Her mother had listened to the idea too. She could normally be relied upon for support, someone who could gently cajole her father into changing his mind. He, after all, would often say *no* but relent: her choice of university, her choice of holiday venue, her choice of boyfriend even. But this time, not even mother looked sympathetic.

"Tell me why it wouldn't work, Daddy. Why!?"

"Sweet child, it just cannot be done. Leave it."

"But Mummy…"

"Anna, I said leave it," affirmed her father. Eva pursued her daughter from the room but in an attempt to comfort not encourage her.

Anna would not leave it as had been requested.

Later that evening, she spoke to the man whom she

saw as being the key to the Cohen's future – Andreas, her boyfriend. She relayed her idea and awaited his reaction. As with Anna's parents, it was one of incredulity. *She had to be joking. She just had to be.* It was not until Anna began to cry that he realised that she was being serious. Her suggestion was extraordinary but she meant it nonetheless.

Andreas' initial mocking turned to angst not just because of the realisation that Anna was being earnest but because the ramifications of the SS visit were digested. Anna explained that the family had misread the situation. They had anticipation that the Germans might make their lives more complicated but not that their very liberty was at risk. Andreas acknowledged the danger that the Cohens faced. He too had been listening intently to the radio and had even bought a newspaper that morning to follow events, as the German Occupation extended into Vienna. Why, Hitler himself was due to visit this week and was expected, the *Viennese Herald* said, to get a rapturous reception. His message was one of anti-Semitism. Some even said ethnic cleansing, disguised under the banner of national unity and the emancipation of the working classes.

Andreas had been Anna's boyfriend for several months. Anna had met him at a café bar that adjoined both the Musical College and the Art school where Andreas was in his third year as an Arts undergraduate. He was talented, Bohemian in outlook, and handsome as well. His blond hair was long and often unkempt. He wore ill fitting, second hand clothes but still looked like a fashion model. It was easy to see why Anna had been instantly attracted to him: his dark brown eyes contrasting with his hair but matching his skin tones. Anna had previously been surrounded by young Jewish suitors all from successful families in this close-knit community. They were mostly smart and educated, keen to make an impression with Anna who remained self-deprecating. The fact that she was an heiress to the Cohen's substantial fortune genuinely didn't matter. The young men were drawn to her energy, her sense of rebellion. It was a powerful attraction.

Anna knew little of Andreas' background. Though born in Italy, he had not lived there since the age of four when his parents had moved to Vienna. They were economic migrants with his father working in the docks as the commercial transport by river blossomed.

Isaac was, to put it politely, disappointed by his daughter's choice of boyfriend. He had hoped that the relationship would be a short-lived infatuation. If anything, however, their bond had grown stronger. This had lead him to question Eva's advice to just let the relationship run its course. No need, she said, to express his objections; objections that were easy to discern from Isaac's demeanour when in Andreas' company anyway. Andreas was not Isaac's ideal vision of a future son-in-law: poor, unsophisticated, and a Christian to boot, a non-practicing one at that!

Andreas relayed back to Anna her own plan. He was still incredulous that she was even suggesting it:

"You want me to forge your art collection and hand that to the Nazis instead of the originals?"

"Put simply, yes, save that it would only be a part of the collection – the post-impressionists."

"Oh, *that's* alright then." Andreas threw his arms open and pursed his lips.

"Can you at least give me a couple of hours to rustle them up?

Anna frowned.

"And your father *agrees* with the plan?"

"Well, Daddy is not quite on board yet but Mummy thinks that he will be when he sees what you can do," embellished Anna who had yet to bring her mother on side.

"What do you mean: sees what I can do?"

# CHAPTER FOUR

Anna's head appeared from behind the half open door. Her mother looked up from her tapestry and smiled. Anna proceeded to pirouette on one leg into the room managing to carry out two turns before losing her balance.

"You should never have given up ballet classes, Darling." Eva patted the cushion alongside by way of invite.

"Mummy, Madam Schmitt was a beastly instructress. Even you said so."

"Well, she set high standards, shall we say. Eva remembered fondly those early years in Vienna. Isaac had worked very long hours developing the business which meant that she and Anna spent many an hour together often just as an observer as Anna tried a variety of activities. Ah yes, Madam Hyde. A well-meaning tyrant in ballet tights. Then there had been the horse riding, the Viennese Girl Guides and finally the piano lessons, where Anna had excelled under the softer tutoring of Frau Visch, a gentle spinster whose tolerance for underperformance could only but impress. Isaac had moaned that their piano was more expensive than her show jumping pony but had also enjoyed her ensemble to dinner party guests as her skill evolved. Anna would never have the patience and commitment to become a fully-fledged concert pianist but she had played for many a Viennese dignitary on the Steinway Grand Piano that dominated the cavity below the spiral staircase in the entrance hall to their home.

"Come child, Come," reiterated Eva.

Anna gave her final rendition from Sleeping Beauty and plonked herself as indelicately as she had danced onto the vacant cushion.

"Careful, Anna Dear," said Eva, as she held on to the reels of coloured thread that were slowly coming together to complete the tapestry.

"Ooppps sorry mother. Here let me help." Eva freed her arm up to put it around Anna's shoulder as she kissed her gently on the cheek. Anna moved in closer and Eva repositioned the cushion tray supporting the cloth so that they could both work on the floral design.

"Take this red thread and try and finish the rose buds for me. And be patient child."

Since Anna had started university they had spent less time together doing little but enjoying each other's company, be that a game of cribbage or doing the Austrian Herald crossword. They were at peace together; a mother and daughter separated by a generation of different views, ideas and aspirations but as one.

"Mummy…"

"Yes Anna…let me guess? Andreas perhaps?"

Out of exasperation, Anna's mother agreed to a compromise. She would *not discuss it with Daddy just yet.*

Andreas had therefore reluctantly agreed to come to Anna's house the very next morning. Isaac had set off to his main factory on the northern outskirts of Vienna and Eva had made her way to meet up with her sister in the city. Isaac could not recall missing a day's work in over a decade but he had struggled to leave Eva who had sobbed intermittently through the night. It was his suggestion that she see her sister with whom she could discuss issues in a supportive environment.

Andreas arrived as Henry was clearing away the untouched breakfast. Andreas looked at the table and rubbed his hands together.

"Time enough for a spot of breakfast perhaps, Anna? This is the earliest I've been up for many a week." Anna's grabbed his shoulders and shook him in mock disgust at his lack of urgency.

Henry brought them fresh coffee and toast.

After refreshment, Andreas set himself up in an adjoining room from where he wouldn't be disturbed. He had all day to work. Isaac was not due home until 6:30 pm that evening.

In fact, Isaac returned home later than usual; he was surprised to find his wife and daughter waiting to greet him in the large entrance hallway of their home. It was not a good sign, he thought, but at least Eva had stopped crying.

He had seen that smile on Anna's face too often before to take comfort. His suspicions were confirmed as Anna took a hand and led him into the drawing room where Andreas awaited them. He was sitting nervously on the edge of the chaise longue. He stood up straight away as much out of trepidation as respect. There was a waltz by Johann Strauss, *Oracles*, playing in the background on the gramophone. It was one of Isaac's favourites and this further aroused his suspicion. For a moment, Isaac assumed that he was about to be notified of their engagement. He took up a favoured defensive position with elbow leaning on the fire place mantle. *Surely not – his country was at war. Everything they stood for, all that he had worked so hard to establish was at risk. Yet, here was his precious daughter about to announce her impending marriage, to a lazy gentile at that. He would just say no.*

Anna took up position at the other end of the fire place. She tried to mirror her father's stance but was too small to comfortably rest her elbow on the marble mantle.

Therefore, there was a sense of relief when Isaac realised that marriage was not on their agenda. That relief was short lived. Anna had barely started to speak before her father intervened.

"I said no, Anna. No! It is out of the question"

Andreas shuffled uncomfortably, not sure if he should return to sit on the chaise longue.

"Boy, is this your idea?!" said Isaac sternly, pointing his finger accusingly across the room. Before Andreas had a chance to utter a nervous word, Eva shuffled over to stand beside her husband. It was now her turn to hold his hand.

"It's Andreas, darling, Andreas. Come, Isaac, at least look at what Andreas has produced."

Isaac instinctively yielded to his wife's gentle persuasion. He shook his head. How could his loved ones be so foolish? He was angry too that his wishes had been disobeyed.

From the drawing room, they made their way along the

carpeted hallway to another smaller reception room. Anna produced a large dark metal key from the pocket of her floral dress. Attached to end of the key was light green silk tassel. She inserted the key it into the lock. It was the first time that Isaac could recall seeing the room locked. Anna pulled the door handle towards her, whilst simultaneously turning the key clockwise.

She partially opened the door but beckoned her father to enter first. Apprehensively, he peered around the door. He was dumbfounded by the scene that faced him: There, resting precariously against the window sill, was his prized Rembrandt self-portrait, a priceless masterpiece, being treated less sensitively than one of their framed family photographs that adorned the baby grand piano in the corner of the room. Alongside the Rembrandt was a make shift easel upon which rested a much smaller canvas. It was surrounded by messy tubes of oil paint, used rags, and an array of brushes, the latter being held in one of Isaacs favourite china tea cups. Isaac's gaze was drawn, not to the cup, but the creation on the canvas. Though only 6 inches square, it was instantly recognisable as a section from the Rembrandt – a small section, yes, one capturing a shaded area of his face and its darker surround.

Nobody said a word. Isaac lifted the smaller canvas from its resting place. He could see that the paint was still wet and could smell it. He pulled down his glasses for inspection and studied the partial portrait. He then held it directly alongside the original, comparing shape, colour, and brush stroke. He turned to look at Andreas. His pursed lips did not reveal the begrudging admiration he had for the work of the young artist. Reaching into the left-hand drawer of the small corner desk, Isaac pulled out a magnifying glass. He used it for studying his impressive stamp collection which was stored in green and brown leather-bound albums on the shelving to the rear of the piano. It was a hobby his late father had encouraged and it had become Isaac's passion too in later life. Isaac moved his magnified gaze slowly between the original and the copy, muttering imperceptibly as he went.

Anna could not restrain herself any longer.

"Daddy, I told you Andreas could do it. He's a brilliant artist." Anna wrapped her arm around Andreas' neck. He fidgeted uncomfortably. He was not used to such public praise nor her open affection. He was also conscious that Isaac had not yet given any appraisal of his work.

"It's out of the question," declared Isaac finally. He headed out of the room seeking to avoid further discussion.

# CHAPTER FIVE

In his main factory at Floridsdorf, on the northern outskirts of Vienna, Isaac had two offices. One, he used for more formal meetings. His preferred second office was the one that afforded him a view over the factory floor. It was noisier and too hot in the summer but this was where he spent most of his time. He wanted to live the business, see it in action. He would often stand and look out of the window taking in the 30 rows of weavers and seamstresses. The looms would work throughout the day and night whilst the 200 seamstresses were only employed during daylight. Although the machinery reduced the costs for the wide range of clothing produced, invariably, the garments had to be finished off by the talented sewing and stitching employees. Nearly all were women. His father, Levi Cohen, had also been in the rag trade but never had the aspiration nor educational advantages of his son. At his peak, Levi employed a team of twelve, two of whom were on the sales side.

His father had moved around Europe having been born in Austria. As a family, they had moved back to Vienna when Isaac was in his late teens.

Both his father, Levi, and his mother, Maria, valued education. Isaac had been privileged to have a private education from the age of eleven. His parents were therefore furious with him that he did not wish to attend university. He had secured a scholarship at the University of Vienna to study history. Though it was a subject that had fascinated Isaac through school, his greater passion was for the world of commerce. He had worked during the school holidays at the family business. He considered himself to be reasonably skilled with a sewing machine. He could put the finishing seams to a dress or pair of trousers good enough for subsequent retail. Though, it was in the area of sales that he had excelled. Even at the age of seventeen, he had been able to secure meetings with clothing outlets. Isaac had noticed that he often had to cajole his father to attend those meetings and, on a couple of occasions, he even substituted himself with success.

His father had begged him to take up his place at university. He accepted also that his son had a rare talent in the fashion production and sales arena. It was rare to see this skill set combined. Regrettably, Levi had died when his son was only twenty years of age. Even then, he was showing signs of being entrepreneurial and a sound manager. These qualities were beginning to create conflict between Isaac and his father. Levi's death had been a bitter blow to the family. However, from a business perspective, it had been the making of Isaac and the company. The business had flourished and evolved. They quickly outgrew their first factory before adding others as sales increased and profit margins grew.

There was not a job in any of his five factories that Isaac didn't understand and couldn't do himself. He would occasionally join the ranks of seamstresses. He would sit at a sewing machine station just to prove to himself that he hadn't forgotten the basics. This endeared him to the staff even if he set very high standards for quality control.

Today, as Isaac surveyed the frenetic activity from his viewing gallery, he was distracted. His focus was not on the completion of an order of five hundred blouses for shipment to Poland as it should have been. His thoughts were on the rising political upheaval. He paced up and down the room like a caged tiger.

*What should we do? Is Eva strong enough to evacuate to Switzerland and start a new life? What of Anna? Dearest Anna. She had her whole life before her. Was the position as bad as their Rabbi had reported?* What of all their *friend – Surely hey couldn't abandon them?*

Isaac had taken a call earlier that day from his best friend, Joseph Litzman, who asked that they meet up back in the centre of Vienna. Litzman was an academic at the University of Vienna. He was a professor and head of the humanities faculty. His speciality was in Mediaeval and Renaissance culture. Isaac and Josephs worlds of influence were distinctly diverse. It was this divergence, they agreed, that had bonded them so closely. Neither really understood the other's job yet each respected what the other had achieved. Isaac referred to his friend as a *boring boffin*. Isaac was derided as a *rags to riches barrow boy*. Their contrasting lifestyles provided them with endless material to tease and torment each other. On the more serious front, both wielded influence within the community. Professor Litzman was a prominent figure particularly within the Jewish sector. He was a regular public speaker, someone often turned to by the media for comment on issues relating to academia and culture as well as Judaism. As for Isaac, his influence was more widespread. This was because of his wealth. Though he didn't financially support any one particular political party, he was often courted by individual politicians. His generosity across a range of charities attracted attention albeit it was not something that motivated Isaac. His philanthropy was just that, not a means to an end.

They had known each other for over twenty years. They were the best of friends yet Isaac could not remember an occasion in the last decade where they had met up during the day of a regular work week. Joseph did not want to speak on the phone but sounded distressed. There were none of the normal irreverent exchanges. Isaac did not hesitate to agree to the meeting. He asked for his driver to be ready to take him to the city centre at ten o'clock that morning.

Had they been meeting after work for a carafe of wine, invariably, they would have met in Judenplatz Square. Though within the Jewish quarter, the area was multicultural and vibrant. It was possible to drink wines and beers or teas and coffee from day break to late evening. The restaurants in the area were small but the food was always freshly made with care and proportions were generous.

As the political tensions had mounted, so the number of visitors to the area had declined. There had been isolated but well reported incidents of Jews being abused verbally. More recently, the attacks had been physical. Graffiti had appeared, anti-Semitic and vile in nature. It had found its way onto shop front shutters. There was an air of uneasiness.

It was because of these concerns that Isaac had agreed to meet Joseph in Museums Quarter at Café Cristina which they had frequented occasionally during the period of their friendship. It served the best Leberknodelsuppe or beef broth in town.

Due to unexpectedly heavy traffic, Isaac arrived just after ten thirty. His friend was waiting for him. Isaac's car pulled up on the perimeter of the pedestrian only square. He agreed the pickup point with his driver, Otto, and walked swiftly to the entrance to the cafe. The door was ajar.

He could see Joseph seated in at the far end of the twenty-cover cafe. Joseph stood up as Isaac bounded over towards him, apologising for his lateness.

Isaac noticed that he had not bothered to remove his coat even though the weather was relatively mild. Joseph's eyes were red and there were tears running down his face and into his grey manicured beard.

"Good Lord, Joseph – what on earth is the matter?" His friend was unable to speak at first and Isaac pressed gently on his shoulders to get him to retake his seat. As he did so, the bar owner approached. Without engaging, Isaac quickly asked for two white coffees before taking up a seat himself. He readjusted the table which was covered in a worn but freshly laundered checked tablecloth.

"Joseph, tell me what's the matter. Is it, Maria?" he asked, concerned that something may have happened to his wife. Joseph shook his head still unable to speak clearly.

"Good God, tell me that Zachariah and Eliana are fine?"

"No, no, Isaac, it is me. I have been dismissed from the University this morning."

Isaac felt outraged already and he didn't even know the reason.

"What do you mean, Joseph? For what? By whom?"

"There was a letter on my desk first thing this morning signed by the Vice Chancellor. He said that my services were no longer required and that my contract had been terminated forthwith. No sensible reason given, not a word of gratitude, let alone anything by way of compensation."

Isaac listened in disbelief. "I had to clear my desk within the hour...." Joseph began to shed another tear.

"This cannot be so – this cannot be right!"

"We are Jewish, Isaac, persecuted Jews, and I am just another victim. There's nothing I can do about it. I now know I am not alone. Three other senior lecturers have also been summarily sacked. All of the Faith. What am I to do? This is my life."

Before Isaac had an opportunity to reply, the drinks arrived and were placed on the table. Both men smiled politely expressing their thanks. Courtesy had been in short supply of late.

"No reason given at all?"

"The Vice Chancellor simply said that there had been reallocation of resources...." At this, Joseph reached inside his jacket pocket and produced a letter. He handed it to Isaac to unfold and read himself. Isaac did so shaking his head. He wanted to rip the letter into tiny pieces.

"There have been protests at the University, as word spread of the dismissals. But listen to this, Isaac, there were as many supporting the moves as opposing them! And these, our most educated young people, our future leaders..."

Isaac banged the table with his clenched fist, catching the attention of others seated nearby. Isaac looked over towards the bar and, catching the owner's eye, ordered two schnapps.

"This is intolerable. I will make some calls this afternoon, Joseph. I will visit the principal himself if needs be. Is it not still…Eric Wolfen? Will he have forgotten so soon my donation towards the new arts wing?"

"Isaac, you are a good man but you too must be careful. We live in dangerous times. Sanity may not prevail. The new order is not rational, not open to debate."

Isaac tried to interrupt but Joseph stopped him.

"No, my good friend, hear me out. We Jews know the history of persecution, do we not? For generations, we have been told about it. We have read it in the bible and the history books. We are now living it. We will become tomorrow's history. Make sure that we are there to tell our grandchildren. That is where our duty lies not in matters of principle or useless gestures of defiance. Isaac, promise me you will put your family first."

# CHAPTER SIX

The following day saw Hitler himself visiting Vienna, the *Fuherer's place of birth*. It was billed in the *Austrian Herald* as a tribute to the union with Germany and Austria. Isaac's chauffeured journey home from work had been severely disrupted by the huge crowds that had gathered. Alserstrasse, Karntnerstrasse and Renweg, the main roads in central Vienna, were completely blocked. Isaac could discern a fervent edge to the atmosphere as supporters made their way to the main Plaza. It was here Hitler would deliver his speech. This was no festive carnival but a fanatical political rally. Those previously disenfranchised starting to sense a change in the power structure. There was chanting and overt hostility. Isaac's Bentley was kicked, rocked, and spat upon before Otto could find a route to circumnavigate the city centre. Isaac had not associated this aggression with him being Jewish for, although some said he portrayed stereotypical facial traits of the faith, he was hidden behind a raised newspaper as a precaution.

This was not a day to be relaxing in the bars of Sterngasse, the traditional Jewish quarter. This was as much a public uprising against the wealthy and successful from those who had suffered through years of austerity. That said, it was the Jewish business community that had become a focus for the aggression. Irrational thoughts were turning to hatred. Hatred to violence. It was, of course, this suffering and inequality that Hitler had targeted on in his rise to power from the early 1930s in Germany itself. Those who have little to lose buy too readily a false promise. It was ever thus. For Isaac, the journey was unsettling in its less exuberant moments and frightening at the more aggressive end of the day's spectrum. Reports of looting from the city's gothic cathedral, the Stephansdom, were muted; attacks against socialist protestors brave or stupid enough to openly display their opposition were unrecorded. The numbers turning up to the rally were exaggerated by the press but, from what Isaac had witnessed, the figures were still depressingly high.

That evening, Isaac and Eva begrudgingly listened to the speech given by Hitler in the front of Hofburg Palace. This stunning backdrop itself caused offence to them.

*How dare he say that this pillage is God's work? How dare he call on the Lord in aide of this affront to humanity! How dare he! This was nihilistic.*

The events unfolding that day had concluded with an interview Isaac had tuned into on the BBC World Service radio station. The Austrian media, Isaac had observed, had become increasingly biased or at least constrained in what they broadcast and printed. The apparent universal support for the annexation was indicative of that fact. The silent minority were being ignored and suppressed. The left-wing newspaper, *Presteigne*, which, to be fair, Isaac had little time for, had been shut down only days earlier following the orders of the Government on grounds of subversion. Isaac may not have agreed with their political views but he respected their right to comment. No longer a right, it would appear, for political commentary become a patronage: one gifted by the State.

Independent views were therefore difficult to come by and even the weekly editions of the *London Times* in Isaac's club reading room were out of date and in limited supply.

The BBC interview had deeply disturbed Isaac; he had not previously been naive about the position but still had found it hard to comprehend such a dramatic and immediate transformation of his country, his business, and his family life. Eva had adjourned early to bed and Isaac had stayed up, pouring himself a brandy before settling into his favourite leather armchair, a treat normally reserved for special occasions. The arrival of Hitler in Vienna had been a special occasion, he concluded, even if one that reviled him. The radio interview with the General Secretary of the International Council of Zionism, Zac Motzkin, had been chilling.

*"The situation in Austria is fluid, fasting moving, and uncertain. Let there be no doubt that the Nazi's stated ambition of obliterating the Jews is an active one. We are receiving, by the day, unverified but exponentially increasing reports of abduction, intimidation, and property sequestration…"*

Isaac had shuffled to the edge of his chair, putting his head in his hands.

*Lord Why? We do not deserve this – Anna does not deserve this.*

Isaac shook his head, challenging the wisdom and fairness of his God.

Isaac slumped back into the armchair, picked up his brandy glass and gulped from it barely tasting the rich cognac.

The remainder of the interview did nothing to ease Isaac's fears and his mind was made up to at least investigate Anna's scheme further. There was a major downside. If their attempts to deceive the Nazis failed, it would certainly cost them their liberty and may cost them their lives. The plan was simple to describe but extraordinary difficult to deliver. Perhaps too difficult?

# CHAPTER SEVEN

Isaac could hardly believe that he was contemplating an attempt to fool the Nazis. *Were things really this desperate? We need the money.* The paintings were an international commodity, worth substantial sums anywhere in the world. Like gold, a universal currency. Isaac had sat at his desk and having shaken his fountain pen, tried to work out on the gold leaf family headed note paper how much wealth he could smuggle out of Vienna or already had abroad. The accounts in Switzerland had modest deposits. He needed a guaranteed income. They could try to bring jewellery and cash but would they be searched. He would raid his stamp collection. The rarest stamps should be easy to hide but philately was a very specialist market. *We don't have enough – we need the paintings.*

Isaac threw his pen across the room and screwed the sheet of paper up, gripping it tightly in his fist before hurling it aimlessly towards the door.

He had not told Anna or Eva that he was reconsidering his decision. He couldn't bear to see their misguided enthusiasm at what was a very high-risk strategy. *Too high, Isaac. Too high.* But, with every news report, the danger to the family grew. Isaac felt like a man deciding on his method of execution; different means but the same result. Hope, concluded Isaac, could be worse than helplessness. When fate was determined, there was less to worry about: only time to pray for a higher salvation. But there was hope. Anything to give his family a chance. *Best wait, see what happens, Isaac.*

Isaac would try and get his wife and daughter out of the country first if needs be but for now a contingency plan was required.

Isaac had forced himself to sit down with Andrea and discuss a plan of action. *Discuss young man – not implement.* Both Anna and Eva were excluded from the conversation.

Isaac *tried* to be objective. He even began to call it *the project.* By treating it more like an order for his factory than a life-threatening gamble, Isaac was able to bring a degree of practicality to the challenge. Be it a painting or a suit, there was a process to follow: design through to production and on to delivery. In this case, the design had already been undertaken as the paintings were very much in existence. Andreas faced a barrage of questions;

*How would he decide which paintings to copy? How many of them? How long would it take? Where would he paint? What materials would he need?*

Having flushed out the practical issues, Isaac move on to the more emotional of the project.

*Why did he want to help?*

*What if he failed? Could he live with failure even if it cost him our lives? He had to face up to that question. He couldn't ignore it. Did he understand that he was in real danger too? He could walk away. He wasn't Jewish. Italian Catholic.*

His life under the Germans would be unchanged. Hitler admired the Italian leader, Benito Mussolini, who himself had not been averse to land grabbing in Africa. German Italian relations were strong. As an Italian living in Vienna, Andreas was not under any immediate threat from the German invasion. He knew that if he was found to be complicit in the fraud that his punishment was likely to be severe.

Finally the personal challenge for Andreas:

Isaac had seen that the young man had talent. His partial copy of the Rembrandt self-portrait had been highly impressive but it was a huge leap of faith to assume that he could produce three or four fake paintings within a couple of weeks that would deceive the Nazis. The deceit only needed to last for a short of time in order to secure an escape.

*Could he pull it off? If it was impossible, he should just say. No one would think any the less of him – no one, especially Anna.*

The more Isaac probed the more he thought it was unfair to Andreas. *Too big a weight on young shoulders.* To his credit, Andre's primary concern was to try and help Anna. Though he didn't need to say it to Isaac, he loved her. But that was the problem: *love distorts perception.* Isaac needed an honest assessment, one unencumbered by irrational hormonal attachment.

Putting aside technical ability, Andreas was concerned that the fake paintings would look too fresh. Indeed, he said that the oil paint itself may take up to a month to dry out completely. Andreas knew, from even his limited knowledge of the history of art, that both the canvas used and the oil paints themselves had changed significantly over the years and this itself could be fatal – literally in this case.

Artists also mixed paints with different pigments to gain the tone and thickness the artist sought to create. The mix might include dust and grime from the streets of Paris, flour from the mills, or even a dash of absinthe. Matching colour and consistency was a huge challenge. The range of colour reflected the difficulty of the task. For Andreas, these weren't red, white and blues but sophisticated variations: carmine, corn silk, celeste and cyan. Subtle changes that defined the paintings, an assault of colour.

# CHAPTER EIGHT

If forging the paintings would be difficult enough, the actual selection process was fraught with complexity. In total, there were thirty paintings to choose from. Most, though not all, were from the post-impressionist period. Some of the collection was out on loan to institutional museums but the bulk remained on display at the Cohen's home or locked away in the secure unit in the basement. Andreas had asked Anna to find out from her father which were the most valuable paintings as these should be a priority. Isaac himself had thought it right Andreas carry out the first review of the paintings without him. After all, he was the one who had to paint them. He would be best placed to judge the skill level required.

Andreas arrived at the Cohen's home in the mid-afternoon. Though his visit to the family home had become more frequent, he felt it sensible to use the side door, the tradesman's entrance so as not to generally announce his arrival. He and Anna had chosen a quieter time during the day to carry out the itinerary inspection. Given that her mother was out attending a charitable lunch and her father was at work, this meant that the staff were less engaged around the house and suspicions would not be raised. Anna did not for one moment doubt the trustworthiness nor loyalty of the household team but, if anything, wanted to avoid putting them in a dangerous situation.

Andreas was greeted with a passionate hug and kiss from Anna. Andreas sought to truncate the embrace given that the butler, Henry, was present though this did not seem to deter her in the slightest.

Anna held a black leather-bound notebook which contained plain sheets of Manila paper. She waved her Mont Blanc pen in front of her face, indicating that she was ready to record his every thought.

They started their tour in the first reception room. Here, there were two paintings of interest. The first was by Toulouse Lautrec, listed in Anna's notes as *Moulin Rouge Dancers, 1890.*

"This Lautrec is a definite no, Anna. It's just too large," said Andreas admiring the quality. "It is simply too big and would take too long to complete." Anna paused before noting the conclusion in her pad. She smiled at him as though in complete agreement. They walked diagonally across the reception room to the smaller painting above the desk table. "Let's put this down as a possibility for now. The size is good. Do you know about its value, Anna?"

"I do indeed, Mr. B," she said gleefully, flicking to a further sheet of paper at the rear of the notebook. "Remind me, who it's by?"

Tut-tut. Anna, shame on you. It's by Henri Rousseau. He did a whole series of similar works.

"Yes, yes of course." She ran her pen down the list.

"Leave it. It is worthless." Rousseau's *The Dream*, which was worth more than a row of houses, was dismissed out of hand.

The couple moved into the main dining room. There Andreas sighted the two Cézanne paintings hanging in their glory. He inspected them briefly. He had seen these paintings before, shortly after he started dating Anna. It still remained a thrill to be able to look at such great works of art so close up. He even felt empowered to touch them gratuitously, explaining to Anna that he wanted to try and assess the thickness of the oils.

The two paintings personified Cézanne's range of work. The first, *Bathing Beauty*, presented a distorted view of human form, challenging the viewer's perceptions. The second, a mountain landscape, more Cubist in structure, *Col de Galibier*. Both paintings were relatively small. The post-Impressionists movement away from fine detail brushwork would again be an advantage to a forger short on time.

"Yes to both." He did not need to ask as to whether they were of value. He knew they were worth a fortune.

It came as no surprise to Andreas that the third painting in the room was by Paul Gauguin. Although the style of painting contrasted with that of Cezanne, he knew from his studies that the two had spent time at together in Paris. They appeared in photographs with the likes of Degas and Matisse. *It must have been quite a party.* Indeed, Cézanne had painted several portraits of Gauguin before he moved to Haiti for the wilder part of his life.

The painting, *Tahitian Princess*, depicted a beautiful native Tahitian, captured nude as she lay in the forest, enjoying succulent water melon. Andreas smiled to himself for he knew that Gauguin's reputation for drinking and debauchery had been a hallmark of his career. Andreas felt that he would not be entirely unsuited to the lifestyle.

"Don't pay too much attention to the nudes, Andreas. I might get jealous."

"Purely professional interest, Anna. Put the Gauguin on the list as well. What is it worth by the way?"

"Let me see. The Gauguin…*Tahitian Princess*…acquired at auction for $475,000! Wow, Andreas!"

"Yes, that should do nicely then."

In the Cohen's main bedroom were two masterpieces. The first was by George Seurat. Andreas did not know the title but it depicted a Parisian scene with the Eiffel Tower in the background. Andreas much admired his work. Seurat, he explained to Anna, was as much a mathematician as an artist. He had developed a style known as pointillism. A combination or art and science.

"It is a fantastic piece of work, Anna, but it would take a lifetime to reproduce. Come closer. Have a look with me. Can you see that it's all made up of individual dots of colour?"

"I can see. How clever."

"Too clever for me – next."

The second painting hanging over the bedroom headboard was a magnificent piece by Manet. Entitled *Café de Paris,* the painting was a large one depicting a vibrant restaurant scene at the turn of the century in the heart of Paris. Rich gentlemen supping fine wines and being entertained by younger glamorous and promiscuous women dressed in finery. Andreas pondered briefly before Anna stepped in.

"It's far too large and too detailed, Andreas. We will just have to give this one to the Nazis."

"Agreed. Strictly speaking, it's not really Post Impressionism. A tad too early. Notice the detail as compared with, say, Cezanne."

Anna was impressed.

"Where are the Van Goughs? Any old student can rustle up copy of some sunflowers."

"No sunflowers, I'm afraid, Andreas. Even Daddy wasn't prepared to spend that sort of money. Obscene as it may seem, the Van Goughs are both in the basement at the moment. Daddy likes to rotate some of the paintings and I'm afraid the Van Gough's are off the menu at the moment. Come, let's go downstairs and take a peek. It is dark on the stairs going down so you might need to hold me tightly."

Andreas raised his eyebrows to the sky but then tickled her waist playfully, forgetting temporarily the enormity of the task before him.

The inspection in the basement had taken longer than it should have. Andreas was less sure than Anna that their amorous engagement in the basement had not been had overheard by members of the household. That said, the exercise had been worthwhile because a Van Gough had been at added to the list which was now ready for review by Isaac.

# CHAPTER NINE

Isaac was sitting at his desk in the study when Andreas arrived with his short list of paintings for review.

Isaac invited him to join him in a glass of red wine. The half empty bottle of claret looked tempting and the gesture was helpful in relaxing both men.

"Anna tells me that you have drawn up a possible itinerary."

"Indeed, Mr Cohen."

"Call me Isaac for goodness sake, Andreas." This was the first time Isaac ever remembered using Andreas' name to his face.

Andreas reached into his trouser pocket and began to unfurl a sheet of paper that had been folded rather haphazardly. He recognised Anna's immaculate hand writing. Isaac inspected the list.

"No Seurat?"

"I thought about it, but the work is so complicated. It would take forever... Isaac."

"How many can be produced, I wonder? Depends on the time available, I know that. I doubt that we have a month. Is that a -impressionist works only but I don't trust the Nazis. They will want problem?"

Andreas didn't reply but his face reflected his concern. Isaac blew air from his puffed cheeks as he assessed the position.

"I'm told that they want the post more, maybe all of the collection."

"Yes, I've limited the list to the period. We could debate Monet's inclusion, I suppose. He crossed the timeline." Isaac smiled because the lad was right and discussing art over a glass of decent claret would normally have been rather appealing. For another day, perhaps.

"Did you see the Manet?"

"In your bedroom? Magnificent!"

"No chance of including it, I suppose?" For Isaac, Manet's *Café de Paris* was special. He had acquired it as a fiftieth birthday present for Eva and she adored it too. Isaac accepted that it would be a challenge but this was his favourite piece and at auction it would fetch a substantial sum. Yes, he wanted to maximise the prospects of deceiving the Nazis but at the same time he cherished the painting. He accepted that the plan was only as good as the worse reproduction. It was no good having three perfect replicas and a poor one. In the end, he knew that it was too great a challenge. Too complicated. He didn't await a reply before moving on to consider each of the works neatly listed by Anna.

Other paintings were considered by the men and rejected. Isaac accepted too that the Pissarro that had caught the Major's attention was too technically elaborate with its intricate series of painted dots. The Rembrandt self-portrait was worthy of discussion. It made its way onto the list given the proficiency that had already been exhibited by Andreas. The next choice was the Cezanne, *Col de Galibier*, painted at the height of Cezanne's fame. It would fetch a fortune at auction if the need to sell was imperative. From the forger's perspective, the broad and robust brush strokes leant itself more readily than the Manet to be copied.

"Anna tells me that you don't have a Van Gough Sun Flower? Shame as it looks a breeze. I'm sure I could fabricate one of those before lunch. Isaac shook his head dismissively. Though he did not tell Andreas, he had been offered a Van Gough painting only a year earlier but had considered the price prohibitive. It may have proved to be a bargain contemplated Isaac as the pair discussed the final painting selection. Upon this at least, they were in agreement: if time allowed, then the final fake would be another, somewhat later, Rembrandt self-portrait.

On the comprehensive tour of the Cohen's collection, Andreas had noted a number of works from lesser well-known artists, which, for obvious reasons, were excluded from the forgery list; some may have been easier to forge than the current selection but would then be worth relatively little. The method of painting selection by definition had to be crude – could it be faked and was it worth enough – so much for art appreciation. However, in dismissing some of the minor paintings, Andreas was able to come up with a helpful suggestion even if it would, in normal times, have horrified Isaac.

"Let's pillage the canvases of the ones we don't want," exclaimed Andreas with a smile on his face for the first time since they had sat down. Isaac looked bewildered so Andre pressed on;

"We have a major problem. If we use a modern canvas, they are thicker, less absorbent, and well…they just look newer – we just won't have the time to artificially age them. So, let's just cut out and use these old canvases." Andreas pointed to two minor paintings hanging up in the study.

Isaac winced.

"What? Paint on top of them?"

"Thin them out first with cheap vodka as best we can and then paint on top. Artists have always reused canvasses even the great masters. When I mess a painting up, I often reuse the canvas."

Andreas' failures did little to boost Isaac's confidence.

"But the sizes will be different, won't they…"

Isaac didn't have to wait for a reply for he realised that the canvas would need to be cut to fit. It seemed one thing to paint over a quality piece of art another to destroy it completely. Putting the dilemma in perspective, the two paintings in the room were painted by Paul Signac and Edward Vuillard respectively. Although the artists had not achieved as much fame as say Cezanne and Van Gough, there were art critics who thought these works more technically gifted and profound. Desperate times indeed.

Two other paintings were selected for destruction or *reincarnation* as Isaac had started to call it in order to appease his guilt. The criteria for selection changed slightly. Size and value (or lack of it to be more accurate) remained but the date of the painting was now significant in order to match canvas and so was the strength of colour, an alcohol rub would only remove part of the painting. It would be hopeless to have a brilliantly faked Cezanne hillside scene which, upon closer inspection, showed an underlying Greek Goddess painted by Titian.

As Isaac poured the last drop of wine from the bottle into Andreas' glass, the list had been finalised. It was time to move on to the next phase of production.

# CHAPTER TEN

Anna's outrage at the way she and her community were being treated was tempered with a sense of self preservation. At the university there had been small pockets of protest to the annexation but these had been met with violence from fellow students and arbitrary arrests. Anna had assured her parents that she would adopt a low profile, which given Anna's general exuberance, was relative.

This morning saw her arriving early for her first practical music session of the week. She had declined the offer of a lift from the family chauffeur, preferring the twenty minute stroll to the main university building via the embankment of the River Wien.

The lawn adjoining the front of the college was full of groups of students reliving their weekend exploits. Partying was a more prominent subject than politics.

"Anna, I love you!" Came the call from the far side of the terrace. It was Charles a fellow music undergraduate. He was the only openly gay man on campus and eccentric with it. Anna had enjoyed being his date on a number of occasions where they had drank Riesling wine and sang late into the evening. Anna waved furiously before holding on to the hem of her dress, pulling it up fleeting, flashing her stocking tops. She hardly broke stride as she then took the ornate steps leading into the university two at a time.

Her destination was room Braun 2, named after an accomplished Austrian pianist and composer who was congenitally blind.

She entered and was not surprised to see most of her fellow students present even though the class was not due to start for a further ten minutes. Their tutor, Peter Von Hoffer, was notoriously fiery and students arriving late, even by a minute were simply excluded from the session and reported to the vice principal for insolence.

Anna sat at the Steinway baby grand piano and adjusted the height of the stool. The first few notes of her recital were lost in the hubbub of noise but the students, whose ears were more highly turned the melodic composition than conversation soon quietened down.

Anna continued to play the German national anthem – but very badly. Her trained fingers deliberately hit the wrong key every third note or so. Without warning her solo was being accompanied by Bernard on his clarinet. The anthem, though clearly discernible, squeaked and truncated, to the joy of Anna's classmates some of whom in a fit of spontaneous parody marched and saluted around the room.

The arrival of Hoff brought the concert to an abrupt end. To everyone's surprise and relief he did not explode, for he had listened to the charade from outside the room and had paused to recover his composure. He was not known for smiling and did not want his well-earned reputation for solemnity tarnished.

"Given your new found enthusiasm for our German neighbours perhaps we should begin the week with Bach's piano concerto Number one in D minor..."

That was enough rebellion from Anna to last the week but she would delight in regaling the detail to Andreas later; perhaps not mummy and daddy.

# CHAPTER ELEVEN

Time was at a premium. The Chancellor had announced a referendum or Plebiscite on whether or not Austrians support the annexation. It did not offer much prospect of a reprieve given the apparently overwhelming support being expressed in the press and on the streets. Jews would not even be entitled to vote! Isaac had also noticed a change in the attitude of his workforce. He considered himself to be a good employer, one that demanded high standards and commitment, but paid relatively well and supported staff that were having a difficult time either through personal sickness or that of a loved one. Annual bonuses were rare in Austrian commerce but Isaac always tried to link his profits to pay and at year end made generous payments to his staff who had remained loyal and motivated – until recently. Isaac had noticed a sudden increase in staff absence and, more worrying, apparent sabotage of the production lines leading to unprecedented levels of garment rejection.

The referendum was but three weeks away. Assuming public support for the annexation, there would, undoubtedly, be an increase in anti-Semitic activity. For the minute at least, he could loan his art on a voluntary basis albeit he thought that the prospect of the paintings returning remote. The gesture would be looked upon favourably for now.

Isaac was used to working under a tight deadline; his buyers were demanding and the lines of clothing produced at the factories changed on a regular basis, not only with the seasons, but also depending on fashion trends. Andreas, on the other hand, had not made an assignment deadline since he arrived at art school. His argument that *good art can't be rushed* had worn a bit thin with his frustrated tutors because it was often clear from his demeanour and appearance that art was very much secondary to his social life. Had it not been for his obvious talent with brush and paint, his absence from the art school, with often ran to days, would not have been tolerated.

It was time for Andreas to begin his huge challenge. Isaac had given him sufficient money to buy all the paint, brushes and easels required. He would also move into another small flat which would act as his studio. He could not afford to have his friends from University popping around hoping to see him.

# CHAPTER TWELVE

As is often the case, finding the solution is easy, it is the enactment of it that is the real challenge. Andreas was just finding that out.

He was working on the Van Gough this morning. Rather than work on one painting at a time, he had three work in progress pieces.

This was partly due to time pressures but also that he had tried to produce a pallet of oils that could be used on several paintings and thus avoided the need to constantly remix. That saved time but also lead to consistency. Andreas knew that if you looked at a number of Cezanne paintings it could be seen that the colours are remarkably similar.

Another factor, particularly relevant to the forging of the Van Gough, was that the oils were often layered and needed time to partially dry before another layer could be added. Time in between needed to be put to good use.

Whilst at college, Andreas had detested copying other artist's work. *I do my own thing*, he would proclaim arrogantly. He had discovered, through his new-found career as a forger, that in trying to replicate others work he learned, painfully in some cases, the different range of techniques being used. Cezanne's brush work looks simplistic and ad hoc. *It is anything but* concluded Andreas who would have been full of admiration had the style not created such problems for him.

The Van Gough was very different. Most of the paint being applied was by way of a palette knife, not a brush. It was a technique with which Andreas was familiar but more for larger, less structured works where accuracy was at less of a premium.

In terms of respect for the masters, he had found Paul Gauguin to be the easiest to copy: simple shapes and simple colours with little interest in background and perspective. Andreas understood that Gauguin's fame arose more out of his exotic choice of subject matter than technical ability. Naked Tahitian women had obviously stuck the right note. His wild lifestyle as a debauched alcoholic had raised his profile and, subsequently, the value of his art.

There was a knock on the door. Andreas jumped and added an extra smudge of yellow paint from the paint pallet.

"Andreas, it's me," Anna called softly as she knocked once more. "Open up."

Andreas removed the table that he had lodged against the door, opened the double lock, and let Anna into his small first floor flat. He waited, checking that she hadn't been followed. The flat doubled as his art studio. Its location was the fringe of the Opera and Naschmarket Quarter, an area more vibrant at night than during the day, probably due to the high occupancy of students. The noisy coffee bars in the narrow, crowded streets disturbed the tranquillity of the residents but drove down rents.

Having re-locked the door, Andreas turned cautiously to Anna who was inspecting the progress. There had been none since she left him yesterday evening and she noticed the empty bottle of wine lying on the floor, his dishevelled state, and unsteadiness of foot. He noted her concerns.

"Anna, it won't work. I cannot copy the masters." He stood alongside Anna and together they surveyed the bizarre scene before them. Set on old but sturdy easels stood an original Gauguin, Cézanne, and Van Gough. Alongside them stood three further paintings from the late 19th century whose canvasses had been scavenged.

"Anna, I've hated destroying these paintings." He knew that reference to "lesser work or minor artist" was relative. He was well aware that the paintings he had to obliterate were themselves worth a considerable sum but his great pain was in destroying quality art that he himself was incapable of matching. Anna swung her arms around his rigid neck and kissed him affectionately and enthusiastically on the cheek.

"Andreas, come on. You can do it. One day, you will be more famous than Cezanne himself. For the moment though, you will just have to pretend to be Cezanne." She giggled at the prospect, which contrasted with her boyfriend's scowl. Anna was in love and that obliterated objectivity. Nowhere within her being was there any doubt that Andreas was capable of pulling off the feat of tricking the Nazis. As for Andreas, there was no doubting his talent but he had never expected other people's lives to be, literally, in his hands.

Anna walked to the side of the room where the sunlight streamed in through the skylight window. From the floor, she picked up one of the practice attempts that Andreas had made to copy the Cézanne; it was still drying. Even she could see that the greens were too vibrant and that the scene had a freshness which could be easily discerned from the duller original work produced by the master, over 40 years earlier.

"I prefer your version frankly," said Anna, comparing the two.

"But that's the point, Anna. You shouldn't be able to tell the difference!"

"An artist like you, Andreas, needs to be treated like a master." She made her way over to the bag that she had laid down by the sofa, which doubled as Andrea's bed. Unzipping the canvas holder, she pulled from it a bottle of vintage Moet and Chandon Champagne that she had already chilled, having borrowed it from the family cellar. She had wrapped two glass champagne flutes carefully in tissue and they chinked together for good effect as she unwrapped them. Andreas shook his head partly out of amusement, partly bemusement. Here, he was trying to save the Cohens, or at least save their fortune, and there was Anna treating him as though he was about to open his own exhibition in Paris.

With the skilled manipulation of somebody used to entertaining, the cork was removed in a controlled fashion and effervescent excesses were avoided by angling the bottle and glasses at 30 degrees. Having delicately poured and topped up the glasses as the initial fizz settled, Anna walked silently over to André handing him his crystal glass.

"I read that Cezanne made love to all of his models to enable him to paint them with more intimacy and understanding," said Anna as she placed her glass down by the side of the sofa and jumped full length on to it.

Without diverting her eyes from Andreas, she proceeded to open the five buttons which held together the front of her light blue, cotton dress. She stretched her arm out to pick up her champagne glass, allowing her dress to fall open. She had thought it particularly Parisian to wear no underclothes and Andreas was startled by her boldness.

Whilst he doubted that he could paint like an old master, he was confident that his lovemaking would not fall as far short.

# CHAPTER THIRTEEN

The second official Nazis visit to the Cohen household was less informal than the first. Henry reluctantly interrupted the family's supper.

"Forgive the intrusion, sir. There is a letter that needs signing…" Isaac sensed the hesitancy in his butler's voice. His hesitation was but a clue to Isaac that all was not well.

"Post this late, Henry?" queried the lady of the house, checking the time on the grandfather clock.

"No worry, dear. Carry on without me."

Henry had not thought the visitor worthy of a place in the reception room and, as Isaac made his way to the front of the house, he saw the uniformed figure standing almost to attention in the hallway. He clicked his heels in a most unlikely manner for an Austrian soldier who had only been under German occupation for a matter of days. "Herr Cohen?" the young soldier enquired with little enthusiasm.

"I have your orders to sign for," he continued, oblivious to the significance of such a request.

"Orders, you say?" said Isaac, with no attempt to hide his contempt.

"Herr Cohen?" ventured the bemused soldier.

Isaac shook his head as if to dismiss the enquiry and reached out to take the brown envelope that was gripped tightly in the messenger's hand.

The soldier held what Isaac could see was a delivery acknowledge form.

"Where do you want me to sign?" said Isaac, gesturing to Henry for a pen.

"Do you not want to read the papers first, Herr Cohen?"

"I do not take orders from the Nazis, young man."

Isaac snatched the sheet away and signed it, thrusting the acknowledgement into the arms of the bewildered soldier.

No sooner had he taken the envelope than Isaac had torn it in two and thrown it on the floor at the feet of the astonished messenger.

Isaac repeated his mantra for good effect:

"I do not take orders from the Nazis, nor should you."

The young soldier was taken aback but remained silent. He was tempted to pick up the pieces but made no move to do so. "You've delivered your orders, now go!" The soldier did not protest. He clicked his heels again as before but this time saluted "Hail Hitler," as well. Isaac was not a man of violence but his anger was about to boil over. Henry stepped in between the two men and ushered the guest to the exit.

Isaac waited until the front door had closed before picking up the two halves of the torn envelope. He slid the contents out on to a sideboard adjoining the entrance hall. He married the torn pages easily enough. Rather than read the detail of his orders line by line, Isaac turned immediately to the list of named paintings on the requisition list. As anticipated, the list was not restricted to his post Impressionism collection. *Bastards! Complete bastards – They want the Manet!* Outrage was followed by relief: none of the four scavenged paintings were detailed. That would have created a real problem. The date for collection was prominently displayed, 28th of April, in just ten days' time.

"Bastards, complete bastards."

Henry could never remember his master cussing in a decade of service.

# CHAPTER FOURTEEN

Anna insisted that Andreas take a break. He looked exhausted. He was exhausted. He had slept less as the days slipped by. He had started to grow random stubble; he hadn't washed and his lovely brown eyes lacked sparkle as the bags under them magnified. As the deadline approached, he needed to be painting more and found that he couldn't sleep anyway. He was paradoxically becoming less productive and the quality of his work was suffering. Anna could see that even if she would never tell her boyfriend in such direct terms. She sat down on the sofa and beckoned him towards her. He didn't resist. She put her arm around him and gently pulled his head down until it nestled on her shoulder. Neither spoke. Anna ran her hands slowly through his long blond hair, massaging his scalp as she did so. He was asleep within the minute.

Having allowed Andreas to rest for an hour or so, she had awoken him by whispering softly into his ear. An enforced and painful shave, a change of shirt to boot, and they were sitting in a nearby restaurant, The Waltz. Andreas' appetite was returning and he felt better for the rest. They sat in a quiet booth, surrounded by dark red velvet seating. Had it not been for the current circumstances, it would have been romantic.

As Andreas tucked enthusiastically into the bread basket, Anna tried to take his mind of the painting.

"Tell me more about your family, Andreas. I don't feel that I know them at all."

Andreas had not spoken much to Anna about his family. He was focussed, he said, *in the here and now,* not the past. He had not sought to deflect her questions too much; he just didn't see why she would be so interested. But as their relationship developed, he began to realise that for Anna family was everything. She spoke endlessly about her parents, with pride at their achievements, or just in diarising their thoughts and movements: *Daddy this; Mummy that.*

Anna knew from what she had been told that Andreas' father had died early in his fifties from a heart attack. As he took the first few sips of the house white, he began to open up more.

Andreas dispensed with his napkin and wiped his mouth with his hand.

"I wasn't as candid with you as I should have been." Andreas looked down for a moment.

"Andreas?"

Regaining eye contact he proceeded;

My father didn't die of a heart attack – He was an alcoholic." Andreas paused and looked off into the distance this time as though conjuring up an image from the past. He readjusted his fringe.

"I would have told you earlier but…well, it was not that I was ashamed or anything. It was just that, from your parent's perspective it was bad enough that I was a poor artist let alone then having come from a degenerate background too."

Anna shook her head vigorously and tugged Andreas' shirt sleeve playfully.

"Yes, you should have told me but I can see that Daddy might have been unimpressed," she smiled at the thought. "Tell me more."

Anna snuggled in as close as was decent in public to hear the full story.

"My father worked extensively as a merchant sailor."

"Does he have a name?" teased Anna.

"Yes, Simone Bellino. He picked up some bad drinking habits whilst at sea. It was a time when sailors were given a daily ration of rum as part of their pay packet. What chance did he have?"

Andreas went on to say that he had been born and brought up in Naples, close to the port. His father would be away from home for weeks at a time but returned full of fantastic stories about strange tribes and animals not even seen in the zoo.

"I would sit and listen in wonderment. Had the truth been known, he had probably just been to London but I cared not. Mother would carry on washing and ironing around us as the tales unfolded. In hindsight, she looked less impressed than me." They both laughed this time and Anna leaned forward and kissed him on the cheek as if to thank him for his candour.

"Life in Naples was tough to be honest, Anna. I stood out a bit with my blond hair. In an area rife with gangs and violence, standing out from the crowd was not a positive trait. Add to that the fact that I was more interested in art than football and I was in for a tough upbringing. I'd stand my ground but took a few beatings." Andreas pulled up his shirt and pointed to a three-inch scar on his left side just above his hip.

"Stab wound," he said, with more than a hint of pride.

Anna rubbed it.

"Ouch!" reacted Andreas in exaggerated fashion.

Although travel by sea became less popular, the growth of trade between European countries saw a huge increase and with it: river transport. Father's employers offered him the chance to work their giant container boats on the Danube. That was when we moved to Vienna. The pay was less but the hours more regular and secure. More time ashore though meant more time drinking. It became a real problem."

"How did your mother take it?"

"Fortunately, he was never a violent drunk but the rows became more frequent and animated. I tried to speak with him but he laughed it off saying that mother was exaggerating."

"And the problem got worse?"

"Sort of. One day, he seemed to go completely mad. Shouting and hallucinating. Nothing would calm him. He was taken to hospital with a diagnosis of pancreatitis and, three days later, he was gone."

"Andreas, your poor mother."

"Never mind mother, what about me?" Andreas looked away indignantly.

"Yes, of course you, Darling, but you know what I mean." She reached for his hand and he took it willingly.

He explained that his mother had, of course, struggled with his fathers' death, blaming herself for not being firmer with him, but she knew in her heart, as I did, that nothing would have changed his addiction.

"What added to her guilt was that we were better off without him. Not only were the household costs less because no money was being spent on booze but his company,

Cevello Shipping, was very generous, making sure we were housed and fed. They funded my art scholarship."

"So, without your father's drinking, you could be on a cargo ship on your way up the Danube now."

"I'll drink to that," said Andreas as he downed the last mouthful of wine and gestured to the waitress for replenishment.

"But I thought that you said that your mummy was in Tuscany. Not another fabrication, Andreas?"

Andreas grinned, displaying his lovely white, if slightly jagged, teeth.

"That's true. I swear. She had been brought up in Tuscany and had in effect been an economic migrant, moving in her late teens to Naples via Rome. Following the work if you like. That was when she met Father in a bar by the port. She said Father was drunk that night and she should have known better. She put up with city life more than enjoyed it. She hankered to return home. I used to go on holiday with mother in the summer break but grew increasingly bored with it. Not a place for a streetwise city kid."

"Tell me you still see her, Andreas."

"I do but not as often as I should…"

"We should go together one weekend. When all this nonsense is over."

"Yes, we should, Anna."

He was relieved that the waitress had arrived to dissipate the intensity of their conversation.

# CHAPTER FIFTEEN

Isaac had not been able to bring himself to view Andreas'
work before its completion. Though he said that this was to
avoid suspicion, given that he would never be normally seen
in the more salubrious quarters of the city, the reality was
that he could not bear to face failure. The burden that had
fallen to Andreas was overwhelming; *unacceptable and very
dangerous.*

As for Andreas, he was pleased to be left alone save by
the increasingly frequent visits from Anna. He was by now
exhausted, both physically and emotionally. He had barely
slept. He had insisted on a last-minute extension in order to
try and finish the final painting but had accepted defeat and
the half-finished Rembrandt now lay abandoned at the side
of his unmade yet little utilised sofa bed.

Andreas' feelings were mixed. He was satisfied that he
had given his all to the attempt. On the other hand, the
quality of his work troubled him. Every time he compared a
fake with the original at close quarters, he saw flaws. He had
tweaked, fiddled, and corrected but time had run out.

His next task was also challenging. The fakes had to be transferred into the original frames. This was important as it would add to the look of authenticity. Framing itself was a skilled task and not one taught at college. Previously, most of his work had remained unframed and the few pieces that had required it were sent off to the faculty's technical department for completion.

Andreas and Anna had discussed seeking the help of one of the college assistants but such a move was quickly dismissed as being too fraught with risk. Instead, Andreas had befriended one of the technicians by showing an interest in his work and asked him to be shown the process. It had been his first visit to the college for a week and he deftly avoided any contact with his peers or lecturers. He arrived early in the evening. He knew that none of the artists would work late.

The most difficult task was stretching the canvas sufficiently and uniformly. How much should be factored in for drying? What equipment is used? Should it be pinned straight away? The questions flowed.

A stretcher tool used for the task discreetly found its way into Andreas' satchel and that evening, with Anna's assistance, the next stage of the challenge began. It transpired that the hardest task was the removal of the small canvas nails or tacks for their reuse. That was essential for authenticity. They were fragile and partly rusted. Some were beyond using again and this compounded the fitting problem. Each painting took over an hour to fit. Two required refitting for the canvas had sagged.

The wooden frames themselves were old and subject to wear and tear. They had been decorated with plaster and gilded in gold leaf. They were though prone to move as pressure was applied to fit the canvas in position. One frame needed reinforcement with modern threaded screws. That in itself might be enough to alert Nazis suspicion.

Along the way, the original masterpieces were carefully laid flat in an old, paint splattered leather portfolio folder that Andreas had used for his own work. He would utilise any spare or discarded frames when it was safe to do so. That might not be for a long while yet. Anna helped by sandwiching each of the copied paintings between sheets of newspaper partly to avoid damage and partly to hide from unwanted, prying eyes.

The portfolio would remain for now with Andreas. It was too risky to move the newly framed fakes by foot let alone public transport. Little thought had been given the transporting of the paintings. Isaac decided to send his driver at the appointed hour to collect the pieces from Andreas' flat. Anna had ensured that they were wrapped in ample layers of newspaper for they were too large and heavy to fit into a box. It would be pretty clear to the driver, Otto, that he was collecting art work but why not given that Andreas was indeed an artist. Not even the trusted family butler, Henry, was aware of the plot. There would be little mercy shown if the plan failed. The fewer who knew of the operation the better.

# CHAPTER SIXTEEN

Although Isaac had intended to inspect the fake paintings prior to their collection by the Nazi, he had not expected the sight that greeted him that evening. His arrival home this Tuesday evening from the factory had been early. Indeed, Isaac had been leaving the factory earlier with every day that had passed since Annexation.

As before, the unusual gathering of Eva, Anna, and, this time, Andreas brought with it trepidation. Andreas looked pensive, Anna eternally optimistic, and Eva like a mediator, trying valiantly to appease everyone.

Anna grabbed her father's hand.

"Papa, come with me but shut your eyes; I will guide you."

Isaac's protests were not heartfelt and he was guided into the drawing room where Anna stopped. She turned her father 45 degrees and declared that he could reopen his eyes. He knew that in so knowing that before him were likely to be the forgeries for inspection. He had not though anticipated that they would be hung on the wall, on display as though there to adorn the household. Two of the paintings were in their original spot and the third, the Cezanne, which had normally resided in the main bedroom, had been swapped for another drawing room piece.

Isaac therefore took a deep breath and obeyed his daughters wish, opening his eyes and seeing for the first time the finished works. He remained motionless save for a gentle swivelling of his head to scan the room. He could contain his emotions no longer and tears ran down his cheeks as with one hand he grasped his wife's hand and hugged Anna with the other. He nodded to Andreas before gently disengaging with his family in order to shake hands vigorously with the young artist. Isaac made no attempt to inspect the individual works of art. For the moment, he wanted to just acknowledge the achievements before him. The sight was overwhelming, the quality stunning. He would defy any art scholar to tell from seven paces that the works were anything but priceless masterpieces. Given that each painting was adorned by a beautiful, ornate gold leaf gilded frame, the deceit was credible, just about credible. Isaac still had reservations, of course, but what were the alternatives? The grip of the Nazis tightened daily. Reports of anti-Semitic behaviour were muted in the press but very real on the streets of Vienna.

Tonight would be one of celebration for the Cohens. There was little that could be done about the future but, if Isaac was going to lose his fine wine collection along the way, he would have a decent attempt at drinking some of the better vintage Claret. Yes, he thought, it would be rather wasted on an art student more used to cheap plonk but this was not the time for wine snobbery.

# CHAPTER SEVENTEEN

Isaac was unsure how to behave on the day of collection. If he broke his usual work routine, would that look suspicious? He was desperate for Eva and Anna to leave the house at least. They had left the night before to stay with his sister-in-law, close to the city but far enough away to buy time in the event of disaster striking. It had occurred to him that, in the event of trouble, communications might be difficult and therefore they were not to return home until she read an entry in the Births, Deaths, and Marriages column of the Vienna Times:

Wolfgang Henrik, first born son of born 3$^{rd}$ April 1938.

Anna, unsurprisingly, had wanted to stay at home; for her, this was still an adventure. The naivety of youth thought Isaac. This was a rare occasion when he insisted on her doing as she was told.

Isaac himself decided to be present. He had an excellent knowledge of all the paintings and might be able to distract and divert attention if need be. Given that his staff were still ignorant of the plot, they could not be relied upon to assist.

Isaac also wanted to take personal possession of the exit visas being traded in exchange for the art in order to check that they were accurate.

To his surprise, Isaac had managed to sleep reasonably well which he put down to an indulgence of single malt whiskey. That said, he was up early but declined Henry's offer of breakfast. He would take tea in the lounge instead. Before doing so, he inspected for the umpteenth time the two wooden chests containing the paintings. There were ten paintings in all. Four had been forged. Isaac had wondered in what order to plant the fakes? All together? At the front? Near the back, perhaps? The decision felt like an important one but, as it transpired, it was taken from his hands because Henry would not contemplate his master sullying his hands with what was clearly domestic work. Russian roulette it would be. The paintings were neatly secured in its own vertical draw which slid upwards for inspection and removal. The cases had been supplied by the Viennese National Art Gallery a couple of years back when he had loaned them several pieces by Vienna artists. They were perfect for transporting but lended themselves too readily to inspection. In order to combat too close an inspection, Isaac had ensured that each painting was wrapped in brown packaging paper taken from the factory. Isaac had written the name of the artist and title of each painting across the wrapping at the top of their frames. Even recording the name of the duplicate paintings created tension as Isaac was paranoid that his writing would somehow be different. Finally, the crates were secured with a padlock.

He could do nothing but wait.

# CHAPTER EIGHTEEN

When the front door bell was finally rung, Isaac's stomach churned. It knotted further as he made his way to the hallway where Henry had admitted the visitors. He knew that this was not the time to show weakness. Isaac strolled, as casually as he could muster, into the hallway.

Before him were three uniformed German soldiers. Young, Isaac observed, junior in rank. Excellent news, clearly no suspicion, no plot to deceive perceived, just orders to follow. *My God! This may just work.*

"Henry, help these young men to load up perhaps…"

The soldier who had been inspecting the casing interrupted.

"Nein, Herr… Cohen," he hesitated as he checked his note book for the name. "We must check the list first."

Isaac remained calm because the prospect of a young soldier knowing the difference between a Cezanne and a Gauguin, real or fake, he concluded, was remote.

"Open up, please." Henry caught Isaac's eye. Isaac nodded.

As Henry fiddled with padlocks, Isaac's confidence was further jolted when another soldier produced from his satchel several papers and a set of photographs. Isaac could see that the top photograph was of his Pissarro. At least this was an original. As the soldier flicked through the papers, it was clear that he was holding a complete set of photographs depicting each of the paintings. Isaac realised that this information, as before, had been obtained from the insurers. They had photographed his collection a while back for their records, ironically to identify them in the event of theft. The Nazis had used this material to identify the art in the first place. Isaac did not want to appear to show too much interest but it appeared, to him at least, that the quality of the photo was poor. The black and white grain could never capture with any accuracy the colour range. Given that Andreas' biggest concern was the vibrancy of the forgeries, this method of verification was, on balance, helpful. Point for their side.

Henry stood back having opened up the crate.

The soldier counted the number of photographs.

"Acht, neun, und zehn," he declared, inviting his colleague to count the ten paintings. He, in turn, ran his hand along the top of the covered frames.

"Funf und Funf – Zehn."

Ten on the list. Ten in the crates. The first hurdle overcome.

The soldier waved the Pissarro photo in front of Isaac. He didn't speak as his request was clear.

"Allow me, sir," said Henry.

"Thank you, Henry. The Pissarro, Winter on the Seine. As Isaac repeated the title, he couldn't help but recall with bitterness that first encounter with the Nazis officer. *Not now, just focus, Isaac.*

Henry lifted the retaining frame and Isaac rolled down the paper wrapping to reveal the stunning winter scene. All three soldiers glanced at the accompanying photograph.

"Ja." Henry re-covered it and slid it back into place.

The Russian roulette continued. "Next…" The soldier in charge of paperwork flicked through the options. His younger colleague suddenly reached over and plucked a photo. Laughing, he showed the third soldier whose attention had waned to adjusting his lacquered hair in the hallway mirror.

"Ja. Let's see this one."

It was the Gauguin, *Tahitian Princess*, a vibrant nude. Isaac appeared to frown. The soldiers assumed that their childish behaviour was being chastised. Isaac's reaction wasn't that at all but a tell-tale sign of stress. This was a fake.

Even Henry knew the Gauguin, which, in friendlier times, would have been worthy of comment.

The painting was at the front of the first case, which was unhelpful as that afforded a clearer view. As Isaac peeled back the covering: disaster.

There, clearly to be seen on the gold frame, was a smudge of paint, green Paint, patently identical to that of the paintings background. The paint looked fresh. Isaac's heart stopped for a moment.

"Allow me, sir," interjected Henry who reached out to take hold of the frame, his hand deliberately covering the evidence of fraud. Isaac briefly caught Henry's eye. *Bless you, Henry. Bless you.*

All three soldiers admired the nude. The fact that this was no Aryan beauty seemed to escape them. The soldier that had previously been grooming himself started to lean forward to get a closer look. Isaac stopped breathing. Henry gripped tighter.

"Ja…lovely body."

He turned away satisfied. Isaac forced himself not to hyperventilate and, with steady hand, Henry slid the drying canvas back into place.

Sensing the soldiers' impatience, Henry moved to the next piece in line. *No, Henry, No! Another forgery.*

"Nein, enough. We have seen enough. Lock the boxes up."

Henry duly obliged. The boxes were good to go. Two of the soldiers gripped the handles at opposite ends of the container and turned through 90 degrees to face the door.

"Wait," exclaimed Isaac, placing his hand on the chest of the lead soldier.

"What about my visas?"

"I know nothing about visas, just paintings."

Nothing within the soldiers' tone hinted at any misinformation or deceit.

Isaac removed his hand before it was removed for him.

"Visas aren't our concern. Try the Department for Foreign Affairs. Step aside."

Isaac quickly tried to assess whether or not he should stand his ground.

"I said, step aside."

The rise in tone literally spoke volumes. Isaac may have had moral authority but he and Henry were no physical match for these young uniformed intruders.

Isaac stepped out of the way. The nod of the head from Henry affirmed his decision.

Henry opened up the shiny black front door and the first box exited down the steps. It was lifted into the rear of the waiting Jeep. Soon, both boxes were on board.

As the soldier returned with signed receipt in hand, Isaac walked away instructing Henry to shut the door. He couldn't tolerate another Nazi salute in his home.

# CHAPTER NINETEEN

Isaac's calls to the Department for Foreign Affairs had been frustrating at best and deliberately obstructive at worse. Information regarding exit Visas could not be given over the telephone he had finally been advised, having been returned to the telephone exchange operator on five occasions for redirection.

That afternoon, he had been driven down to the Department Offices in the Administrative Quarters less than three miles away. As the car turned into Burgring Street where he had been directed to on the telephone, the queue of people was immediately evident: three deep, men, women, and children, some carrying bags and pushing makeshift trolleys. All Jewish, like him, looking to flee.

*No stomach for the fight. No, Isaac, No! No choice, no chance.*

The line must have stretched for over fifty metres. He asked his driver to cruise slowly down the road. The sight was pitiful, compounded by the grey sky above and gentle drizzle. As the car approached the front of the queue, there were a group of four young men standing in the road. They were carrying sticks or broom handles. Isaac watched as one of the men taunted an older man in the queue who cowered from the prodding and threats. These were anti-Semitic thugs. Another joined in the baiting this time striking the man on the head causing him to fall to his knees. There were three police officers also standing in the road due to the log jam of people. They were less than ten metres away but did nothing to intervene.

"Run them down, Otto!"

"Sir?"

"Run them down. Do it."

For a moment, Isaac just didn't care anymore. Like a condemned man.

Otto turned to look at Isaac. He could see that he was serious. Otto began to toot his horn, long sharp bursts, and steered the Bentley to the curb side heading straight towards the group. He accelerated sharply towards the attackers who were distracted by the sound of the horn and the revving engine. They realised the imminent danger. There was insufficient room on the pavement for them to escape so they sought to cross the road but had to pass in front of the vehicle. Otto hit the brakes at the last minute. He was trained to avoid accidents not cause them. The skidding tyres brought the car to a halt but too late to avoid the first of the bully boys finding his way on to the lengthy dark blue bonnet. He looked startled but unhurt. Otto accelerated forward ten metres with the additional passenger then hit the brakes. Given that Otto diligently polished the car's bodywork every day, the gleaming surface quickly saw the assailant dispatched from it. He fell on to the road out of Otto's sight. Reversing for a further few meters until visible, Otto revved up again. The look of horror on the racist's face as he thought Otto was about to finish him off settled a score for Isaac.

"Time for home, Otto, I think."

"Sir."

It was time to leave, for the policeman who had been so passive towards the attackers of innocent, unarmed Viennese citizens, were taking a keener interest in Isaac's attempt at vigilante retaliation. As they accelerated away, they passed the bully boys running up the road.

# CHAPTER TWENTY

As Isaac fiddled with his scramble egg and toast, Henry entered the dining room.

"I have your post Herr Cohen."

Isaac did not look up but reached over to the tea pot with a view to topping up his breakfast cup.

"Stick it in the study for later Henry. I'm already running late. Is Otto good to go?"

"The engine's running and ready Sir."

Henry instead of exiting made his way over to the table.

"No, that's fine Henry, I can pour for myself."

"It's not that sir. I thought that you would be interested in seeing the mail *this* morning. There was the faintest hint of enthusiasm in Henry's voice. Isaac looked up, Henry stood before him holding out the four or five envelopes on the palm of his hand.

There it was on the top of the pile. A brown coloured envelope unlike the other manila and white letters. It was embossed with the Austrian coat of arms, the double headed eagle which had once been a symbol of pride.

Isaac avoided the temptation to snatch the envelope.

"Why, thank you Henry, you may well be right."

"I will leave you to it, Sir."

"No, stay Henry, perhaps pour that tea after all."

Somehow Isaac did not want to be alone when he opened what he hoped was their tickets to freedom. *Would the authorities really just send the paperwork in the regular post?* It seemed insulting. Eva would have reprimanded him for wiping his egg stained knife on his napkin but he worried not as he slid the blade under the fold of the envelope and carefully cut it open. He reached inside. Just one sheet of folded paper. It was the most valuable paperwork he had ever seen. *Priceless? No, we have paid heavily for it.*

The Visa itself was straight forward enough. They listed the names, dates of birth, and address of those granted permission to travel and exit. They listed the border point for crossing; there was a date stamp and a further section stating in capitals that the authorisation was valid for seven days only. Crucially, there were two additional stamps, one in black ink and the other in red. They were official seals on behalf of the German and Austrian States. The former including a large *APPROVED* imprint.

"Thank you Henry. Any sign yet Frau Cohen?"

"I will ask Christina to check Sir."

"Tell Otto that I will be out in ten minutes?"

Isaac folded the paper back up into the envelope, leant back in his chair and enjoyed a sip of Earl Grey tea, no milk but a hint of lemon.

# CHAPTER TWENTY-ONE

Matilda, a house maid, opened the front door for Isaac to let him in. That was unusual as Henry would normally be ever vigilant for his return from work.

"Thank you, Matilda. Is Henry on a rest day?"

"No, Mr Cohen, he's in the lounge comforting Mrs Cohen." Isaac quickly handed his raincoat and hat to Matilda and hastily headed to the lounge.

Eva was sitting on the edge of the sofa. She looked distressed. Henry was busily wiping up tea that had spilt from Eva's cup and saucer onto the sofa.

"Ah, sir…" He didn't need to say any more.

"Oh, Isaac, thank goodness you're back. Henry, thank you for looking after me."

Henry took his leave having poured a further tea for both the Cohens.

Isaac joined her on the sofa. He noticed the tremble in her hands which he held to steady her.

Eva needed no encouragement to talk.

"Eliza has been to see me. Mathew has gone missing. She fears that he has been abducted by the Germans. Isaac, she is at her wit's end." Mathew was the eldest son of Eliza and Uri Levin, dear friends of the Cohens.

"Is this possible, Isaac?"

"Slow down, Eva. When did they last see Mathew?"

Eva struggled to get the words out as she relived Eliza's pain.

"Two days now. He had gone into town. Eliza had warned him to be careful. She said he was defiant, unable to stand by and watch his community ripped apart. He never returned home. Uri is out looking for him as we speak, starting at the hospitals, just in case he has had an accident. Isaac, you must do something."

Isaac handed her tea but Eva's hand tremors led to more spillage and he took the saucer carefully from her. Isaac had read of the Germans carrying out internment of citizens without charge but couldn't believe it was actually happening.

*There must be another explanation…*

The ring of the telephone disturbed the silence and startled both Eva and Isaac. Isaac put down his newspaper and put his hand on Eva's knee to assist his rise from the comfort of his chair.

Covering the receiver he whispered to Eva, "Its Eliza." Eva made her way over to the phone as Isaac continued.

"Oh Isaac. It's Mathew. They have him. Our Mathew."

"I'm so sorry Eliza. Yes, Eva told me. What is the latest news? Is David there?"

"He is down at the police station trying to find where Mathew is being kept and why. Isaac why? why?"

Eliza's voice tailed off as her grief and anxiety overwhelmed her. Isaac passed the receiver to Eva.

*Why? Why, indeed.*

Eva tried in vain to comfort her friend. Eliza, through intermittent sobbing, told Eva that a friend of Mathew's who had been arrested at the same time as their son had just been released. He had come to see them straight away.

Eliza relayed that three of them had simply been plucked off the street near the University to be questioned. Though he didn't say so, it was clear that the friend had been beaten up. His offence? Fraternising with Jews. His grounds for release: not being Jewish. Mathew had no such defence nor did his other friend who had also been detained. The telephone connection had been lost

Isaac tried to call Eliza back but the telephone exchange said that they were unable to place the call at this time. Isaac thought he was becoming paranoid because he assumed that the Austrian Telecommunications were now also under the control of the Third Reich and restricting access. *It made sense? It made no sense. Nothing appeared to be what it once was.*

*Was it time to run? Run without dignity. Was that worse than appeasement? It could be Anna next – then what?*

Isaac looked at Eva as she wiped a further tear away. They both knew that it was time to go.

There wasn't even time to say proper goodbyes. It was hardly a case of organising a party for this was no celebration. The Cohens were also conscious that the fewer people who knew of their impending departure the better. It somehow tempted fate or would lead to greater scrutiny. Only they knew about the paintings but *they felt* as though their deceit would be discovered and with it their escape from the Nazis would be foiled.

Isaac first needed to tell Henry, the head of the household. It was not only right that he and the staff be told but they would be actively involved in the packing and preparations. If it were not for the fact that it would have made Henry uncomfortable, Isaac would have asked his butler to sit with him in the lounge. Protocol seemed so meaningless in times of adversity but Isaac would do nothing to compromise Henry's professionalism and so stood as well.

"You called, sir. More tea, perhaps?"

"Thank you, Henry, I'm fine. Tell me, Henry, how long have you been head of the household?

Henry looked quizzical but not unperturbed.

"Funny enough, the cook asked me the same question last week. Fifteen years this coming August. Lady Porterhill, God rest her soul, died that spring and I saw the vacancy advertised in *The Lady* magazine, of all places, a month later. I then travelled to Vienna from London where I met Mrs. Cohen."

"We've all grown a bit older since then, Henry. I'd like to think wiser but I'm not sure some days."

"Indeed, sir, indeed."

"Henry, I'll get to the point. You are no fool, far from it. You will have followed events as much as anyone, no doubt with equal alarm. You didn't need to be Jewish to despair. Your discretion has been exemplary but I know that it will come as no surprise that we are going to have to move away. For a short time, anyway, until we get some more political stability. We will travel to Switzerland.

Henry bowed his head a tad.

"Just tell me when, Mr Cohen, and how many staff you would like to travel with you."

*Good old, Henry. He was treating it like a long weekend away to the Austrian lakes in Tyrol.*

"We shall leave this Wednesday but travel alone." Isaac could see Henry's confusion.

"We will need Otto to take us to the border but you must stay and look after the house, Henry. We have booked into to the Grand Hotel in Zurich. The service isn't as good as yours but it's not bad for a five-star Hotel." Isaac smiled, trying to ease the burden on Henry, who was just starting to comprehend the wider picture. He was a tall elegant man but, in those moments, seemed to shrink as though withdrawing into his light weight morning suit that he usually wore with such style.

"Henry, this is important." As he spoke, Isaac moved over to the side table. He picked up one of his business cards and wrote quickly on the back of it.

"Take this and hide it out of the way. Memorise it ideally. It is the code to the safe…" Henry was about to interrupt but Isaac was determined to finish. "In it, you will find sufficient cash to keep the household running for several months. I will also arrange for more money to be sent from Zurich. But, Henry, if for any reason, you have not heard from us by, say Saturday, I want you to clear out the safe. Take everything: cash, gold jewellery, and all of the papers. Do you understand, Henry?"

"I do and I don't, sir. You mean that if we don't hear from you…"

Isaac didn't hesitate to interrupt.

"Yes, Henry. This means that something may have gone wrong. Strip the safe and hide its contents. I can rely on you to use them wisely."

With that, Henry extended his hand to Isaac. They shook firmly. Protocol had given way to humanity.

They just couldn't escape without telling anyone. They just wouldn't. They would be discrete. Less people less risk.

The news of their departure had been met with hysteria by Eliza Levin whose son Mathew was still being held without charge. Yes, she was upset about her good friend's departure but it appeared to her that Isaac had been her last refuge of hope. Someone who was influential, someone who could at least find out where her son was being detained. If the Cohens were fleeing, what hope for the rest of them? Part of her was angry. *They should be staying. They should fight for what is right.*

Eva did all she could to allay Eliza's fears but worked in vain. *They would be back. They would help from Zurich.*

*No, they would be gone along with their beloved Mathew.*

\*

Isaac had not missed a scheduled day's work for decades. He would take family holidays but, even then, he would return early and allow Eva and Anna to carry on without him. Yet, he was about to walk away from the factory, leave it without him at the helm, without succession planning, without notice. He stood by his desk window, looking out for the last time on his commercial empire. He watched the looms rhythmic fall and rise as he had done on many occasions. He could see the rows of seamstresses with heads bowed, busying themselves with the latest batch of clothing for completion. He had scheduled a meeting with his ten most senior staff for 9.30 am. *What was there to say? He could pretend that he was going to have a short holiday? That a relative had fallen ill, perhaps. But his staff needed to take over his position, assume that he was not coming back, otherwise the business was bound to fail.* How he wished that he had delegated more. Their challenge would then have been less onerous. Whilst the team had, of course, been aware of the increasing anti-Semitism, they, like Isaac, had counted on the fact that his wealth would be a source of immunity. Nothing could prepare Isaac or his senior staff for that meeting. No agenda or minutes would ever capture the magnitude of their shock and distress. The owner of ACC had left the factory within the hour of the meeting.

Isaac's meeting with his lifelong friend Joseph had been more uplifting. Joseph was a realist. It was he that had encouraged Isaac to put his family ahead of issues of principle and justice. *There will be no justice in destruction and destitution.*

They were even able to laugh, reflecting on how their lives had altered direction so dramatically. The more schnapps they had, the funnier it became: a facade of humour but a powerful protective barrier in times of emotional turmoil. As they prepared to leave the café, Isaac handed Joseph a small velvet draw string bag.

"For you, Joseph. Take it. Treat it as a loan if you like but take it."

Joseph was surprised at the weight of the small pouch. He carefully untied the string and looked inside. Gold coins. He discretely lifted one half way out of the pouch. There was nothing with such an alluring colour as 18 carat gold. Joseph knew that he would desperately need financial help. They were such good friends that pride didn't distort the practicalities of having no income.

Joseph smiled. "What sort of rate of interest?"

"Lunch is on you when I return from Switzerland."

"That's a deal." Joseph tightened the draw strings and placed the pouch safety in to his coat pocket. Both men stood and hugged each other, knowing that the debt may never be repaid.

# CHAPTER TWENTY-TWO

Anna had said her goodbyes once already to Andreas. The day before handing over the paintings could have been their last together. They had treated that day as if it might have been. Had it not been for a timely intervention by Henry, it could have been.

They lived out a lovers' pact: commitment, adoration, and tender words. Love making without vigour: slow, very slow, as though climax itself would mark the end of their time together.

Tonight would be her last with Andreas before the Cohens set off for Switzerland. It would be a long car journey but it was a transient parting. It was more of a celebration. They had a future together. The Nazis had been fooled. They had only needed to be deceived for a short while. Enough time for the exit Visas to be issued. Success!

They had discussed their plan to be reunited. It would be soon. Anna would telephone, write, or just turn up to collect him. Next week? The week after? It mattered not as it would be imminent. Isaac had made sure that Andreas had sufficient cash to travel and, if need be, go into hiding. To that end, they both felt secure.

"What would you like to do tonight, darling?"

Andreas appeared to ponder before grappling her waist and rolling her on to his sofa. "No, Andreas." She laughed. "After that!"

Andreas took her hand and lifted her up. "Tonight, Anna, we shall dance." And with that, he put his right hand into the small of her back and, with his left, extended her arm.

They began to twirl with accompaniment from Andreas. His version of the Strauss waltz lacked depth of tone but he could just about match the rhythm with his feet.

*Da da da di da*
*Da da di dum*
*Da da da di da*
*Da da di dum...*

Anna accepted his dubious lead and squealed with delight. Having twirled and twisted, they soon returned to the intimacy of the sofa. It was Andreas that broke away from their passionate kissing.

"Do you think that the forgeries define our relationship?"

Anna, who was surprised to have their embrace interrupted, looked bemused.

"What on earth are you talking about?"

Andreas sat up. "I mean, if all this hadn't happen do you think that we would still be in love. Is it the drama, the fear, the excitement that has distorted our view of each other?" Anna sat up too.

"Distorted?!"

"You know what I mean. What will it be like when life is back to normal? I might become boring. I couldn't bear that. You might crave excitement not me."

Anna placed her hands on Andreas' cheeks as though cradling his head.

"Dear Andreas, I would love you even if you decided to be a librarian, quit drinking and took up collecting... butterflies. This whole episode has brought us closer together for sure but only in that it has magnified our strengths and accelerated our emotions. Distorted? Never. Now enough of these foolish thoughts, we have less than an hour together. This is not the time to be question our love. Embrace it; embrace me darling."

# CHAPTER TWENTY-THREE

Unlike many who would be queuing to cross the border that day, the Cohens were able to travel relatively light. They had arranged for an extended array of cases and boxes to be delivered to Zurich via the Austrian postal system. The destination for their property was the Zurich Palace Hotel, pending the short-term lease of an apartment in the centre of a city. It was to become *God willing,* thought Isaac, a short-term bolt hole whilst political turmoil resolved in his home nation.

Their staff of six lined the hallway as the Cohens made their way to the waiting car. Cook was crying, as were both the maids. Even Henry was fighting back the tears. Eva hugged each in turn, exalting the fact that they would soon be back. She believed this to be true. Isaac wanted it to be true but didn't believe it. Anna, as always, was the most positive of the three, describing the trip as a holiday, an adventure at worse. Isaac awkwardly ushered his wife and daughter through the open door and into the waiting Bentley. It was early morning and the streets quiet. The returning shift workers and passing cleaners paid no attention. Eva and Anna waved vigorously to the staff as the car pulled away, whilst Isaac bit his lip in anger and distress, staring straight ahead. He reached out instinctively to clutch his wife's hand, this time for his comfort, not hers.

The drive would take several hours. As they drove through the city towards the main highway west, the Cohens were quiet, taking in the beauty of their stolen capital. This might be the last time they would see Vienna. The feeling was surreal just unimaginable. *A lifetime of memories distorted. A future destroyed. Just surreal.*

The city passed into suburbia and the then on into countryside with mountainous backdrops. Cook had packed a picnic for them but no one was hungry. Anna was content to chat in an animated fashion with the driver leaving Isaac and Eva to some privacy in the rear of the limousine. Isaac had felt Eva trembling next to her. He asked for the heater to be turned up but they both knew that it was fear and not cold that was the cause. He took her arm and linked it through his.

"My angel, all will be fine. A short spell in Switzerland before order is restored."

Eva knew that he had no confidence in this happening and feared much worse but she still took comfort from it.

She began to recite a favourite poem of theirs, one that had been read at their wedding forty-eight years earlier.

*Ten o' clock, the broken moon*
*Hangs not yet a half hour high,*
*Yellow as a shield of brass,*
*In the dewy air of June,*

*Poised between the vaulted sky*
*And the ocean's liquid glass…*

Isaac joined her in the final verse:

*Yet we feel them floating near,*
*Know that we are not alone,*
*Though our open eyes behold*
*Nothing save the moon's bright sphere,*
*In the vacant heavens shown,*
*And the ocean's path of gold.*

Isaac took out a handkerchief and wiped a tear from Eva's cheek before dabbing his own eyes. He replaced the handkerchief and took out his tan leather wallet. Reaching into the last of the silk lined compartments, he removed the three photos that had been with him for the better part of twenty years. They were small black and white photos, creased and faded over the years but just as meaningful as they were when first captured. They had looked at them often and Isaac shared the pictures one more time. Their wedding day had been a relatively modest affair given their current wealth and standing but Isaac and Eva were surrounded by friends and family. The sun shone and the day marked a recognition of love that would survive the decades. She pointed as she usually did to his mop of curly hair and him, in turn, to her cream satin shoes that she had borrowed for the day but had been too tight and caused blistering ahead of their wedding night.

Anna may have disliked her baby photo but it always brought a motherly sigh from Eva. Anna dressed in an elaborate and long dress complete with knitted mittens and hat. She was but 6 weeks old, chubby in cheek with eyes barely open. It would not enhance any modelling career but was a special photo.

Finally, there was a surviving photograph of Isaac's parents on their wedding day. Eva had always been struck by the warmth with which she was initially greeted by them and subsequently integrated into the family. She knew that Isaac and her father had not always been aligned on the commercial front but those disagreements never once spilt over into family life. Eva's parents had been less supportive of her and that created a special bond with Levi and Maria Cohen whom she readily called Mother and Father after her union with Isaac. In turn, she had been treated as their daughter.

Neither Isaac nor Eva spoke. They didn't need to but it was Isaac this time that broke the silence, singing quietly for Eva an old Hebrew song that again had featured on their wedding day celebrations.

*Hava nagila,*
*Hava nagila,*
*Hava nagila,*
*Venis mecha.*

*Uru, Uru achim,*
*Uru achim belev sameach,*
*Uru achim belev sameach,*
*Uru achim belev sameach,*
*Uru achim*
*Uru achim*

*Belev sameach.*

Eva knew the melody well but was overwhelmed at hearing the song sung by Isaac. She tried desperately to fight back tears so as not to alarm Anna.

# CHAPTER TWENTY-FOUR

The border between Austria and Switzerland stretched over 60 kilometres. Most of it was mountainous and inaccessible. Isaac had read of attempts being made to escape via the Alps: indicative of desperation. It was unclear how successful these attempts had been. The visas granted authority for the Cohens to exit Austria at Martina, a village more than a town. Its access was limited to a single road which made for easier border control. The ground between Austria and Switzerland was separated by a short but critical distance: fifty metres between Nazi occupation and a freedom of sorts. The border patrols had been reinforced significantly on the Austrian side in the past few weeks. In years gone by, there was but a battered sign identifying the border but little else. The residents of the nearby villages would cross between countries without cause for concern, let alone a visa. Their wallets would contain a mix of Swiss Franc and Austrian Schilling.

The Cohen's car passed at least two hundred fellow refugees in the final mile alone. Most were on foot pushing wooden trolleys stacked high with essentials; case upon case, piles of clothes, and blankets. How they had even got this far remained a mystery to Isaac as there were only few cars abandoned at makeshift car park on the edge of the village. This was policed by armed soldiers to ensure that no one tried to ram their way across the border. Upon inspection of their papers by an Austrian guard, the Cohens were allowed to drive to within a hundred metres of the border before finally being told to stop and alight their vehicle. The instruction this time came from a German solider standing alongside an Austrian army officer. They were working as a team; allies, concluded Isaac with shame. The German's tone was not aggressive, officious perhaps, but no hint of the hatred against the Jews that had been so evident in Vienna. No one said a word. An outstretched hand, a quick glance at Isaac's papers, and a nod in the direction of the border sent the Cohens on their way, metres from a forced freedom but a freedom from persecution none the less.

The border was marked by a raised red and white wooden barrier. On either side of the barrier were identical wooden structures, more huts than offices. Unlike the weather worn barrier, they looked new.

The Cohens were ushered into a relatively short queue. There was so much at stake for those who were entering the checkpoint zone just metres a new life in Switzerland. The mood was a subdued one, exhaustion rather than fear. Certainly not a hint of exhilaration. Not even from Anna.

The final border patrol consisted of four soldiers: two Austrian, one German, and the other Swiss. Each uniform worn was similar but the insignia and different colour tones revealed their respective allegiance. Isaac gripped the family's authorisation papers tightly, like a drowning man to flotsam, fearing the lifeline might somehow be taken away. The queue moved quicker than the Cohens might have expected. Whilst those in front of them had their identification inspected, it was only a cursory glance by the Austrian soldier.

Isaac had brought their passports with him in order to formally identify themselves alongside the exit visa.

Isaac removed his arm from around the shoulders of his treasured women and stepped forward presenting their papers. Out of polite instinct, he offered a greeting. "Gentlemen, good morning to you."

Rather surprisingly, both the Austrian and Swiss soldiers responded positively, having been met with little civility whilst on the border patrol. The German soldier, however, failed to acknowledge the greeting with his attention drawn to the papers being held by the Austrian guard.

"Show me," he said, grabbing the papers clumsily. The German eagle stamp on the letter of passage seemed to have caught his attention. He inspected it closer.

"Identification," he demanded. Isaac took the Austrian passports from his coat pocket and handed them over without comment.

The German soldier looked at each passport in turn, daring to lift up Anna's chin in order to verify her photograph.

Isaac ushered his wife and daughter forward as though trying to speed up the process. The Austrian guard was frustrated by the unnecessary delay.

"Come, Come," he said, at the same time as gesturing to the Cohens to pass. The Swiss Guard smiled at Anna having for the first time noticing her attractiveness. Anna's attempts at a smile in reply lacked conviction for even she was now nervous. The Austrian reached out to take back their papers from the German.

"No wait!" he called with a degree of assertiveness, looking up to take in the faces of the Cohens once again. "Wait here." The guard disappeared into the adjoining hut. Isaac could see that he was using a telephone but he could not overhear any conversation.

"Let us through," said Isaac to the remaining guards. "Please let us through. We are good people. We have done no harm. He focussed particularly on the Swiss Guard who seemed to be sympathetic, even if only to Anna. "We have been promised safe passage," he continued, trying to sound authoritative but lacking real conviction, his voice revealing a slight quiver.

The German guard had been away for but a couple of minutes, long enough for another family to be vetted and approved. Parents with two young crying children. The father looked back at Isaac almost apologetically, trying to offer comfort, for he knew the burden of responsibility that had now fallen to the head of the family in these uncertain and dangerous times.

The Nazi soldier reappeared from his hut waving the entry papers in one hand and opening the holster to his hand gun with the other. He did not withdraw it but the intent was clear. Then came the dreaded declaration.

"There is a problem with their papers. They must be detained."

"No! No! This cannot be so. Let my wife and daughter through," pleaded Isaac as Eva dropped to her knees in despair and Anna gripped her father's arm in a state of complete vulnerability. Isaac felt a sense of wretched helplessness.

# PART TWO

TUSCANY, 75 YEARS LATER

# CHAPTER TWENTY-FIVE

Alex chided his work mate whose footwork was distinctly unimpressive this morning.

"Luigi, you are like Ronaldo: couldn't hit a barn door from ten paces."

Luigi, with a gesture of defiance, gently jogged after the football, which bobbled lamely to the right of the barn where the men would be working later that morning. Luigi put his ineffectiveness in front of goal down to the uneven surface that doubled as their pitch as well as the partially-inflated ball. The missed strike on goal brought the men to a natural coffee break.

It was still well before 8 am and the strong black brew was welcomed as were the home-made bread rolls that had been indelicately wrapped in newspaper and slung into the back of the workmen's van. Luigi returned with the ball, wiped it down the front of his off-white vest, and nonchalantly headed it into the back of the van. This incited further derision from Alex and Georgios, his younger assistants. The three men sat on the vehicle's tailgate, which was positioned in the shade of two Cyprus trees and slurped their refreshment whilst discussing anything but the day's toil ahead of them.

Their breakfast was disturbed by the sound of a vehicle approaching up the long overgrown drive. Even though the men were not expected to have started work yet, there ensued a speedy downing of coffee and a covering of the football, as the silver Mercedes drew up alongside them.

Luigi, being the eldest of the trio, clumsily assumed the role of team leader and greeted their client for the day.

Luigi thought about offering up his hand to shake but it was still covered in oil from yesterday and Signor Portelli looked too well-groomed in his beige linen suit.

"Good morning, Signor Portelli. My boys are feeling strong and awaiting your instructions."

Luigi thumped his chest and pointed to Alex and Georgios, who looked less inspired than both Luigi and Signor Portelli would have hoped. The crew had worked for this local lawyer before. Both occasions had involved house clearances following the death of one of Portelli's clients. As for many provincial lawyers, there was more money to be made out of death than life. In the small town of San Miniato where Portelli's office was based, litigation was virtually unheard of; disputes were resolved either by communal ostracising or a fist fight in the pitch of darkness at the back of Alberto's Tavern. Though he pretended otherwise, Portelli's practice would not have been commercially viable without the funds he had inherited from his parents. He had status but lacked a steady income. He therefore was pleased to be instructed to deal with the Will and Probate of the late Signor Andreas Bartelli. Signor Bartelli had died in hospital a few weeks back. He had fallen at home, fractured his hip, and contracted pneumonia. It was a pathway to Heaven that many elderly folk had suffered.

The lawyer was surprised to read in his will that Andreas owned this isolated warehouse for he had seemed to be a man of modest means. Portelli had hunted through the deceased's belongings for a key to the lockup and he had brought with him several possible candidates, each gathered from a variety of Andreas' draws and storage containers that cluttered his small apartment. Portelli threw the plastic bag containing the five keys to Luigi. He looked at the keys and walked towards the rusting lock and chain that blocked the access to the warehouse entrance. He was not optimistic. He had brought with him his large cutters just in case. After attempting a couple of keys in the rusty lock, Luigi grew inpatient and attempted to use the cutters. Having called on his younger assistants to help, extra leverage was applied and they were able to cut through the rusted chain. Just as it had taken three of them to break the lock, all their efforts were required to open the thick oak doors whose hinges had become heavily rusted and stiff. The hinges squeaked under pressure then screamed as the men pulled. Luigi encouraged his troops with a final

"Uno, due, tre!"

The effort didn't so much open the doors as cause one side to collapse from its frame. In a display of deceptive agility, Luigi escaped major injury, though made it clear that he had not bargained on danger when they had taken on the job. Brushing aside Luigi's dramatics, Signor Portelli moved forward to enter the warehouse. He stopped just inside. It was dark and the only chink of sunlight came from two partially boarded up windows. With less effort than had been needed with the front doors, the window guards were swiftly removed, throwing further light on the internal chaos. Signor Portelli was anxious to assess the extent of the deceased's affects. The sale proceeds were directly linked to his fees. As his eyes adjusted to the light, his fee expectations diminished. He took in the scene: a clapped-out Fiat motor car without wheels and partially stacked on crumbling bricks, half a dozen tea chests over-flowing with old newspapers, and a sundry heap of moulding curtains upon an equally dilapidated sofa.

Portelli approached the first of the tea chests. He picked up the yellow stained newspaper that spilt from its edge. It was too dark for him to read the main print but the bolder headline told its own story:

"Chamberlain in Peace Deal"

Disdainfully removing a cobweb from his linen jacket, he delved further into the box. It was his duty to make an itinerary of the items but, looking at the contents, he would be safe enough to delegate that task to Luigi:

*broken china tea cups – 3,*
*lamp with shade (partially damaged) – 1.*

He moved to look in the remaining boxes, which were equally ungratifying: a few photographs, more newspapers, and some letters that were loosely held in their envelopes. Nothing of value. On his way towards the exit, the lawyer prodded the folded curtains with the wooden handle rake that had littered the barn floor. The material split apart on contact revealing only the horse hair stuffing on the sofa beneath it. There would be little to auction beyond the warehouse itself.

"Prepare a list of all items for me. Have it on my desk by tomorrow. Take the junk to the tip and stack up the rest. We will put any decent pieces of furniture or crockery in the auction at the end of the month in Midino – if there are any!"

Luigi acknowledged his task and again contemplated offering his hand as a farewell gesture but, noting the cobwebs already on Portelli's jacket, decided against adding his own grime.

As the Mercedes could be heard disappearing into the distance, there was time enough for further coffee and another kick about before work began. Luigi earlier had gained the impression from Portelli that there may have been be a substantial amount of lifting involved. It now looked like a pretty straight forward job: certainly, time for more football. As Luigi made his way towards the open barn doors that now formed the new makeshift goal, Alex drove the ball past him into the barn, clattering the battered Fiat.

"One – Nil Milan!" he exclaimed, as he raised his torn T-shirt on top of his head to celebrate with arms fully extended.

Luigi was irritated to see that the ball had rolled under the car chassis alongside the bricks that supported it. Before kneeling to retrieve the deflating plastic, he took the opportunity of looking inside the car with a sentimental sigh. It had always been his father's unachieved ambition to own a Fiat like this, a 500 Topolini. He wiggled the giant steering wheel that had more play in it than his own delivery van which itself was badly in need of maintenance. The keys were still in the ignition. He turned them feeling a sense of nostalgia.

He jumped back as the car moved forward scrapping on the bricks. He smiled, noting that the car had been left in gear.

Looking at the back seat, he saw more of the curtain material that draped the worn sofa. Even in the dim light, it was clear that this time the curtain was being used as a protective wrap. In the meantime, his fellow players were becoming restless.

"Come on, Luigi. It will be half time soon."

"I'm coming, I'm coming," he called though his voice was muffled because his head was leaning through the car window. His hand stretched towards the back seat. The two objects he lifted were just too big to make it through the wound down window. He therefore pulled vigorously on the back door. It reluctantly yielded but at further cost to the support bricks.

Walking towards the sunlight, Luigi held up his find in the manner of a trophy winner. His pals came to inspect the two paintings that he proudly displayed.

Alex was not impressed:

"She's fat and ugly."

Luigi cuffed Alex around the back of his head.

"Far from it. She reminds me of my Bella."

Laughter flowed from the three of them.

"This one is even better," said Luigi.

"Yes, that's good. Haven't you got one like that in the kitchen?" reflected Alex, Luigi's nephew.

"Do you think that they are worth anything?" enquired Luigi.

"Only to you, Luigi. Bella can now appear naked for all to admire."

More laughter, more hitting. Luigi tossed the two

paintings carelessly into the back of the van. They had a combined market value of over $100 million.

That, as Luigi would have said to his Bella, was a lot of lira.

# CHAPTER TWENTY-SIX

That evening, Luigi returned home and parked the van haphazardly on the driveway. The men had indeed been able to finish the unpacking job earlier than expected and Luigi had proceeded to enjoy the late afternoon in the cool of Tavern Bellini in the village. The jug of house wine may have lacked the sophistication of the commercially bottled regional wines but it did wonders for the soul and an aching back brought on by years of heavy manual work. Luigi knew that his wife, Bella, would be annoyed that he was late for the evening meal. Her mother dined with them on Fridays as well. This would add to her angst. Tonight though, he felt that he held the upper hand, given that he had brought home the paintings found in the car. They were a present for his wife. The extended rest break at the tavern had given him an opportunity to wipe off the cobwebs that had stretched across the frames. With a liberal sprinkling of the house white on the canvasses, he was able to bring out a decent show of colour on the landscape and the tanned coloured flesh on the portrait.

As he entered into the kitchen, his heavy footsteps noisily echoed on the tiled floor. Bella did not turn around from the sink where the ravioli was gradually losing its freshness on the stove beside her.

"Take those dirty boots off."

Luigi complied but, still in jovial mood, kissed Bella playfully on the back of the head. He invited her to turn around. Far from being responsive, she shook her head disdainfully. She noted not only the unusual display of affection but the telling odour of plentiful cheap wine.

"Bella, my darling, I have bought these for you," he said, offering up his spoils. "It reminds me of you as my young bride."

Bella turned to face the nude.

"You are disgusting, Luigi! It is filth," said Bella, crossing herself lightly on the top of her large chest. In the corner, her mother was, by her own standards, positively enthusiastic about the piece but the portrait was ushered away by Bella who now inspected the Cézanne landscape. The scowl turned to a smile for she did, indeed, have a similar print in the dining room.

"Luigi, that is much better; it is like that Da Vinci next door. Look Mamma." She sighed, as she turned to her mother who was seated at the table. "Does it not remind you of our time with Papa in Tuscany?"

Mamma tutted. She remained more interested in the nude.

"I bought them from an art student in the market," lied Luigi with an ease acquired through much practice.

"Well, you can take back the rude one. The Da Vinci, you can hang up after dinner."

She laid the $60 million Cezanne down by the dog basket where Bendi, the family pet, was stirred from his canine slumber. He smelt the canvas inquisitively and then licked the white wine coating until reprimanded by Bella's foot. It was time for the well-cooked ravioli.

# CHAPTER TWENTY-SEVEN

Luigi was up earlier than usual for a Saturday. Bella was surprised to see him shuffle into the kitchen before 7 am, his slippers half on, half off, soles sliding against the tiled floor, a habit that Bella moaned about endlessly.

"Pick your feet up." She scolded.

"Anyway, why up so early? Couldn't sleep and looking to get on with tidying the garden as you promised to do a month ago?" The garden had been a dump for most of the year.

"Shhh, Bella, I will get round to the garden but today I'm going into town with one of the paintings to try and make our fortune." As he dreamed of a better life, he playfully patted Bella's bottom. Bella raised her eyebrows dismissively both at his optimism and endearment. She returned to the stove where the kettle boiled. Luigi took up a seat at the table, awaiting his first cup of coffee of the day.

"In to San Miniato? Perhaps, I can come too and pick up a new frock for Alex's wedding?"

"No, not Miniato but Lucca." Luigi frowned for the thought of having Bella joining the excursion rather spoilt the plan. More specifically, it reduced the opportunity for him to indulge in an extended oyster and wine lunch.

"Oh. Why Lucca?"

"They have the best art people there," remarked Luigi, sounding authoritative. The reality of the situation was that Luigi was unable to go to the local town for fear that Portelli, the attorney in charge of the warehouse clearance, might discover that he had "borrowed" a couple of the items.

He didn't quite know who he was going to approach but Lucca was a bigger town and it was bound to have more options including the flea market in the town square at weekends. Luigi's expectations were low and, if he could get enough euro to cover the cost of petrol for a short holiday to go to see his brother in Lake Como, then it will have been time well spent. If he got enough extra to treat Bella to a new outfit for the forthcoming wedding of his nephew, then this would be a welcome bonus.

"Lucca is even better for shopping," said Bella cheerfully, "let's have breakfast then I will then come with you. Clean out the front of the van first. It's a disgrace."

It was that, even Luigi had to admit.

# CHAPTER TWENTY-EIGHT

The traffic into Lucca was busy and the passage slow. The aircon in Luigi's van had stopped working effectively several weeks back and they could not afford to have it repaired. Bella began to sweat profusely and tried to cool herself with a makeshift fan made from an old newspaper found in the cluttered seat well.

"Luigi, drop me off here if you will. It's 10 o'clock. I will meet you in the main square by the clock tower at say, 11:30, when we can buy me a coffee and a cake. That should leave you enough time to sell the masterpiece." Bella giggled and Luigi chuckled as he pulled over briefly to the side of the road to let Bella out so that she could begin her shopping trip.

Luigi eventually found a parking spot. He had parked so close to the vehicle next to him that it was difficult to get out of the car let alone retrieve the painting. As he pulled the canvas out at an angle it scraped along the side of the red adjoining Fiat Uno. Luigi slammed the van door in annoyance and looked at the canvas to make sure it hadn't been damaged too much. No tear anyway. He would describe it as minor scuffing. He put a little bit of spittle onto his at index finger and, following some less than nimble rubbing, he was able satisfy himself that no real harm had been done. Luigi set off to the market square with the painting firmly tucked under his arm. At auction, it was probably worth in excess of US$50 million. But he had no idea about that. He would be delighted to get €100 for it.

The weather forecast had been good for the whole weekend and this had helped to swell the number of visitors. As ever, there were more people looking than buying but there was an energy and vibrancy to the square as people mingled and snaked their way at random through the stalls. The market itself was broadly divided into two sections. On the side of the town hall, itself a grand affair with adjoining clock tower and turrets, were the major stallholders who were present all week during the summer season. Each had a separate awning to protect from sun or rain. The range of products was varied but new clothes were prevalent as too were food stalls. The artisan stands attracted much attention normally because the owner of the stall would carry out their craft as they waited for their next sale. Some would have a long wait. The marketing of leather goods such as belts and purses was stronger than say wood etchings of the town hall or mosaics of the local countryside. No one doubted the talent required to produce these works of art but supply outstripped demand. This did not seem to deter the crafts people themselves who were happy to engage in discussion about their trade with tourists and locals alike.

On the far side of the square, where Luigi headed, stood the flea market. Here, although stall holders used tables as well, most of the second-hand goods were placed on the cobbled stones in front of the stalls. It would be wrong to say that all of the items were toot. Far from it, there were some bargains to be had but there were few discerning punters and Luigi certainly didn't fall into that category. As for the provenance of the goods, nobody asked too many questions. None at all actually. It was rather hoped that most of the items had been stolen as this was the best way of securing a good price in the first place. Although the police might occasionally wander into the square, their interest was also in in finding a bargain rather than locating a stolen item. There were very few stalls which had a central theme. Certainly, there was no one stand selling just paintings, second-hand ones at that. There might be a preponderance of clocks, a cluster of old fireplace utensils, and one stall had numerous old cameras for sale. However, even among these stalls, there was vast diversity of goods: golf clubs with carbon, steel, or wooden shafts, costume jewellery aplenty, military medals, lamps, and Luigi even spotted an old, though presumably still functioning, porcelain cistern in pride of a place on one stall.

Luigi strolled a tad uncomfortably between the rows of tables. He was feeling a bit out of his comfort zone but was encouraged when one market trader called out to him.

"A nice piece you've got there, Signore. How about this to go with it," he said, offering up a smaller canvas painting. There appeared to be no correlation between the works, given that Luigi's Gauguin depicted a naked Tahitian and the new offering was a portrait of a Spanish Cavalier. That said, both were oil paintings.

"Actually, I'm trying to sell it," replied Luigi with enthusiasm.

"As you say, lovely isn't it. Will you make me an offer?"

The market trader's friendliness subsided a morsel as he morphed from seller to buyer.

"I'm here to sell not buy, Signore. Remember that I have had to pay for this pitch."

Luigi acknowledge the point and continued his stroll waiting until he was out of sight of the disgruntled Cavalier seller. Luigi was attracted to what he thought was a more up market stall. There were fewer people inspecting the wares but the owner looked better dressed than most of the other stallholders. He was wearing Corduroy trousers and a shirt. The buttons were even done up.

This compared with the normal dress code of shorts flip flops and a T Shirt.

"Excuse me, Signore. I have this painting for sale, might you be interested?"

The stallholder put down the pocket watch that he had been polishing and ushered Luigi forward. He took the painting from Luigi, extended his arms to fully take in the scene, and tilted the canvas upwards to block out the sharp sunlight.

"Paul Gauguin," he said "such a top artist. It's what we call a giclee reproduction. Not cheap, you know."

"You like it?"

"Yes, I do like it. I do indeed. I'll give you €40 for it." As he made the offer, he reached into the money belt. He could see Luigi was hesitant and before any counterproposal was forthcoming made an increased offer of €50.

Luigi was tempted to make the sale but had liked the idea that this was a good reproduction and also thought that the market trader was too quick to increase his offer. Luigi would try his negotiation skills:

"I was looking for €100," he said, sounding more nervous than confident.

"You'll be looking a long time, young man. You need to remember that although it's a good quality copy there are lots of them around and it's a bit battered as well. Look at the state of the frame. I'll tell you what, I'll go to €60, my final offer, take it or leave it."

Luigi hesitated. He would be chuffed to be able to tell Bella that that he had been able to sell the painting but now sensed that it really was worth €100.

"I will think about it."

"Don't wait too long. It may be worth less later on, especially if I sell one of these I watches."

The posh stallholder waved him off. There was no offence taken at the failure to secure a deal. Luigi felt buoyed up by his trading exploits and decided to take a time out. A well-earned comfort break. He checked his watch. He still had an hour before his reunion with Bella. Time enough for a glass of grappa.

# CHAPTER TWENTY-NINE

The bars on the periphery of the square were not only crowded but more expensive than those off the side streets of Lucca.

Luigi therefore made his way past the town hall, walking up the hill towards the cathedral. Turning right down a narrow-cobbled street, he saw an ideal venue for a comfort break: several bars and cafes, one with empty tables and in the shade.

As he made his way along the road, he passed an antiques shop. He looked through the window but could see little but crystal chandeliers for sale, dominating the view. Outside, he noted the old mirror leaning against the window and then a painting of a horse pulling a plough. He couldn't resist looking at the price tag. At €150, it looked expensive even if twice the size of his nude. He decided that he would call in on the way back.

Having placed his order, Luigi sat outside, content to sip a generous glass of Nardina Grappa and a double espresso. A copy of the La Gazzetta Dello Sport newspaper added to the experience. Having assessed Juventus' prospects of retaining the Serie A championship, he was refreshed and ready for another attempt at selling the piece. The bar owner himself had offered to trade the painting for another round of drinks but they agreed that the painting would be incongruous surrounded by the football photographs and pennants that covered the bar walls.

"Anyway, it might offend the Signorinas," said Luigi in a rare display of political correctness.

"No worry. They are banned from here, Signore!"

They both laughed heartily with Luigi's gender awareness campaign having quickly evaporated. Luigi looked again through the antiques shop window and this time saw the proprietor adjusting a statue in the shadows. The owner spotted Luigi and beckoned him in.

Luigi noted his welcoming smile and felt less apprehensive at entering. As he did so, he was startled by the loud bell that affixed to the top of the door.

"Signore, come on in out of the sun. Feel free to browse."

Alberto, the proprietor then noticed the painting under Luigi's arm.

"Oooh, let me take a look at that."

Luigi perceived straight away that his one hundred euro target was achievable.

Alberto had not sought to disguise his enthusiasm. Luigi offered up his wares but as Alberto looked at nude captured so vividly by Gauguin back in 1898, he paused.

"Wait one moment. Let us look at it properly."

Luigi held onto the painting whilst Alberto lifted a nearby still life depicting a vase full of dried flowers from its display easel and placed it carefully on the ground. Luigi saw the price tag for the flowers: €100 (excluding frame). *Happy days.*

Alberto pulled the wooden easel, which itself was for sale, closer to his desk and taking the painting from Luigi placed it on the designated plinth.

Unexpectedly, he began by focusing not on the painting but the frame in which it was contained. He pulled out a magnifying glass from the table draw adjacent to the easel and turned the work so that it was face down. Alberto worked his way systematically along the ornate framework. Luigi would have to accept that the frame was a bit battered and the further damage he had caused getting the work out of the car earlier probably hadn't helped.

Alberto took a pair of tweezers, again from the table draw, and held them like a surgeon about to commence an operation in theatre.

"May I?" he enquired, looking at Luigi from above the ridge of his spectacles. Luigi nodded compliantly, not sure as to what he was agreeing but wanting to be cooperative.

Alberto used the corner of the tweezers to rub away a tiny section of the frame's top coat. He then produced, like a conjurer, a loupe from the breast pocket of his green paisley waist coat and slid out the lens with a flamboyant flick of the wrist. He carefully inspected the small amount of debris created by his scratching, letting out a deep "ummm" sound which revealed nothing to Luigi of Alberto's deliberations.

He then looked carefully at the rear of the canvass, focusing on every marking. It was only then that he turned the painting over to take a look at the Cezanne itself.

The silence was broken by Luigi.

"I'm looking for…120 euro," he blurted out, hesitating as to whether or not to reassess his aspirations for the target price.

"Ahhhh…" was still all that could be extracted from

Alberto who was now looking intently at the oil painting itself. His indifferent response caused Luigi to wish that he had stuck at the €100 and not been so greedy.

"May I ask how you acquired the painting?" The question was not posed in an inquisitorial fashion; Alberto didn't even look up from his inspection of Gauguin's signature at the bottom of the masterpiece. That said, the question troubled Luigi. It had not been a concern of the market traders earlier and after all, in Luigi's mind, it had only technically been stolen. He hoped that the slight delay in replying had not alerted Alberto who then temporarily deferred inspection and looked up at Luigi expectantly.

"From my wife's auntie who passed on recently. A great lady who loved art and even painted a little herself."

Luigi respectfully performed a cross on his chest, hoping to appear more convincing.

"I'm sorry to hear of your loss. Was she a lady of, shall we say, substance?"

"Substance, Signore?"

"Was she a lady of wealth? If I may be so bold as to ask."

"She certainly worked hard for all she got in life," replied Luigi, not really understanding the direction of the question. Alberto nodded. He put down his loupe and raised his glasses on to the top of his head where they rested comfortably. He gestured to Luigi to take a seat alongside the table. Luigi brushed down the back of his trousers and sat in the mahogany chair with high armrests and a spring upholstered, brown leather seat. For Luigi, it felt luxurious as he sank into its core. Alberto sat in its twin chair behind his desk as they exchanged names. A good sign concluded Luigi. *He means business.*

"Luigi, I am not an expert when it comes to paintings.

Now, give me a grandfather clock and I would be far more confident as to its authenticity and value. I have no doubt that this is a really good piece of art. The frame alone is of high quality and this should be a clue. Why display something of limited value in a frame worth more than the canvas? It obviously isn't painted by Gauguin but I do wonder, given its quality, whether it could have been painted by one of his more junior artists, an apprentice, if you will. This often occurred back then. This would still make it worth a lot more than the €120 you are asking for Luigi." Luigi smiled.

"This," continued Alberto, "is what I think we ought to do. Let me hold on to the painting for a week or two whilst I carry out some research on it. There are experts in this field who I can contact. This way I can offer you a fair price. Antiques dealers have a bad reputation, Luigi, but I am a man of honour and will be straight with you. The only thing I would ask is that if the painting is worth more than expected, rather than me buying it from you, I would arrange for it to be sold to an art dealer. The standard commission for me would be 20%. How does that sound?"

Luigi did not like the idea of having to handover the painting. Antiques dealers did have a poor reputation and for Luigi there was no honour among thieves. He expressed his reservations.

"Do not take this in the wrong way Alberto but my wife, Bella, who, strictly speaking is the owner of the painting, would not want me to leave it behind." Luigi felt awkward at expressing his lack of trust and was torn between an instant sale and waiting for a better price.

Alberto understood Luigi's reluctance and sought to compromise.

"I understand, Luigi. Leaving her auntie's painting with a complete stranger. How about, as a gesture of good will, that I give you today, a non-refundable €150? If it then turns out in a week or so's time that the painting is a straightforward modern copy, then you get to keep the money and I will even give you the painting back. If though, as I suspect, the painting is worth a bit more than we think, then I we sell it to a dealer and I get my commission. I can't be fairer than that."

The deal sounded too good to be a true for Luigi but Alberto looked and behaved is a straightforward way. Perhaps, he was just naive thought Luigi. He recalled the words of the market trader who said that it was a good quality copy. If that is the case then he still gets €150, much more than he had been expecting and gets to keep the painting. *What's not to like about that?* "That's a deal," said Luigi, thrusting his large hand across the table to cement the agreement. Alberto gratefully took his hand and a shook on the deal.

"I should say that I have another painting that auntie left us: one in a similar frame but of fields not naked women."

It was Alberto's turn to think he was being conned and he laughed nervously as he counted out the €150 from the notes he had taken from his wallet.

"She was quite a lady your auntie. I can see that. Let's see how we go with this one first."

"Let me take a few details from you so that I can write you out a proper signed receipt – all above board." *Nearly anyway,* reflected Luigi to himself.

With cash and receipt in hand, Luigi and Alberto said farewell.

Luigi checked his watch; it was just after 11:30 am and he was late for Bella. He picked up the pace downhill and whistled as he did so, a sure sign that he was in a good mood.

Bella would forgive his discourtesy when she heard his tale and especially when he bought her a new dress for the wedding. Time for coffee, cake, and perhaps another grappa.

# PART THREE

# CHAPTER THIRTY

It was not unusual for academics from different institutions to engage with each other. Peter Brinsden and Simon Braithwaite both taught art at Cambridge University, though at different times. While they were commercial competitors, in the sense that they worked for different auction houses, their degree of specialisation meant they could benefit from each other's knowledge. With one conversation, they might verify their own thoughts or advanced their own theories. They also had no compunction in ganging up on other art critics looking to break into their world or to question the conclusion of those retained by other smaller auction houses throughout the world.

Each of the major auction houses would perhaps have three significant auctions a year: one in London, one in New York and increasingly, as the Asian markets flourished, one in Hong Kong. "Significant" meant an auction that had within its list of lots, pieces of art, primarily paintings, with an individual value in excess of £250,000. The auction houses retained Brinsden and Braithwaite by way of a consultancy fee, meaning that they were free to take on additional work from a variety of sources. Brinsden had retained his more formal academic career as professor of art at Cambridge, whereas Dr Braithwaite had a more public profile. He wrote regularly for both the *London Evening Standard* and the *New York Times*. The rewards were modest but served to prop up his ego and enhance his status on the social circuit. Every new gallery or exhibition would want him on their opening party guest list, even if he was being paid to attend. He was content to sip champagne with the wealthy, famous and beautiful, often using such occasions to promote his private services on a variety of art related issues.

Braithwaite found that his more controversial articles, particularly those attacking contemporary art, helped with his commissions, even if they attracted significant social media criticism from others who considered themselves more sophisticated. Braithwaite was happy, for example, to challenge publically the Tate Britain Trustees for buying a pile of bricks for £300,000, which he described as being *symbolic of nothing but a building site*. As one abusive critic had retorted:

"Braithwaite, why don't you stick to evaluating post-impressionist – it's an era in which you are stuck!"

He would be happy to do so if such consultancy work had paid better. The expert therefore supplemented his income by working on behalf of wealthy buyers, either to make recommendations as to paintings that might usefully sit within their art portfolio or by promoting up and coming young artists. Both he and Brinsden were hired guns and both were highly regarded with over 50 years' experience between them. It was true that occasionally they disagreed on the authenticity of a particular work. That however was rare and tended to occur when debating the works of a "lesser artist" for whom there was less material available to compare and contrast.

Braithwaite had enjoyed a lie in that morning as he enjoyed the sunshine streaming through his London apartment windows. The block, Neo Bankside, afforded views of the Thames, the dome of St Paul's Cathedral and Tate Modern. The galley had acquired iconic status since its conversion from a disused power station into housing one of the world leading art collections. Braithwaite was happy to publically criticise a number of the trustee's acquisitions but he enjoyed the status that came from the 6th floor apartment. Braithwaite had nipped down to the ground floor artisan bakery and ordered a croissant and flat white before sitting on a stool and opening up his iPhone. The email that he had received from Dr Peter Brinsden' was, on the face of it, innocuous enough:

*Simon Hi,*

*All well?*

*I thoroughly enjoyed your Royal Academy review in the Standard last week – outrageous as ever!*

*Can you help with a query come across my desk? Am I right in saying that you were the authenticator of Gauguin's, Tahitian Princess? I ask because I have been contacted by an Italian antiques dealer who seems to think he has a masterpiece on his hands – don't they always!! The video clip he has sent through to me of the painting looks to be to a high standard (attached). Do you know whether Gauguin or his apprentices produced a couple of similar versions? What*

*do you know of the original's provenance? All I can see was*
*that it was sold privately back in 2010. You couldn't tell me*
*on the quiet who bought it up could you? They might be*
*interested in adding this to their collection even if it's "house*
*style" rather than by Gauguin himself. I'd see you alright, of*
*course, old boy!*

> *Best,*
> *Peter*

The authentication of paintings was a role they both undertook intermittently. It was an important one to the extent that the owners, potential purchasers or auction houses had a lot at stake. The difference between a painting *out of the school of* a particular master and it being painted by the master himself, could run into millions of pounds.

Braithwaite wiped the sweat from his brow and picked up his phone but it was not Peter Brinsden's number he dialled. The ringing tone was an extended one, an international call.

# CHAPTER THIRTY-ONE

If it were not for the fact that he was required to do so at law, Harold Reidler would have not displayed the name nor the nature of his business. For a Swiss attorney, his offices were certainly stylish from within but presented a low-key exterior. Based in the down town region of Zurich it was an unpopular venue for those in the commercial sector. From Reidler's perspective the offices were ideal, providing anonymity within a secure working environment. This was not a law practice that attracted passing trade. Reidler's entry within the Swiss Bar Council List of Practitioners was short and vague: *Reidler, Harold Hans; qualified 1975; educated University of Bonn and Balliol College Oxford; Commercial Practice – intellectual property.*

The fact that he infrequently took on new clients, in no way detracted from the success of his practice let alone the strength of his bank balance. His select clientele were demanding but rewarded generously for his input. The service he provided was not so much good, as unique. That business model ensured repeat business. It was not that clients did not moan bitterly about his fees, for they did often, but they would never complain to the Swiss Attorney's Association nor seek alternative legal advisors.

His clients made for an impressive CV but it was never a list that he would promote. Reidler was a fixer; at best a broker. Though his speciality was paintings, stolen ones to be precise. His professional armoury ran to antiquities, old bullion and stamps. Despite these illicit deals, Reidler was actually an attorney of some repute. His professional area of expertise was in jurisdictional disputes for the return of Nazi procured art. Reidler was always acting for the defendant in such actions, either for museums or private individuals seeking to retain possession of their prized artwork of dubious provenance.

As Braithwaite tucked in to his morning pastry, Reidler was in a meeting with three trustees from Harbour Point Museum in Zurich. He had been instructed to act on their behalf in resisting an attempt by the Jewish Repatriation Society to recover a painting by Matisse, The Purple Singer. The court proceedings had been commenced in the New York Fifth Circuit for the recovery of what was described in the court papers as *Nazi plundered art*. The action was being brought against the museum by the aggrieved descendants of the Mandel family, who argued with some force that the painting was plundered from their home in Paris, shortly after the German invasion. The trustees had been happy to travel to Switzerland to meet with Reidler as it would remove any unwanted publicity.

From a moral perspective the case looked a strong one. There was documentary evidence that the painting was indeed owned by the Mandels. Records showed that the family had been sent to Struthof, France's only concentration camp. The plaintiff's in this court case where the great grandchildren of Ethan Mandel. The papers filed at court set out that the family wanted the museum either to return the artwork to them or pay restitution damages, which the family placed at approximately $35 million.

For Reidler, the task had been made far more challenging following a U.S. Supreme Court decision of *Republic of Austria v Altmann* in 2004. Up until that time the US courts have been very reluctant, not so much to acknowledge the original ownership of the art but to apply retrospective retribution. Reidler was in no doubt that had *he* been instructed to act on behalf of the defendants in the *Altmann* case, the claim would have been successfully defended. Although the case itself had made the current matter more challenging, Reidler's skills were more in demand than ever as both private individuals and institutions nervously sought to protect *their* property. The *rogue* decision of the Supreme Court, as Reidler saw it, had further galvanised several of the Holocaust charities that existed, including the Holocaust Art Repatriation Group, which was based in Zurich. This charity had seen a threefold increase in donations following the Supreme Court ruling and they were now active in supporting more lawsuits, particularly in the US, where a lot of the plundered art had ended up. The prospect of being in front of a sympathetic plaintiff jury in Manhattan brought no pleasure to the Harbour Point trustees.

Reidler's fee structure was unusual for a lawyer. He charged by the hour at top city rates but he also charged a success fee or what he described, in his retainer letter as *a reverse contingency fee*. He took a percentage of the money that was *saved* in successfully defending any action, as opposed to the normal plaintiff attorney arrangement of a contingency fee based on a percentage of the damages actually recovered. Reidler was more *no fee, no win than no win, no fee.* The percentage, non-negotiable at that, was 20% of the insured value of the painting or other work of art. Given the insurance estimates were often inflated, this always worked in his favour too.

Reidler surrounded himself with a small loyal team of attorneys. There were no other Partners in the practice, but his team of five associates with supporting paralegals were better paid than most partners working in other city law firms. It was easy enough to buy loyalty when a senior associate could be paid $1 million.

Although repatriation trials were becoming more popular, they still remained relatively rare. Sometimes the mere instruction of Reidler caused underfunded plaintiffs to withdraw from a case, knowing that they could not compete against what appeared to be Reidler's bottomless funding pit. Reidler *never* took on cases that weren't funded to the hilt by his clients. Even the increasingly well-supported charities were nervous of his involvement because an unsuccessful four-week trial would not only prove to be very expensive but would include a barrage of unfavourable publicity. There was a delicate balance to be achieved between pioneering on the part of those families who had endured the Nazi indignity of pillage and targeting more receptive opponents such as the major international institutional art galleries. These galleries, in the main, had developed protocols with regard to establishing the provenance of any work displayed and acknowledged earlier ownership. Such an acknowledgement did not automatically lead to compensation, as in some jurisdictions, actions for recovery were time barred at law. For example, in the UK, the National Gallery Act 1992 provides immunity from action in such circumstances.

Quite often, Reidler's advice would be to settle a case on compromised terms, thus avoiding the publicity that a court hearing brought with it. It was not unusual for that retention of anonymity was an important driver for the current owner of a major work of art. There was invariably a correlation between such ownership and wealth. Sometimes this wealth had been acquired through less than transparent means. The last thing they wanted therefore was for their profile to be raised. This assisted Reidler in securing a negotiated settlement; one which always had a confidentiality agreement attached. This fear of public scrutiny often meant that the mere threat of litigation brought forth a settlement, even when the case could be successfully defended. If say, a sculpture by Rodin has a market value of $20 million, the claimant may be more than willing to accept a without prejudice sum $1 million. Reidler knew only too well that often the plaintiffs were far less wealthy then their ancestors who had been able to acquire the artwork in the first place. To those ancestors $1 million was an awful lot of money. He had read on countless occasions that the issue was not about the money but one of principal and seen on as many occasions a modest sum in settlement accepted. Money could heal wounds.

By contrast, wealthy claimants were the most aggressive and troublesome to deal with. They were far more likely to take the matter to trial and for them principle *was* the key feature. Upon accepting instructions on a new matter, one of Reidler's junior associates first task was to investigate the finances of the claimant. The result of that report would drive strategy.

There was no doubting that Reidler was not only a wealthy and successful lawyer but a ruthless and talented one. He was never nominated for an award, nor invited to address his peers. He was despised by human rights lawyers but his understanding of the cross jurisdictional issues meant that he was the leading lawyer in this field.

Reidler's success was aided by the fact that he cheated. He had no compunction in doing so. He saw the law itself as but a tool, one of many. Information about opponents was far more valuable. It was easier to assess what sum ought to be paid to settle a matter if one had been able to bug an opponent's meetings, especially one where your latest offer to settle was being discussed. Reidler was not subtle in his methods but he might be with his negotiating tactics. He would never propose exactly the level of settlement that had been discussed and agreed at the plaintiff's meeting, often offering a more generous amount to see an end of the case. His client we never aware of his tactics, or rather, they never asked about them. He assumed that they didn't care either. Although Reidler's reputation was enhanced by running a successful trial, cash flow was more readily achieved by early resolution. Given the reverse contingency fee arrangement that he put in place the less time he actually spent on a matter the better: 20% of a $10 million saving, equals $2 million in fees if the case is resolved within six months or three years. He preferred the shorter route and it was rare for a client to complain that he hadn't been value for money.

Reidler knew that the more complex the ownership trail, the harder any case would be for the plaintiff family or group.

He was able to provide, at significant cost of course, extended ownership packages. He had shell companies and offshore trusts in The Virgin Islands, Panama and even the more respectable Channel Islands of the UK. Much depended on where the current owner of the art lived or where the claiming ancestors were resident. Either could indicate different law and therefore a different strategy. Norway was one of Reidler's favourite jurisdictions because statutes prohibited any reclaim. If it could be shown that the piece had been owned in the country for 10 years. Such ownership was easy to arrange.

Although the preliminary financial review of his opponents was carried out by a junior associate, often the most valuable research was carried out by one of his private investigators. He was not be so naive as to instruct them directly but did so through his web of contacts. The investigator would thoroughly research not only the plaintiffs themselves, but their lawyers and as was often the case, any key benevolent supporters who were helping to fund the case. Whilst Reidler was interested in finances he was more interested in foibles. If it was necessary to employ blackmail to achieve the results, then so be it.

The recent bringing of a child sex abuse claim against one such supporter immediately saw the withdrawal of funding and with it the abuse allegations were withdrawn. Reidler's case concluded – fees paid. The last person who refused to pay Reidler's fees regretted their decision. A successful media magnate had instructed the attorney to carry out negotiations with the Egyptian authorities for the release of a marble statue of the *Goddess Osiris*. The negotiations were not protracted due to the generous bribe offered to the relevant officials at the Interior Ministry. The *Certificate of Release* was forthcoming within days of Reidler that having been retained and the fee of $75,000 due. The recipient of the *Goddess* defaulted. The subsequent divorce resulting from the release of a compromising gay sex photographs of the Goddess' new owner, cost substantially more than the fees that were owed. It was Reidler's way of working.

He preferred not to use violence to attain his goals, not because he had any moral abhorrence to aggression but he prided himself on his intellect and strategic know how. To that end, violence was sometimes necessary, partly to gain respect and partly to achieve goals where paperwork alone was ineffective. His "heavies" were as well-paid as the senior associates. Their work was sometimes brutal but held to a high standard and he needed to ensure that they were not corruptible by an outside source, be that an enemy, of which there are many or the National Crime Agency. Reidler was on the Interpol database not because he had actually been convicted of a crime but because he had been implicated in several. Investigations carried out by them and The FBI had quickly come to a halt, with suspicion never resulting in hard evidence. The authorities had met with an impenetrable wall of silence; one that this lawyer had acquired at significant expense.

Underperformance was not treated lightly but this was nothing compared to an act of disloyalty. It was disloyalty, Reidler feared, that would one day bring about his downfall. He had well-rehearsed contingency plans. If a quick escape was ever needed, he would have ample funds available, not only to disappear but to continue to live the lifestyle he enjoyed and thought that he deserved. He wished to avoid or at best defer having to take such evasive action and the most likely way of doing so was to be cautious, trust few, pay well and punish harshly. It was a formula that had served him well thus far.

Only that very morning Reidler had to assert his authority. He had been on the phone and in a state of agitation.

"We have agreed the delivery date. Excuses are unacceptable!"

It was clear that the recipient of his wrath had been in some difficulty with the latest transaction. Reidler was relentless. He was not in the mood for renegotiating deadlines; his demand had an air of menace.

"If Mehmet has failed, then replace him. You will be met at the docks in the usual manner. I will extend your deadline to midday on Tuesday but no longer. Do not let me down."

Reidler had replaced the telephone receiver feeling less anguished. He was optimistic that the delivery would be made. He cared not for Mehmet, who, on this occasion had failed to deliver his assignment. The target for Mehmet had been the theft of minor Egyptian antiquity from a private collection in Cairo— an ancient statue, *Tawaret*, a goddess of fertility. Mehmet's capture meant for him the end of a distinguished career as an antiquities thief. There would be no trial or appeal of sentence. The authorities, certainly in public, were anxious to reduce the relentless drain of ancestral works from the country even if their supply, was a valuable source of private income for those in public office. Mehmet's attempt to steal from a private collection as opposed to one of the numerous municipal museums was an error that he would regret, given bribery was less effective in the private sector. He would not be afforded the harsh state justice system but a more brutal private one. Even before Reidler had replaced the telephone receiver, punishment had been inflicted upon Mehmet; the hammer had fallen more than a dozen times upon his tied hands. He could no longer be a thief and with every bone in his hands and wrist broken, amputation was a distinct possibility without urgent medical attention. Mehmet's employers were not in the habit of providing private medical care and his tears reflected as much his fears for the future of his family than the agony of his injured work tools. Reidler cared not.

Reidler had two active projects on the go this week, each very different in nature. The first was involved preparing to defend the New York gallery from a well-funded attack by the Nazi retribution League to recover the stolen Matisse. All attempts at negotiations had failed thus far and intelligence received suggested that plaintiffs were prepared to go to trial to recover *The Purple Singer*. The gallery itself had seen a healthy increase in visitor numbers since the dispute became public with the filing of court papers but the loss of the painting by the gallery without compensation, would be a dreadful blow as, along with an early Turner scene of London, this was a star attraction.

The second project involved facilitating the private sale of a stolen Persian carpet. Not any old carpet from a Moroccan bazaar but an 11th century rug carelessly lost from an Iranian temple. Arranging for the transportation of the rug had not been without danger, at least for the underpaid mule, if caught, he could not expect formal judicial processing.

He was ten minutes into his meeting with the gallery trustees when Reidler's mobile vibrated.

"Will you excuse me? I need to take this call." He stood

without waiting for a reply. He adjusted his purple Hermes tie and slipped back on his petrol blue tailored suit jacket. Its silk lining and top pocket handkerchief perfectly complimented the tie. "Whilst I'm away, ponder whether or not you could run to two million U.S, spread over, perhaps, five years."

Reidler exited the meeting room into the adjoining corridor where he could speak freely. He had been pleased to see that the call was from Simon Braithwaite from whom he was awaiting an *authenticity certificate* in order to progress a private sale of a Manet. He liked Braithwaite, a leading authority in the field of Impressionism – world-renowned and crooked too, an ideal combination for Reidler.

"Simon, I'd prefer you not to use this number but have you authenticated the Manet?"

"Mr Reidler, we have a problem, a big problem…"

# CHAPTER THIRTY-TWO

The vintage *Bottega* prosecco *was* flowing freely in Milan's Museo de Arte Miani. Roger Kirtley adopted a low profile; as best one could ever do as a wheelchair user. His task was made easier by the surrounding company: celebrities and art critics mixed with the wealthy and successful from the world of commerce, many forthright in dress and opinion. The gallery had been closed to the general public for weeks leading up to this launch. Tonight was the first of several private viewings. Invitations were hard to come by. Roger sipped on his sparkling water and rested his glass between his immobile legs. He smiled politely at the waitress who awkwardly gestured her offer to hold the drink for him. He was alone in avoiding the expensive fizz. Roger was on duty and despite the convivial atmosphere, there was still a lot at stake for him. The exhibition was to run for a month and it was expected to attract over twenty-five thousand visitors.

From an art insurer's perspective, the greatest risk was accidental damage to a piece on show. Over the years Roger had witnessed damage to oil paintings from both red wine and cigarettes. Water colours were particularly vulnerable to spillage and expensive to repair. Recently, at a show in Madrid, his insurance company, PNP had been left with having to make a €100,000 payment for a damaged sculpture knocked from its plinth following a boisterous scuffle towards the end of a private viewing for Italian art critiques. It had been described as *a lively affair*, in the reviews that followed— indeed. For all that, the traditional exhibition headaches, transportation and installation had, for this Post Impressionism exhibition, been relatively trouble free. A Pissarro, presumed missing on route to Milan from New York, had turned up in Frankfurt airport; it had a rather inflated financial reserve placed upon by the U.S. financier who owned it and therefore its recovery was certainly a relief to Roger's employers, though less, he suspected, to its owner who, had with a degree of undue haste had sought and received an interim payment pending final valuation.

Roger appeared to be scrutinising at close quarter the detailed brush work of a Monet, turning his chair side on to the painting. In reality, he was checking the vibration gauge fitted to the frame. The device was ultra-sensitive to any movement and would readily trigger an alarm. Not all of the fifty two paintings were afforded special protection, only those on the *priceless list*. The other pieces were generally protected by CCTV cameras and security guards. He stepped back and took in the scene. There was no natural light but this enabled the lighting experts to maximise focus on the exhibits in a manner that best captured the artist's portrayal. Some were enhanced by spot lights, other by lights immediately above the frames. The gallery had dedicated the entire first floor to the exhibition, which had been years in the planning. The floor was divided into sections by a number of stud panels. This, the catalogue said, was meant to *add to the intimacy* of the viewing, not a word that readily sprung to Roger's mind as the throngs jostled for a better view of the art and the prosecco waiter's eye. The professional photographer's flash sought out suitable shots for society periodicals, *Vogue, Vanity Fair* and Milan's own *Femm.*

Roger's concentration was more shattered than disturbed by the scream that came from the corner of the gallery floor, fifteen metres from where Roger sat. He turned, his eye drawn to the sound. The young woman, dressed confidently in a red Japanese print silk dress, now looked far from assertive as she covered her mouth and looked intently in front of her. Despite the drama, Roger couldn't help but notice her bright red manicured nails, which perfectly matched her dress. His eyes moved quickly to the cause of the drama. Two men, smartly dressed from the neck down in blazer, collar and tie but with their faces covered by black woollen balaclavas. Roger had a better view of one of the men; he was wearing gloves and holding a black matching hand gun. The hubbub of social intercourse had drawn to a close, replaced with an eerie, but temporary, period of silence, not extending beyond a few seconds. Silence was replaced with the less convivial sound of fear and panic come to life in an odd mix of gasps, screaming and shouts of inquisition and disbelief. Much like the screams from a theme park roller-coaster ride that runs into mechanical difficulty, the volume of noise remains the same but the nature of the screams change, a change for the worst.

Roger cautiously rolled a few metres to his right to get a better view. He could now see that both men were armed.

The thinner of the two, whom had been obscured from his vision, stood up on the leather bench that ran parallel to one of Monet's *Water* Lilly scenes. The comfortable seating area designed for restful contemplation of Monet's *Givenay Garden* was now anything but tranquil. The man waved the gun above his head and rolling up the bottom of his balaclava shouted out.

"Everyone, face down on the floor! Do it now!"

The voice revealed little about the man. Roger could see that despite some stubble, the man was well tanned and had the hint of an Eastern European accent. Those immediately in front of the once again fully hidden face did not hesitate to get to their knees and lie down. Others, more like reluctant worshipers, hesitated before following suit. Roger was at a distinct advantage in joining the prone gathering. He had though become agile at transferring from chair to floor over the years but space was limited. Several guests had also tucked in behind the chair, hoping, rather optimistically, that either Roger or his chair would afford protection. There was the crash of glass as one of the waitresses who had been serving alongside Roger lost control of her tray. He watched as the remaining half bottle of prosecco flowed rhythmically from the top of the bottle. Almost instinctively another guest reached out with his hand to upright the bottle. Even in a moment of crisis it seemed a shame to waste good fizz.

"Down! Everyone stay down and you won't be hurt." This time the command was delivered with equal assertiveness but less venom. Roger leant forward ducking down as best he could. He remained very much above the proverbial parapet and caught the attention of the assailant. He pointed the pistol in Roger's direction but in turning to do so he could then see that Roger was in a wheelchair and he raised his hand in acknowledgement. It was a paradoxically humane gesture given such aggression. In the far corner behind the elevated assailant, his chubbier colleague was hard at work attempting to remove a painting. From his position, Roger could not see which one. He knew though from the fact that an alarm had not instantly sounded that it was not one of the exhibitions three most prized exhibits—all Monets. These pieces were very reluctantly insured by PNP. Hence they were afforded extra protection. Looking at the terrified face of the waitress alongside him, it seemed cruel for Roger to take any comfort from the fact that the main exhibits were, so far at least, intact.

He offered up a hand of comfort and she clenched it tightly, her whole body shaking with fright.

The sofa-bound assailant broke his gaze from the gathering before him to look over his shoulder in a frustrated fashion at his labouring colleague.

He encouraged him in parochial terms to complete the task with more vigour; both men had thus far remained calm and professional but they both knew that there was a limit as to how long, in the heart of Milan, a hundred normally dynamic and independently minded people could be kept at bay. Further fraught wrestling with the picture frame saw it finally freed from the wall. Roger was still unable to identify it.

Roger saw a uniformed security guard peering from behind of the diving walls trying to get a better view. It was unclear if he had line of sight of both men. Roger tried to get his attention by tapping his water glass on the spokes of one of his wheels, but to no avail. Had he seen that one of the men was armed? Roger saw that the guard was short and portly in stature. He had removed his blue cap and had put his radio to his ear. The security guard leant at a more extreme angle, assessing the position.

"Go! Go! Go!"

The guard, without warning, dropped his radio and sprang from behind his surveillance post, heading straight toward the larger robber who by now had wrenched the painting from the wall and had placed it under his arm. Roger watched two other guards about to join the fray. All three were now shouting, albeit incoherently. A battle cry. Seconds later, the galley reverberated to the sound of two gun shots. The noise was accentuated by the low ceiling. It numbed the ear drums temporarily.

Counterintuitively, Roger sat up again to get a clear view. The bullets had found their target. Two guards lay on the floor; Roger's portly neighbour lay motionless and the other guard writhed face upwards, holding his side. His light blue shirt was covered in blood. The third guard was backing away slowly, hands raised. He was shaking violently. As quickly as the gun fire deafness appeared, it subsided. The ringing in the ears was replaced by screaming.

There were no further instructions from the robbers who were now making their way past Roger to the narrow entrance through which the guests had entered and collected their first drink of the evening. One held on to the painting and the other waved the gun randomly in order to ward off any have a go heroes who were in short supply given the fate of the guards. The painting's canvas was pointing towards Roger. Although the portrait was upside down Roger identified it easily. Paul Gauguin's style was unmistakable.

*Tahitian Goddess,* not the most expensive masterpiece on display but a masterpiece nonetheless with a price tag to match.

As the painting disappeared out of sight two further shots echoed in the hallway. No one set off in pursuit.

# CHAPTER THIRTY-THREE

Roger switched on the main lamp to his eleventh floor executive hotel room. He briefly looked out of the full length window, down on to the twinkling lights of Milan. He transferred skilfully from his chair, utilising his toned shoulder muscles to lift and swivel in one movement and sank back into the armchair alongside his suitcase rack. He reached out to pick up a glass of Reme Martin brandy that he had poured from the overpriced mini bar. It would not be his last. The only other source of light came from the large television screen, offering an array of *in room* entertainment and the LED bedside clock. Had he been interested, the clock would have informed him that it was well past his normal bedtime but only an hour since the conclusion of his interview with the police officers who had taken over the investigation into the gallery robbery.

He was in an unusual position on this occasion and not one he enjoyed: an interested professional party as an insurer, with a significant loss but also a witness and in some ways he felt, a victim, of what had been a brutal robbery. Just being present had disturbed and sickened him.

His statement to the police had been concise and professional, lacking in emotion. The police, he suspected, had little interest in the recovery of the Gauguin. To them paintings were *but rich men's toys*. The focus of the police was catching the attackers. Roger's professional interest lie in the return of the masterpiece. *Of course he wanted those bastards caught too*. The capture of the robbers and the recovery of *Tahitian Goddess* did not necessarily go hand in hand. Roger had seen the problem before. Only last year all chance had been lost of the return of a significant heist of jewels when the police tried to intercept ransom monies as part of their operation to arrest the thieves. To be fair the robbers had used significant violence to force the owner to reveal the code to his safe but in the end, the insurer paid out, the criminals remain free and the victims remain nervous. For Roger cooperation was strategic.

Roger twisted the metal cap on his second brandy and reflected. He was still shaken by events. He had taken some comfort from the fact that both security guard were alive even if one was said to be critical. What Roger just could not fathom was why the robbers would take such a risk. A raid in front of so many people, with cameras and security everywhere. Why would you take such a chance? There was every reason to assume that these were professionals too – calm under pressure – a well-executed job given all the unfavourable circumstances. It didn't make sense.

Roger leant forward and pulled off his brown slip on shoes and finished his brandy. The drink may not assist his deliberations but would aid sleep. He would sleep in the comfy chair tonight, he hadn't the energy or desire to transfer back into the wheelchair and then on to the bed. His formal written report could wait 'til the morning. He had advised head office in London of the theft straight away. Charles Bradley, had reluctantly taken his call on his mobile phone, complaining that he was at a formal dinner party. The news was met with silence followed by "Fuck it. Fuck it!" Roger's wellbeing appeared to be of no consequence.

"Do you know what the reserve will be, Roger?"

"Yes, I've checked the policy schedule on line…35 mill US."

"Fuck it!"

"Who's the owner?"

"Pavlo Stets…yes, fuck that too."

"Roger?"

"Nothing, Charles – rather you than me having to tell him."

"Don't kid yourself, Roger. Get a full report into me tomorrow and the get back to London to see Stets ASAP. Sorry, Roger, I should have asked, how are you? Roger? Roger, are you there…?"

# CHAPTER THIRTY-FOUR

As with all large loss claims, it was PNP's protocol for the lead investigator to meet with the insured who had suffer the loss. This served several purposes:

First, it was good for PR – an insurer being seen to be taking the claim seriously, understanding the distress that can be caused by the loss or theft of an item of such sentimental value; they always say that it is, no correlation, of course.

Another primary reason is to try and manage expectations as to how much the insurer will pay out and when. One needs to be as delicate as a Middle Eastern diplomat; to suggest either that the circumstances are suspicious or that the valuation placed on the item by the owner is inflated, can cause offence and with it complaints at board level. It's the law of social connectivity—someone who owns a Rembrandt is far more likely to know someone who can make your life a nuisance. Three degrees of separation magnified.

Roger had flown back into Heathrow from Milan Malpensa first thing following a restless night. The Italian police were happy for him to fly back and agreed to keep him in the loop if anything significant developed regarding the recovery of the Gauguin. Rather than go to the office first, he decided to head out to meet Pavlov Stet who had already been made aware of the robbery. His formal debrief with his director, Charles, could wait.

Roger collected his adapted car, courtesy of the *Motability Scheme* from the *meet and greet* service. The BMW 5 series Estate was a far cry from the limited choice of a decade earlier. Any car was capable of having hand controls fitted. Indeed, Roger had met a hedge fund manager whilst visiting his spinal unit as an outpatient who had converted a Lamborghini. Roger wasn't sure how he managed to get in and out but wow, once at the wheel, he was king of the road. As a Blue Badge holder the financier also had privileged parking facilities. As if enough heads weren't turning already as the yellow Huracan pulled into the motorway service station.

Roger's route out to the Wentworth Estate from Heathrow, where the mansion was situated, took in some of the country's finest housing stock; the Crown Estate in Oxshott off the A3, past St Georges Hill at Weybridge and down to Virginia Waters. Roger turned left onto the Wentworth Estate, famous for its golf course. He was greeted by barriers manned by a uniformed estate employee.

Roger slowed down and then drove up to the manned booth. His car window lowered to be greeted with a non-officious, genuine, "Good morning sir."

"I'm here to see a Mr Stets at Goring House. Yes, Mr Kirtley, you're expected. Roger was impressed. Johnstone, the security guard, was used to witnessing visitors' reaction by now. "Number plate recognition system, sir."

Roger nodded.

"Drive slowly onto the estate and keep left at the fork towards the golf club. Take the next right down Bunker drive and Goring House is the second house on the left. I will notify them of your arrival."

The Wentworth estate, which encompassed the world-famous golf course, was a symbol for the wealthy. The thirty-two houses that formed the elite residential collection covered 150 acres. Whilst the estate was probably most famous for having housed General Pinochet during his controversial house arrest in the United Kingdom, it housed a few celebrities but most residents were overseas businessman with an eye for discretion, security and anonymity.

Pavlo Stets fell into the *one out of three* category. For although he sought security, discretion and anonymity were not words commonly associated with his lifestyle. There was though, no doubting his extraordinary wealth. This house alone had been purchased for £30 million but two years ago. The fitting out and furnishing ran to over £5 million.

Roger had found little in Stets' Wikipedia entry to verify the provenance of such wealth. Over the last five years, Stets had made many high-profile acquisitions. Those acquisitions certainly extended to the art world. A record payment at auction for a Renoir, two Degas for a combined total of a £48 million. The Henry Moore *for the back garden* for a further £2 million. The list was not endless but it was certainly significant and very public.

Stets described himself as a '*successful entrepreneur*.' His profile listed a number of directorships in private companies from a diverse range of industrial sectors. He was less suited to the more regulated public markets. The publicity that surrounded his removal from the board of Encombe PLC filled the financial section of the broad sheets for many weeks and in its latter stages, even made the *red tops*. It was clear that the regulations imposed by the stock exchange far from suited his autocratic style, in particular his propensity to blend company funds with his own.

They may say that you cannot buy patronage but many have tried and many have been successful. Philanthropy is meant to be selfless but is often driven by desire to be recognised and rewarded. Whilst many industrialists obtained knighthoods, primarily the New Year's honours list acknowledged citizens for their services within the community. Yes, lollipop ladies, dustbin men and church workers have received their MBEs but the higher awards nearly always reflect a significant contribution, more financial than physical, to the charitable sector. Stets was determined to receive official recognition.

The problem for him was an outsider; one craving acceptance in elite society circles. He even employed his own personal PR team to assist with the challenging process. As a charitable benefactor, there would've been few better publicised donors. Any cause attracting public attention would end up being supported. This extended to disasters, dogs, cancer research and most recently of all, *a generous offer* to send Siamese twins to America for life-saving medical intervention. Informal approaches by his intermediaries for him to become a trustee for the Opera House, the Victoria and Albert Museum and finally the Tate Modern, were all withdrawn quickly. Whilst his money was attractive, his personality was not and the risk of brand damage to any partnership was significant. Stets had lived in the country for nearly a decade but had made little inroads into the upper echelons of a British high society. He attended polo at Windsor, had a box in the Ascot Royal Enclosure and to his credit had even been invited once to the Queen's Summer Garden Party but there remained suspicion surrounding his intent, motivation and background. These suspicions were enhanced by dissident campaigners who had identified him as being involved, indirectly at least, in the supply of arms to mercenary Russian forces in the Ukraine. It was alleged that he had, in the early days, taken brutal measures to stamp out any criticism. Bribery and corruption in Belarus were rife. Protesters were arrested. Journalists were dismissed and at least two had disappeared, feared dead. Each death in isolation might have appeared accidental but when combined as a cluster there was genuine cause for concern.

The first thing that Roger noticed on the estate were the magnificent rhododendrons that were at the height of blossom. Bushes extended to great heights with beautiful flowers detracting from all of the opulence surrounding them. Roger had played at the West Course at Wentworth many years ago, before the accident that had rendered him paraplegic. He would've preferred to carry on down the drive to the golf course but he no longer allowed such reflections of his former self to affect him for more than a fleeting moment; comparisons were unhelpful, life now was just different, not necessarily worse. That philosophy was best expressed by Roger celebrating the accident date anniversary with enthusiasm equal to his birthday bashes.

Roger turned in towards the entrance. He had barely come to a halt, when the wrought iron gates began to open. A gravel drive extended before him with a dogleg left on towards a roundabout, which marked the front of the house. The roundabout itself was a modern water feature – a stone surround with copper and glass inserted within. Shards of water shot intermittently at various heights into the air. The theme was unclear, the cost less so.

As Roger drove around to the front steps, a member of staff, dressed in blue blazer and White chinos, encouraged him to continue on the driveway around to the side of the house, where Stets parked his Range Rover *Autograph* and his *regular use* sports car, the Lamborghini being afforded underground protected parking. Roger lowered his window and pointed to his wheelchair which rested on the back seat with its wheels removed. The assistant took one look and Roger watched as his face flushed with embarrassment; an all too familiar reaction. His demeanour improved little as Roger nimbly pulled the frame and wheels from the car and assembled the chair as quickly as an F1 pit stop technician. Chair at 90 degrees to the car, brakes on, shoulders engaged, lift and swivel – good to go. How Roger detested these gravel driveways. The thin tyre profile caused the wheels to sink and the chair jerked forward requiring considerable force to move in a straight line. Fortunately, the distance between the parked car and the start of the granite terrace was but a couple of metres. In front of him the next hurdle; two steps six inches in depth before a level access to the mansion.

The 'small drawing room' was, perhaps not surprisingly given the scale of the property, nothing of the sort and larger than most one bedroom flats in London. It was opulent. The centre of the ceiling was dominated by a modern glass chandelier and reminded Roger of an attractive and colourful version of Medusa's snaked hair piece. Ten to fifteen crimson, orange and ruby red thin shards of hand blown glass extending from a central nub or head. Roger probably wouldn't mention the analogy to his host. There were no carpets as such but a large red and orange rug, subtler than Roger's bland description afforded it. Again modern, and more a work of art in its self. It was lush and thick on the perimeter with tighter yarn towards the centre. The white leather furniture was centred on a spectacular marble fire place flanked on each side by two full-sized bronzed pumas, black with golden spots and green emerald eyes – real jewel stones at that. The mottled marble surround competed for attention with two elongated glass vases filled with fresh and vibrant Strelitzia, orange and birdlike flowers, the perfect accompaniment to the rug and chandelier. The hearth, though filled with logs, looked as though it had remained unused.

Roger was invited by the butler to 'make himself comfortable,' a paradox in terms, given the setting, with whom he was meeting and the circumstances of the meeting. He did not take up the offer but instead wheeled his chair to inspect a painting that dominated the area above the black marble top table on the wall opposite the fire place. He recognised the artist but not the piece itself. Again, the orange and red colour coordination sprang from the canvas. Which came first? Roger puzzled, the rug or the painting.

"Picasso's, how you say, Mr Kirtley, two a penny?"

Roger was unsettled by the unannounced entry of his host. He was clearly light on his feet for someone of such formidable framework.

Gathering himself quickly Roger smiled.

"An early piece, I'd say – pre-cubism – a fine specimen too."

"It should be given what I paid for it."

Roger rolled confidently towards Stets and shook his hand. As he did so, he noticed that the tyre wheels, still dusty from the gravel drive, had left tell-tale tram marks on the edge of the orange rug. If Stets had noticed he was unperturbed and was warm in his greeting. His handshake was more in keeping with his bulky body than his nimble feet. He squeezed, crushed and dominated. To his credit Stets made no mention of the fact that he was in a wheelchair. Such a reaction was, for Roger and most other chair users a rarity. Reactions varied; some people were embarrassed unable to make eye contact, others curious; often too curious (*what's wrong? how did it happen?*). The worst were the sympathisers (*oh, you poor thing*) just ahead of the optimists (*there will be a cure one day*). Stets was unphased.

"Come, let's take coffee or would you prefer to join me in something more enticing?" asked the Belarusian, gesturing towards the two-half full cut crystal decanters on the marble table.

Roger avoided the temptation to check his watch, for he knew it was not even 11 am but clearly for Stets, a limited-edition whiskey or brandy was an acceptable mid-morning diversion.

As though summoned telepathically another blazer clad member of staff appeared in the doorway with an ornate silver tray which he placed robustly on the coffee table situated at an angle between one end of the sofa and an adjoining arm chair. Roger was guided this time by Stets, to tget closer to the sofa.

Stets nodded to the blazer, indicating that his pouring services would not be needed. He then picked up the white porcelain coffee pot, his large hand struggling a tad to grip the more delicate handle.

Roger responded to his cue.

"Thank you, Mr Stets, black. No sugar, please."

As he poured the coffee, which was thick and opaque, as Roger himself liked, Stets' tone changed from that of his affable introduction.

"So, you've lost my fucking painting, Mr. Kirtley. I generously loan a loved one to the nation, your nation, and it has now disappeared. That is a very expensive error, Mr. Kirtley. Sixty million pounds worth of cock-up when I last checked."

This was clearly a solo not a duet and Roger waited for a definite pause before starting to reply. As he did so one of Stets formidable hands reached across and lightly gripped his arm.

"No, Mr Kirtley, no. I do not want any bullshit. No apology, no excuse or explanation. Just a signed company cheque." Stets removed his hand from Roger's arm. The solo was at an end.

"I understand your anger at the loss, Mr Stets."

"Then you understand nothing. I am not angered just expectant; inpatient and greedy, maybe, but not angry."

"The police are optimistic of recovering the painting for you," Roger said, knowing he was embellishing the facts from a less favourable report he had received yesterday afternoon. "They …"

"The police!" interjected Stets with mocking derision. "I have no faith in the police. Remember, Mr. Kirtley, where I come from the police are just as likely to have been the perpetrators of the crime as the custodians of justice." He laughed at his own analysis.

"Under the terms of the policy…"

"Fuck policy terms, Mr. Kirtley. They are for fancy lawyers in expensive suits to resolve in my favour."

Roger was relieved when Stets' mobile phone rang. He took the phone from the initialled breast pocket of his pale pink shirt, looked at the screen and stood up without acknowledgement, let alone an apology and headed for the door, speaking, what Roger could only assume, was Russian—a harsh truncated language beyond Roger's grasp.

The returning butler was curtly polite but direct.

"May I pour you more coffee before you leave, sir?"

If Roger had previously been in doubt, there now was no ambiguity, his meeting with Stets was at and end.

# CHAPTER THIRTY-FIVE

As Roger set off from the heart of wealthy Surrey, he reflected on having just met one of the most well-known businessmen in the country – a dangerous one at that. It was a far cry from his earlier career. Rogers's father, Marcus Kirtley, had been a UK civil servant, working in the Foreign Office, in the capital. A diplomat of sorts. High ranking enough to get an OBE in the Queen's Honours list but a long way off a knighthood. Roger had hoped that his father was a spy, but the truth was far more mundane. Though mostly based in London, where Roger was born, the job had involved assignments abroad: Postings in the evolving Commonwealth, in India for a period and even Sydney for a year with a short spell in Gibraltar. It was at an international conference on oil exploration, hosted in, East Africa, an Italian colony, that he had met Roger's mother, Carina, who was part of the Italian contingent's secretariat. This was one of the countless cocktail parties attended that he wouldn't forget. His mother had moved to London and joined the civil service secretariat there, within three months of their first vodka martini together. The Italian influence had remained strong and Roger was bilingual by the age of three.

It was she who had encouraged Roger's interest in the arts. He remembered fondly the trips to the National Gallery and the Tate, followed by a quick stroll in St James's Park, with his father, whose office was a short distance away in Whitehall.

Roger had wanted to become an artist. This was not discouraged. He had even begun a degree foundation course in applied arts at Earls Court College, in West London. The accident changed all that. He would never be the same again. His drunken attempt to cycle a *borrowed* bicycle down steps at Waterloo Bridge down to the Embankment below seemed, at the time, like a fun idea to both Roger and the other students with whom he had been drinking that evening. Roger had descended the first set of steps rather deftly given his intake of beer but the decision to attempt the final section with hands raised in the air was a mistake...

These days, he *celebrated* November 15th with as much vigour as his actual birthday. But as he lay endlessly on his back, unable to move his legs at the National Spinal Centre Stoke Mandeville, celebrating that day felt unimaginable. Roger could, still to this day, clearly visualise his charismatic consultant, Mr Gardner, telling him, without alarm or drama that he would never walk again – he was a paraplegic. Roger had waited until the clinical entourage had left the ward before he sobbed quietly for several hours. His world felt at an end. However, as the months of rehabilitation ensued, Roger's mental outlook changed. He was helped on journey by many of the staff but in particular an inspirational nurse from Northern Ireland called Tracey. Her smile itself was worth a month of physiotherapy sessions. He too was surrounded by many in a much worse position; tetraplegics, unable use their hands effectively and even a couple of patients on a ventilator, unable to even breathe on their own. Camaraderie on the unit was good. Most of the injured were of a similar age; motor bike accidents, horse riding falls, toppling ladders at work. Spinal cord injuries were the domain of the young and adventurous. Trips to the local bowls club were popular in the evenings; cheap and plentiful beer and a chance to smoke without reprimand. There was a community feel; a false sense of security that would be shattered upon discharge – the ultimate anti-climax. In the spinal unit, you are surrounded by other wheelchair users; the floors are flat and smooth, doors open automatically, corridors are wide and pavements non-existent. Compare that to the real world. He could barely get through his parents front door and he would have to get used to bed baths until the bathroom extension was finished. It was a time that he would like to forget, even if it forged his sense of determination and sheer bloody-mindedness, which would serve him well in the future.

There was no prospect of returning to art school. For one thing the main art studios were all in the basement and wholly inaccessible. Roger's outlook on life had changed too. He wanted to earn a living; wanted to show that he could still make a contribution to society. Although the position has changed significantly with the introduction disability discrimination and even the growth of the Paralympics, employment opportunities were still very limited. Less than a third of wheelchair users even had a job, let alone one of professional standing.

His move into the world of insurance was a compromise. It was not the move into the civil service that his father advocated but insurance was still considered, then at least, a respectable career, one with prospects for progression and diversity. And so it was that Roger Kirtley swapped his paint smattered smock for an ill-fitting suit and joined Lloyds of London. Had he been important enough to warrant a business card it would have said 'assistant underwriter,' which was an impressive title for someone who spent his day carrying paper slips on his lap from one department to another without any input into their production.

Though he never heard the famous HMS Lutine Bell toll on the Lloyds trading floor to announce a major disaster, he took to the work quickly. There was a good social life to be had in the old public houses of the city, most, still dark caverns, with sawdust on the floor and giant old used wooden barrels of sherry blocking out the light. Unlike his life as a student, he even had some money in his pocket. Given that most of his peers had gone straight to work at the age of sixteen, Roger was older, given that he had stayed on at school. He was known colloquially therefore as 'wheels.'

It was not for many years that he began to specialist in art and antiquity insurance. It was perfect for him, allowing his artistic bent to be supplemented with professional input. Given his niche, he was also in demand and moved companies twice before joining PNP seven years ago. His disability also helped his employer's diversity figures.

That morning, Roger pondered whether or not to put on the *Exo Skeleton* – his robotic mobility suit. It had been neatly packed away and its battery put on charge following it most recent use. Originally, the suits were developed for the military. The idea of an infantry being able to run at speeds of over 30mph for hours on end would be a battle game changer.

The concept, on paper, worked but issues with battery size and weight, combined with instability over rough terrain proved challenging. The prototypes were being developed at a time when the United States in particular, was seeing a dramatic increase the number of paralysed soldiers returning from the so called theatres of war; Iraq and Afghanistan. Unlike the Vietnam War, the public were keen to do what they could be help raise funds for rehabilitation and so it was that he robotic suit development changed direction. The Exo was born. It was one of several such devices now on the market each with pros and cons but each empowering its user; the *Rex, ReWalk* or the *Wanercraft*. It was difficult for Roger to explain the sheer of joy he experienced in being able to stand and meet people at eye level. Something he dreamed about, now realised. He called the armour his *weddings and funerals* suit for he often saved it for special occasions. People were often surprised that he didn't wear it all the time but there were limitations – it often took over half an hour to fit and was tricky to do so alone. Battery life was still limited and there remained at risk of pressure sores. Roger had fallen flat on his face once early on when failing to observe the low battery warning. It's a mistake, he said, that you only make once.

The suits do not come cheap nor does the training and maintenance. Roger was humbled when his employer's charitable arm, PNP Foundation, presented him with a grant to cover the full cost of the suit. The cheque, for £150,000, was presented to him at the firm's annual awards dinner. The attendees clapped and cheered, whilst Roger blubbed like a baby for all to see on the giant screen.

He found that the electronic suit afforded him a confidence too and he might need it today. On balance he would do without it given that he hoped to do a decent shift in the office and there were limited charging and changing facilities.

Having utilised his disability parking bay in the nearby underground carpark; a privilege that many paid thousands of pounds for, Roger headed to his office, which was within 400 metres of Liverpool Street Station, in the heart of the commercial district. Upon arrival, he checked that the security guard wasn't watching and rolled his wheelchair backwards on to the bottom steps of the moving escalator that lead to the main reception of PNP's London office. It was a tricky skill, one fraught with risk – tip the chair back, balance on the main wheels and hold on the rail. Though the office had not attracted architectural recognition, the views from further up the twenty eight story block, took in several iconic buildings; The Bank of England off Treadneedle Street, Lloyds, where his career had begun and *the Gherkin* that now towered above them.

The office area had become open plan a year or so back. Given Roger was out of the office so much it didn't bother him, though there had been complaints from some of the older assessors, used to being able to watch cricket on their computers behind closed doors. Privacy was now the preserve of senior management alone.

Roger waved to a few colleagues before rolling into his chairless desk. To his disappointment, he caught Charles, his superior's eyes.

"My office in five, Roger," he commanded, still shaking his head at the thought of the multi million pound loss.

Roger booted up his computer as he listened to the three messages left on his desk phone. One from Charles, asking him to pop in asap; one from HR asking if he was coping following his ordeal – *just about, thank you for asking* – and finally a random call from a corporate hospitality firm offering expensive ticket for the Grand Prix – *thanks, but no thanks.*

The screen showed that he had eighty nine unread emails: *Skip all those where I'm just cc'd – it's always back covering.*

*Ignore all from IT – Yes, I will get around to changing my password.*

*Diary entry for annual appraisal – bad timing!*

Roger noted two *industry alerts* –these related to an insurance industry initiative to share information. The insurance industry was more advanced than most when it came to digital development. The days of the door-to-door salesman from the *Prudential* collecting premiums weekly was from a bygone age. Over ninety percent of all policies were taken out 'on line.' This had advantages, not only in terms of cost, but also data collection and correlation. Insurers even shared data between themselves. The aim was to reduce the amount of fraudulent activity in the world of insurance. Some fraudulent claims were detectible through forensics, such as a deliberate fire at an insolvent factory or suspicions were readily alerted where losses claims seemed incompatible with income and lifestyle (known in the trade as Rolex Syndrome). However, it was not until the market began to coordinate claims that the full extent of the problem was revealed. When assessed individually, claims often seemed very plausible but when analysed from a wider perspective, some fascinating serial claimants were revealed.

The unlucky Nick Ballard from Birmingham, who had been involved in twelve tail-end shunt accidents in two years. Needless to say, none were his fault. The family were generally unlucky because his brother, Finley, had himself endured six such accidents as well. No one though was more unfortunate than the serial widow Veronica Charles, who had just claimed on the life policy of her third husband, all of whom had died *peacefully at home of natural causes* (her words), albeit, *prematurely* (GP's words).

The world of art had also benefitted from this gathering and sharing exercise. It had always surprised Roger how often stolen property was insured by those who had acquired it – even where they may have been aware of the illegal acquisition in the first place! The data also revealed trends that were then helpful in being able to set premiums and insurance reserves. A recent spate of designer burglaries in leafy Oxfordshire had been insightful for the insurers and the police.

Last year, Roger had received notification by email of the theft of three paintings of Sigmund Freud – all three incidents were in different parts of the country. Not only did this lead to a leap in premiums for other owners but warnings were sent out to these collectors, enabling them to enhance security.

Art theft was far more extensive then is often publicised – not a week passes without, for example, a church being raided; an easy target – some thefts were just opportunistic, others well planned.

One major problem was that often the owner has inadequate insurance cover – there is no point in taking out a house hold policy for cover of £250,000 when your art alone is worth £500,000. At the top end, i.e. policies for cover of over a million pounds, additional security arrangements are always a condition of the policy but can be expensive to implement: alarms, locks, CCTV – how often victims of burglary don't bother to set the alarms and complain bitterly when Roger then declined their claim as a consequence.

He would receive three or four alerts a week but he always checked them. They might reveal information or a pattern of theft – all helpful for those setting premiums and considering security issues.

Roger opened the first alert and forced a smile.

*Armed robbery – Museo de Arte Miani, Milan – Theft Paul Gauguin – Tahitian Princess.*

As though he needed reminding Roger opened the attachment and noted the attractive nude painting that was causing his boss such angst.

Roger clicked on the second alert. He stared at the screen, incredulous.

*Theft – Paul Gauguin – Tahitian Princess – Lucca Italy.*

Roger opened up the attached photo and was amazed to see the same Tahitian nude staring at him. *What the...?*

Roger checked the dates. Only a day's difference between them. Lucca first, Milan second. Before Roger had a chance to explore further, he heard a coarse cry from down the corridor.

"Roger...!" It was time to face the music as director Charles Bradley bellowed down the corridor.

Roger raised his bottom a few inches off his chair, in part to avoid pressure sores but also to prepare for the onslaught, lowered himself again and readjusted his tie. He took a deep breath and wheeled as confidently as he could muster up the corridor. The directors' door was shut; always a bad sign.

Bradley fired the first question before Roger could close the door;

"How has Stets taken the news?"

"A mixed reaction I'd say; anger on the one hand and rage on the other."

"Yes, rather you than me on that one. Any ransom appeal yet? They'll never be able to sell it openly, of course, so better to take a few hundred thousand off us and save us good money in the process."

"No, nothing as at last night but I do have a lead I want to follow up on."

Roger proceeded to relay the apparently coincidental notifications received of the theft of the Gauguin within days. After a brief review of the position,

Bradley needed little convincing;

"Get out to Tuscany and follow it up, Roger. There's too much at stake here not to explore further."

# CHAPTER THIRTY-SIX

Roger returned to his desk. He would make the journey tomorrow. He would need assistance from the Milan office. He knew exactly who to call – Pina Venti.

Having checked her direct dial on the internal data base, he waited only two rings before hearing her familiar voice:

"Buongiorno – Pina Venti."

"Buongiorno Pina. Sua Roger Kirtley. Come va?"

"Rogerrr," she enthused.

"Si, sto bene. E tu?

"Bene. Bene. Listen Pina, no you've followed the Gauguin robbery?"

"Roger, yes! I knew London were handling it, but you've got the case have you?"

"Never mind the case Pina – I was there."

"Oh, no…"

"No worry, I'm fine. Nothing a stiff brandy didn't help solve. I do though need your help on the case…"

Pina had been seconded to London three years back and had worked in Rogers's department for six months. On a strict interpretation of HR protocol, he had been her line manager but he had preferred to be seen by her as more of a mentor or a work buddy at least. They had then collaborated on several exhibitions together, reviewing itineraries, cross referencing valuations. It was Roger's role to negotiate the premiums off the back of Pina's valuations.

There had never been anything romantic between them; Pina was a decade younger, not a bar to a relationship but they had different interests. She preferred to be in the outdoors defying gravity as a climber, whilst Roger was more comfortable at home in his lounge quaffing a glass or two of Barolo. They had flirted somewhat in the early hours at a PNP conference in Zurich a couple of years back, but it was just that, flirting without intent. That said they were comfortable in each other's company and both delighted to be working together again.

Roger had been impressed with his *Air Italia* flight. He had been allowed to board his flight ahead of schedule; The lift up to the front door of the plane had been there on time and worked too – not something he took for granted these days having actually been forced to miss two flights in the last twelve months due to what the airlines called 'operational difficulties.' He did not need to wait long for his chair to appear at the other end either. He hoped that his previous record wait of an hour and a half after landing would remain unbeaten for a good while yet. As Roger had made his way past customs control at Pisa airport the arrivals doors opened automatically and he tried to spot Pina among the throng of taxi drivers holding up name boards and travel agents, in more flamboyant dress, seeking to greet their clients. His low eye line made the task more challenging. He surveyed the line a second time. *There she is.*

Pina was diminutive but he had picked out the top of her head and waving hand.

They greeted as old friends with a hug and two kisses to the cheek.

They queued up at the Hertz rental booth before collecting a take away coffee from *Costa* and heading out to *Car Park 2* where there Fiat waited. Pina knew better than to offer Roger help. He appreciated her sensitivity, smiled and sought her help to load his chair into the rear of the Fiat, Her job was then to drive whilst Roger took responsibility for the sat nav.

The hardest part of the journey would be exiting the complex airport network but they were soon on their way travelling north from the terminal building towards Lucca. It was a short drive but time enough to catch up and discuss the case.

"How's your man – James, isn't it?"

"Yes, Jimmy. It's all over Roger, I'm afraid."

"No way, Pina, last time we spoke you had just got back from a climbing trip to the Alps and were madly in love."

"Yes…it was the Dolomites actually and I was in love, as you say – still am really."

"Ouch," said Roger, not sure that he wanted to probe further.

"No, it okay now – I'm over the worst of it," she said, reaching out unsuccessfully to the plastic dashboard to try and touch something wooden for good luck. Pina was relieved to be able to talk about it openly without her family saying that *time would heal*; *there were plenty of fish in the ocean* or worst of all that *she was better off without him.*

"We had come to crunch time really. There was no *let's settle down and have babies'* ultimatum but I wanted more structure to our relationship. He just wanted to climb mountains and have me at his side, or more accurately, five metres below on a rope and belay. He said that he respected my desire to develop my career but would then ask me to join him for a six-week trip to South America to climb Mount Illimani. His idea of romance was sharing a rock face tent half way up a sheer drop!"

"It brings a whole new meaning to the mile-high club, Pina."

"And some," said Pina, blushing just a tad. "It came to a head this summer when he told me that he wanted a crack at Everest and that the Nepalese had granted him a licence to do so. I knew that it was a dream of his but not that it was becoming a reality. I had no idea he'd even applied for a permit to climb it. Needless to say, all of his miserable savings had gone on the venture. *I could join him at base camp.* His very words. Love springs eternal."

"You can't stand between a man and his dreams, Pina."

"It wasn't the dreams that troubled me." She smiled. "We quarrelled then of course. He said that I wanted to turn him into a *boring leisure centre wall climber* and I accused him of needing to grow up and take some responsibility. It got out of hand and I just walked out of our tent at the foot of Mont Blanc where we were having a weekend away and just left him to it. Roger, I love the thrill of climbing but for me it's a sport, for him it's a religion."

"Where is he now then?"

"Trekking to base camp can you believe?"

"Good man – may be when Everest is conquered you can get back together."

"You sound like Jimmy! It's an addiction, Roger. After

Everest, it will be K2 or The West Face without oxygen or without ropes or whatever but definitely without *me*." Pina signed off defiantly by slapping her palm on the steering wheel.

"Oops. I got carried away there for a minute. Now that's off my chest, tell me about our assignment before I smash the car up further."

Roger relayed his story to Pina who was quickly distracted from her former boyfriend's aspirations. She winced as he told of the gun firing in the gallery and looked at him with incredulity at the theft notification alerts that had subsequently been received.

"That just cannot be a coincidence Roger. No way."

"We should soon find out but it's curious if nothing else, I'll give you that."

The traffic into Lucca flowed freely but the town's one way system through the sat nav off course. After two loops of Lucca's narrow roads, Pina and Roger parked up and decided to find the antiques shop on foot. The street cobbles would play havoc with the wheels on his light weight *Quickie* wheelchair but they had time on their hands. By the time they had alighted from the hired Fiat, they had caught the attention of two men enjoying their pre-siesta drinks outside of an adjoining café. Pina strolled over to them and engaged willingly, seeking directions. Roger could see that they were inviting them, or upon reflection, Pina at least, to join them for a tipple. She reached forward playfully to pick up a full glass of beer but then tapped her watch with an exaggerated look of disappointment. The men smiled – they saw few strangers and none as engaging as Pina. She waved before pointing to an immediate left-hand turn which received nods of approval from the elder statesmen.

A sharp right turn twenty metres up the narrowing cobbled street lead them to Via San Filippo. The antique shop was easy to spot, even from sixty metres away. Leaning against the window of the shop were an array of items:

Two gilded frame mirrors; one unframed painting and a French bedside cabinet. The items were discreetly secured. There were no lights on in the shop and given that it was in shadow, it was difficult to tell whether the shop was open or not. Roger thought that the *open* sign pinned to the door gave little indication of the shops actual status. He doubted it was ever turned over to *closed*. The door lock was out of keeping with the old heavy panelled door – Chub locks were not around in the early 19th Century. Roger assumed that this reflected a security upgrade further to the break in. Signor Marconi was aware that they would be visiting that morning but that didn't guarantee his presence.

As Pina turned the brass handle, she was surprised that it yielded readily, opening the door. The bell above the door frame signalled their arrival. The shop was full to the brim of items for sale. Though Roger was no antiquities expert, she could see that the range of items offered covered several centuries, numerous countries and a variety of collector themes: stamps, butterflies, furniture and for the connoisseur, even a stuffed fox and moose head. Roger followed behind negotiating the entrance lip with ease but realising that his movements within the shop would be limited, *bull in china shop,* sprang to mind.

The background music was easy to recognise – Vivaldi's 7th concerto – a relaxing melody for what Roger suspected were long periods without customers or client, as the antiques business preferred to call them.

"Signor Marconi?! Buongiorno Signore!" called Pina

from the front of the shop. From down a narrow corridor, even deeper into the shadows, appeared a large silhouette, transforming into human form, as the proprietor appeared, with a smile on his chubby, ruddy face.

The overdressed theme set by the town's elders continued, for Signor Marconi's thick cotton shirt was supplemented by a tweed waist coat complete with red polka dot hanky (for show, not blow). It vaguely matched the small red rose bud attached to the waistcoat button hole.

*Wow*, thought Roger, *those corduroy trousers must be warm*, even if the 1950s ornate, overhead fan offered some relief. Roger himself was sweltering in his lightweight safari suit – it may crumple easily but was both agelessly stylish and versatile when travelling. Pina still looked ice cool. Her dress was crease free; a royal blue and white pattern with matching jacket – stylish and professional (even by Milan standards);

"Ah… Signor Kirtley and Signora Venti" Signor Marconi took a second look at Roger but was unperturbed.

"Signor Marconi, pleased to meet you," said Roger, handing over his business card out of courtesy rather than for authentication.

"Alberto, per favore," said the antiques dealer, giving the card a cursory glance. I'm surprised that you have come to see me in person. The local Carabinieri didn't seem to care less. Does this mean that the painting is or should I say *was* worth something, as I had suspected? I'd sent the details to an expert in to take a look…a professor no less, Brinsden, specialises in post impressionism. He sounded quite interested at first but I have not heard from him for a few days."

"Peter Brinsden? Based at Cambridge University? Fine chap," Roger said.

"That's the one Roger. My, what a small world it is."

"As for the painting, to be honest we are not sure. The odds of it actually being a Gauguin look remote but it will make a big difference to any insurance pay out."

"Gosh, I hadn't thought of that...will I be covered?"

"If you've got forty million Euro of cover you will be fine," Pina intervened.

"Roger, stop teasing Alberto. He's teasing you. We think that it's probably a good quality painting as you had discerned, but not a masterpiece."

"I never thought that I would be pleased to hear that," reported a relieved Alberto.

Roger looked up and noticed, with disappointment, the damaged CCTV monitor half dangling from the far-right hand corner wall.

Signor Marconi also looked up at the smashed camera and laughed. "Come, come," he said, pointing to his desk. He reached into the pencil pot and pulled out a chunky pen whilst holding up two fingers to his eyes and then directing them at both Roger and Pina. As Roger followed the proprietor, he crashed into a stuffed gazelle which wobbled but it and Roger readily regained their composure.

"Hidden camera," pronounced Alberto with pride, "a gift from my nephew, he love his gadgets. The pen's camera has an in built motion sensor apparently. Whatever next?" Alberto walked back down the narrow corridor from where he had appeared minutes earlier and the pair followed. In front of them was a fine French drawing table complete with metal clad claw feet, green leather inlay and ink well.

The computer screen looked out of place on its 18th century base. Signor Marconi pulled the attached key board towards him and with heavy handed use of his index finger was soon able to pull up on screen a grainy picture but nonetheless one that was clearly a video shot of the shop. Roger noted the date and time on the bottom right hand corner of the image – *1 .30 am, 25th May 2017* – burglary day.

Another firm hit on the keypad and the recording was running – the image was clearer in motion but given the recording was made on an inexpensive piece of equipment, the quality was always going to lack crispness. There was no audio and for ten seconds or so nothing changed on screen.

Then from the front of the shop appeared two men. Neither were facing the camera. As the taller of the men waited the other appeared to be rummaging around the shop. He would disappear from camera shot and then reappear. The visual quality remained sub optimal but the bulkier of the two burglars could clearly be seen showing a painting to the other and then exiting at the top of the screen. This time the other man followed and there was a further period without action.

"I had the painting out the back here so that I could take a good look at it. They will be back in a moment." Sure enough, within seconds the men had returned. This time the taller man is carrying a painting. As he came into vision, facing the camera, Roger leant forward to examine the screen.

"Surely not – pause it, Alberto. Pause it!"

"Roger?" enquired Pina without attracting his attention.

Alberto fumbled with the key board.

"Hold on, I'll have to rewind a tad."

Having done so, he froze the screen.

"Braithwaite, no less!"

"You know him?!" enquired Pina and Alberto in tandem.

"Indeed I do – Dr. Marcus Braithwaite. Art expert."

"Are you sure, Roger?" asked Pina, noticing that Roger was putting his face closer to the screen.

"I'm sure alright – pretty sure, anyway. Play it on further Alberto, per favore."

Alberto complied. *Braithwaite*'s frozen body galvanised and he angled the painting as though to get a better look in the dim light coming from the outside street lights. The squat set burglar joined him and then there was a ray of bright light on the painting, coming from the torch being directed on to the canvas by the accomplice. The glimpse of the painting itself would not have been clear enough to have identified it without prior knowledge but the grained black and white of the naked Tahitian was discernible for all three to see. Seconds later the men had left the line of CCTV sight and presumably escaped from the shop with *Gauguin* in hand.

"Shouldn't we ring the police straight away Roger, given that you can identify this Braithwaite chap?" asked Alberto, reaching over his desk to grab the telephone receiver. Roger was a tad hesitant and had realised that the naming of Braithwaite may not have been the wisest move at this stage given his concerns as to the different focus of the police and PNP.

"Leave that to me, Albert. I will be liaising with them later."

Pina picked up on Roger's reservations and joined in.

"Yes, I will do a full report for the police. This information should help a lot."

"Tell me more about the chap who tried to sell you the painting Alberto."

"Ah, yes, Luigi Bellini. I couldn't imagine a more unlikely owner of a decent piece of art to be honest. That's not to say that he was crooked or anything but awkward, nervous and out of his comfort zone. He told me that he, or as he emphasised, his wife, had inherited the painting from her auntie.

Who's to say that the aunt was not just a discerning lady, perhaps with a few lira behind her? Unlikely but possible?"

"You have his details?" asked Pina.

"I do. He was a bit reluctant at first…" Alberto opened the desk draw and rummaged around.

"Here we go. I don't know the village but less an hour north of here. He doesn't know that his painting has been stolen yet. I couldn't bring myself to tell him yet. He was suspicious of my motives in the first place – he will just assume that I have stolen it. When you said that you were coming, I thought that I would wat and see what you had to say. Does the insurance cover the damage to the door locks too?"

"There is an excess I'm afraid, Alberto, but given that you have been so helpful I'm sure that we can get that paid for you. Send me an email with the details."

# CHAPTER THIRTY-SEVEN

The satnav would be of less use for the second leg of the journey but the aircon would be essential as the temperature continued to rise. The trip to Luigi's house would take less than an hour, passing through more rugged countryside. The roads were less well maintained, unlike the intermittent roadside shrines to Our Lady, which all appeared to have fresh flowers and candles, even though there seemed to be no human inhabitants for miles around. Pina regretted not filling up with fuel earlier as the only garage on route looked firmly closed for siesta, beyond a yapping dog in the forecourt who commanded respect from visitors more for its enthusiasm of voice than its actual size. That said assuming no more detours they should have enough fuel to get them back to the outskirts of Pisa.

The entrance to the town of Balzello was marked by an old sign hanging loosely from a wonky metal post. It offered no warm greeting to visitor.

There appeared to be only one road into the centre of the town thereby reducing the chances of getting a lost. The first house they passed remained unfinished, with rusting metal work extending into the space intended for the first story bedrooms. Though incomplete, the house was seemingly still being lived in, given the eclectic array of washing hanging on the makeshift washing line and the obligatory yapping dog.

The satnav signalled that they had arrived at their destination; it looked a most unlikely venue – a corn field at least four hundred metres from any dwelling. They drove on a further half a mile before entering a small village square. There then came the first sighting of locals; three elderly men seated outside of Giovanni's bar and cafe. The men looked overdressed for the ambient 24 degrees and were afforded little shelter from the crooked table umbrella – on the metal table was a mix of beers and smaller glasses –pastiche perhaps, thought Roger. Having spotted what appeared to be the town's car park immediately adjacent, Roger pointed it out to Pina. Though there was no official parking sign, there were a number of battered Fiats parked, few within the designated white lines. They were clearly not expecting a rush of visitors.

Roger left it to Pina to apply her magic as he remained in the car. Roger saw a shaking of heads, a false trail perhaps. Pina returned to the car.

"No luck, I'm afraid – but they are lying I'm sure – there are probably only two hundred inhabitants in this village, including pets but they say they don't know them – it's the sign of a close knit community, I reckon."

"Well, we do rather look like lawyers or bailiffs even, so you could be right."

"Speak for yourself, Roger. Either way, they are being protective."

Pina thrust her Dior bag onto Roger's lap. "Here, hold this a minute." Roger thought that the bag was a tad like the TARDUS, as she rummaged deep inside. First to appear were the flat shoes which quickly replaced the patent black high heels that were a badge of honour back in Madrid. Having removed, with considerable dexterity, two hair clips, her rich brown hair fell to partly cover her cheeks. The scarf that had attractively decorated her neck was unfurled and flung over her head. Pina looked more set to attend church than interrogate a witness. Roger just watched with bemusement. The final act was to produce a white perfectly folded cotton handkerchief and apply it with precision to the red Chanel lipstick. "There," she declared. "I'm a local."

"An upmarket one maybe," said Roger.

"Find me another group of old men supping beer, please."

It was clear that these small Italian villages had a disproportionate number of bars to residents and the population was an aging one at that. On that basis Roger sighted the next drinking hole, resplendent with obligatory coca cola umbrella, all but two hundred metres further up the cobbled and bumpy road – *Bellinis*. With a final wipe of the lips, Pina winked at Roger, who was still grinning and set off up the road far steadier in her flats – She had more of a challenge this time as there was no one outside to disturb. With a discrete wave in Rogers's direction, Pina disappeared inside Bellinis. There was little time for Roger to enjoy the solitude, for Pina reappeared in under a minute punching the air in the manner in which tennis pros celebrate most winning shots. *She has done it,* reflected Roger.

"Clever girl," he exclaimed, as she opened the car door triumphantly, already removing her head scarf.

"He's a regular apparently and we were unlucky not to find him enjoying a cool larger. It's a short drive away. Sounds impossible to miss: a pink house at the top of the hill with a battered white Nissan truck parked outside. Let's go, Roger," she told him as he taken over the driver's spot.

"I'll put my war paint back on," enthused Pina, waving her Chanel lipstick.

The house was as described, *pink*, as was the truck, *battered*. It was unclear as to which was the front and which the rear door, for each small adjoining strip of garden looked equally unkempt, each with rusting metal work adorning what might once have been a lawn. Their guessing was assisted by the arrival of a docile mongrel dog from one of the doors. With mangy skin but affectionate tail wagging, this was no killer and Roger greeted it with a cautious pat on the head, more concerned about germs than being bitten. Dogs and wheelchairs are not always compatible and Roger had several tails of either being pounced upon or used as, shall we say, a replacement tree or lamp post. The patting gesture was fortunately appreciated by *Bendi*, as his collared tag revealed. The name tag looked to be a gratuitous gesture, as this did not look like a dog that was either going to escape, let alone be stolen for profitable breeding!

Counterintuitively perhaps, Roger and Pina assumed that the dog would have come from the back door and therefore having put the chair back together for what felt like the hundredth time today they preceded to what they assumed was the front of house; either way, both doors were wide open. There was no knocker, no bell either.

Pina peered into the darkness of the entrance and stumbled as she stepped forward, first on the shiny, uneven tiled floor and then by standing on poor Bendi's paw, whose yelp acted as a notification to the Bartellis of activity in the hall way.

"Bendi, shut up you mutt!"

Pina took over, having regained her balance. "Signore, pardon Signore, I did not mean to startle you."

That said, startle she had, as a portly man, recumbent in string vest with baggy trousers hanging below his belly and in need of the braces that hung from his ample waistline to knees. Luigi's surprise turned to Suspicion and aggression – they were not used to visitors, especially those who were unknown to them let alone uninvited.

"Who are you? What do you want?"

"Forgive me," repeated Pina, herself a tad ruffled by his assertiveness.

"We have come about the painting. Did Alberto manage to get hold of you earlier?"

Reference to Alberto and the painting brought a smile to his face. It was as though a 'be friendly' switch had been thrown and Signor Bartelli instantly changed from being aggressive to adopting a far more friendly approach.

"No, forgive me," he pleaded, offering out a sweaty palm to Pina. He nodded towards Roger uncomfortably for he had never known anyone in a wheelchair before and would have preferred to have kept it that way. Pina hoped too that he had not seen her subsequently wipe her hand on the side of her bag. "I have been expecting you." He turned inside for a moment. "Bella! Bella! It's the painting people. Come through and forgive the mess we have been decorating."

There was no sign of paint or brush and Pina suspected that the chaos of papers, cups, cushions and general toot was the norm.

Bella was desperately trying to multitask, removing her cooking pinnie whilst adjusting her hair in an attempt to look respectable for their important guests. Though the apron was whipped off easily the resulting spread of baking flour across Bella's fringe would have disappointed her had she looked in the mirror.

"Come into the kitchen, per favour. Bella will make us coffee."

Bella lead the way into the open plan kitchen whose main feature was a large rustic oak table, as thick as a butcher's cutting block and as well used. The oven was on, though the cake tin on the side had yet to be placed in it. Flour and the remnants of the current and almond mix adorned one end of the table.

"Forgive me," said Bella trying to clear away the baking mix.

"Not at all, Signora Bellini. We should have given you more notice," offered Pina.

Roger was the last to enter the kitchen. Bella looked at him sympathetically, with that, *you poor man* look. Roger halted abruptly when he saw it. He was oblivious to Bella's enquiry as to how he liked his coffee.

There hanging crookedly above the wood burner was a Cezanne. A stunning landscape.

"May I?" enquired Roger as he approached canvas.

"Ah, you like the Da Vinci? It's Bella's favourite isn't it, Bella?"

Bella mumbled indifferently.

"Is this another from your aunt's collection?"

"Aunt?" repeated a confused Luigi.

"Yes, I thought Alberto told us that you had inherited some paintings from your aunt. Isn't that right, Pina?"

Luigi hesitated and Roger noticed.

"Err...Yes, I did say that they had belonged to Bella's auntie. I didn't want to say that I had bought them in the local market. Alberto seems a decent man but if he thought that I had bought them for just a few euro he wouldn't offer me a good price." Luigi glanced across at Bella. He was relieved to notice that he answer had satisfied her.

Roger continued his inspection. Though lacking the academic qualifications of an expert, he had over the years had the privilege and indeed on occasions, professional duty, to see some of Cezanne's work at close quarters. The brush work was distinct the colours vibrant. Roger could not but laugh to himself.

*I thinks it's the real thing. And that means that the Gauguin is likely to be too!*

"You can buy that one too if you like," quipped Luigi with a chuckle.

"Do you mind, Luigi? Remember, that was my present."

"Yes, but think what you would be able to buy with... shall we say, five hundred euro?"

It was time for Roger to chuckle too.

"At five hundred euro that could be a bargain, a real bargain..." Roger's voice tailed off as he straightened up the $40 million painting on the wall.

Having noticed Roger's intense interest in the kitchen painting, she came over to join him. She leant forward to inspect the intricate paint work then stood back to take a broader view. She looked at Roger. Neither spoke. They didn't need to. Pina shook her head almost imperceptibly in disbelief, looking to Roger for reinforcement. He smiled and then raised his eyebrows.

"Signore, per favore," encouraged Bella, as she poured the coffee into the eclectic mix of mugs.

Up until now, Luigi had paid no attention to the business card that Pina had given to him upon her arrival.

He picked it up from the kitchen table and wiped it on his vest to remove the coffee that had splashed from his overfilled cup.

"Hey, it says here that you work for PNP Insurance not from an art gallery as Alberto told me."

Roger angled his chair in toward the table, noisy banging his knee against the bench as his did so. Bella winced but then realised that he felt no pain. He took a quick sip of the coffee.

"Bella, let me explain. It is true that we are from PNP insurers. We have got involved because Alberto's antiques shop has been burgled and your painting has been stolen. Hence, we are involved."

Luigi was unsettled by the news and as Alberto had anticipated, was immediately suspicious. He stood up from the bench.

"Bella, I don't like the sound of that one little bit. It all sounds far too much of a coincidence to me." *Never a truer word,* thought Roger.

"Now that is the bad news, but here is some good news," continued Pina. Roger looked at her intrigued as to how the conversation would evolve.

"Given that the painting is insured, you will be entitled to be paid for your loss. The reason for our visit is to try and get a bit more information from you about where you brought the painting. This second painting will help us a lot to because again, it does look to be of good quality. If we can prove that the… err …Da Vinci scene has been copied by a good artist then Alberto's piece will go up in price too."

"I see," said Luigi with a little more enthusiasm. "He won't want his £150 back, will he?"

"You're safe on that front Signor Bellini," reassured Roger, much to Bella's satisfaction.

As they paused briefly to drink more coffee, Roger's phone rang.

"Do you mind if I take this as I'm expecting a phone call from head office?"

"Per favore, Signore."


Roger deftly rolled backwards towards the kitchen entrance and answered. "Si, Roger…Ah Alberto. We are with Signore and Signora Bellini now."

"Oh, good. I'm glad you found them. How are they about the burglary?"

"I've just been explaining to them now."

"I understand. I suppose you can't speak too freely."

"That's right, Alberto. But how can I help?"

"Sorry, I'll get to the point."

"Your two colleagues have just left the shop," Roger interrupted.

"Colleagues, you say?"

"Yes, not as well dressed as you mind. Must be from the local office, perhaps." Roger turned to his hosts, pointed to the phone and exited into the hallway.

"Did they give their names?"

"Now that you mention it, they didn't. They said that they had run out of business cards. That said they will be with you shortly. I've given them Signor Bellini's address. They said that they would call you on route anyway. The reason for calling was that I gave them a memory stick to give to you of the *spy camera* footage but I'm not sure it downloaded properly, as my computer is showing a fault. I just wanted to let you know."

"Alberto, thanks for letting me know. Exactly how long ago did they leave?"

"Ten minutes? Call it fifteen."

"I must go Alberto. Grazie."

Roger paused, gathering himself. He saw that he had received a text message and opened it. *No way. No fucking way.*

Roger popped his head around the door.

"Pina, can I steal you away for a minute?" His calm tone bellied the turmoil he was experiencing.

Pina joined him in the corridor. She could see from the angst look on his face that this was not good news. Roger relayed Alberto's message in a whisper.

"*Is* there anyone else on the case?" asked Pina a tad naively.

"No, there isn't; if only. We are in trouble here, serious trouble. Take a look at this."

Roger offered up his mobile screen for Pina to read the text from Roger's assistant back in London.

Pina shivered.

*Roger just to let you know that I have tried to get hold of Professor Brinsden as you asked. Sorry to say that he was found dead at home yesterday. The family wouldn't say too much but it sounds like suicide. Best, David.*

Pina held on to Roger's shoulder for emotional support. Roger was right; they were in deep trouble.

"Pina, I don't like this one little bit. We need to get out of here and take them with us," said Roger pointing in the direction of the kitchen.

"What are we to tell them? Come with us you are about to be murdered? They will never believe us will they? We should just call the police."

"We will but we have no more than thirty minutes before *whoever they are* arrive – The nearest police HQ could be an hour away. Let's get them out first and then call the police."

"But how?"

"I've got an idea? Follow me."

They both returned to the kitchen where Luigi and Bella anxiously awaited them, having picked up on the tone of the earlier call and having noted a hint of urgency in Roger's voice. Roger pretended that he was still on the phone.

"…Yes, they are standing in front of me. I can see the other painting from here – a lovely piece. It reminds them of a Da Vinci…" He paused as if listening. "…I know of him. A renowned expert. He'd take a look for us? Oh good! If he assesses the painting, could we would pay out straight away?" He paused again. ".Up to what amount?" Roger nodded an acknowledgement to his imaginary caller. "…anything up to ten thousand Euro, you say." He noted, with relief, the glee on the Bellinis faces.

"The Grand hotel in Pisa? When?…Today?" Roger checked his watch and pulled a face. "That doesn't leave us too much time, albeit we could be with you in the hour, but I don't know what Signor and Signora Bellini's commitments are today."

Roger pulled the phone away from his ear and engaged with Luigi and Bella.

"Sorry about this but our head office have approved the obtaining of a valuation from an art expert who happens to be in Pisa today but need to leave the hotel shortly to catch a flight."

Bella and Luigi nodded eagerly at each other and Luigi gave Roger the thumbs up. Rather gratuitously, so did Pina, suitably impressed by Roger's successful strategy.

"Great. We are good to go. Tell Professor Brinsden that we will be at the *Grand* in just over the hour." Roger regretted referring to the recently deceased academic even if reference to *the professor* certainly impressed the Bellinis.

"Is it okay to take the Da Vinci off the wall? It will be critical for the expert to examine it," Roger said.

"Be my guest, Signore Roger," said Luigi still beaming.

Roger checked his watch again. "Time to go I'm afraid. We can't keep the professor waiting."

"Goodness," cried Bella. "Give me cinque minuti per favore."

"Cinque minuti only, Bella."

"But I haven't even had my hair done."

"Vite Bella! Vite!" called Luigi only to be enveloped by a flour covered apron that Bella had flung at him. The couple adjourned to an adjoining room where Roger could just make out the outline of an unmade bed in the shadows created by the darkness from the curtains that remained undrawn.

"I will call our colleagues and tell them you are coming," called out Pina as she gestured to Roger to join her outside.

"I will call the police now but getting them to take the position seriously let alone quickly will be difficult. What will we do with the Bellinis once we arrive at the Grand?"

"We will tell them that the professor has been delayed and just book them into the hotel on the company account."

Pina and Roger waited in the kitchen and became increasingly anxious as the minutes ticked by. Their estimate was that their *colleagues* were 30 minutes away but that was the problem, based on Alberto's timings, it was just that—an estimate.

After what appeared to be an eternity, both Bella and Luigi appeared through the bedroom, fighting each other to get through the door first. There was no prospect of both fitting for sure. Bella was still complaining that she had not been to the hairdressers albeit she had scrubbed up well for a seven minute make over. She literally wore her Sunday best. The effort made by Luigi was less easy to discern, though the hanging braces had found their way on to his broad shoulders; his vest was still on show through his widely opened and creased white shirt. Had Luigi been a church goer, this would have represented his best effort, thought Roger as he glanced at Pina, who again anxiously checked her watch and encouraged the couple out the front door.

Roger handed Pina the painting that had been resting across arm rests of his chair frame.

"Pina, you go ahead as agreed," said Roger, out of the blue. "I will return to Lucca to discuss the results with Signor Bartelli."

"What are you talking about?" enquired a bewildered looking Pina. She did not wait for an answer. Roger could see from the expression on her face that she had realised what he really meant—that he was going to stay and see who turned up. Pina took hold of his arm and led him further down the corridor, trying to get out of ear shot of the Bellinis.

"No, Roger! Absolutely, no!"

Pina saw the curiosity on the faces of both Bella and Luigi and rather than spook them with her alarm, she smiled at them and spoke to Roger in a casual relaxed tone, disguising her underlying angst. She would make a good actor, thought Roger.

With a fake smile, she continued, "Roger, I know exactly what you are looking to do. Lie in wait for them and try and get identification details" She tossed her head back and laughed as though socially engaged at a cocktail party.

"It's ridiculous and dangerous – I won't have it – leave it to the police to do their job…please, please, Roger." She was about to point out the obvious, that he was paralysed from the waist down and in a wheelchair – she thought better of it, but still thought it.

Roger attempted to replicate Pina's skilled dramatics but was far less convincing.

"Go Pina. I will hide and just try and get another piece of the jigsaw puzzle. I'm no hero, believe me. They wouldn't harm a cripple would day?" he said with heavy irony.

The sound of a vehicle making its way up the hill caused Pina to focus again on the Bellinis who were now waiting outside expectantly.

"Go and go now!" demanded Roger, gesturing to direct her. The speeding car was nearly on top of them and instinctively Pina moved to the front door pointing to the rental car. The approaching vehicle passed the house at pace, though with no menace, a local returning from a day's work at the nearby vineyard. Although the immediate threat of danger had subsided, Pina did not seek to argue further and with a click of her smart key, the car unlocked and she opened the rear door to encourage her guests to enter, before placing the Cezanne carefully in the boot. She explained briefly that Roger was being picked up in order to go back to Lucca and that they would drop him off at the tavern on the way. The Bellinis thought nothing of it; their focus was very much elsewhere. Roger waved them off with a friendly, *Ciao*. Roger had wanted to hug Pina, as much to alleviate his own anxiety as to support her but it would have looked highly unprofessional.

# CHAPTER THIRTY-EIGHT

Roger quickly looked to find cover, fearful that his *colleagues* could arrive at any moment. He certainly didn't want to actually meet them. He saw his mission as strictly information gathering, not one of confrontation. He considered the view afforded from over the road; no, it would be restricted. *But that could do the trick,* he concluded, as he eyed Luigi's battered *Fiat Ducato.* Steering around the garden clutter, he reached the truck door. Sure enough, the door was open. The transfer would be harder than normal because of the extra height of the seats but Roger had worked hard on his upper body strength and this would aid the task. His first attempt failed, as his backside hit the side of the seat and caused him to rebound awkwardly back into the chair. Like a motivated high jumper, he arched his back as he launched himself upwards; success. Stretching down, he removed each of the wheels and placed them in the front passenger seat well. He would need to get out of view and levered the seat back as far as go before sliding into the seat well. His thin, powerless and flexible legs were, for once, an advantage. He took out his mobile phone, pressed the *Camera* button and took a short test video clip.

Roger slid down even deeper into the seat as a vehicle passed. Roger could see that it was a red Fiat. He couldn't see the occupants. This could be a false alarm but unlike the earlier vehicle that had passed, the speed was significantly reduced. Had he been able to lower the van window, he would have heard the vehicle making a U turn back to the house.

There were two men. Roger could see that both were casually dressed and rather too well built for his liking. He suspected one of the visitors resembled the antique shop burglar but he hadn't been able to see clearly enough. Roger was relying more on his mobile phone to video their arrival, than he was his eyes. It was far safer to extend the top of his IPhone 8 than peek out from his position of hiding.

Roger heard the banging of doors. He quickly popped his head over the van door parapet and saw one of the men walking around to what Roger and Pina had discerned to be the back door. Further knocking ensued. Following a short interlude, it must have been apparent that the Bellinis were absent. Roger was hoping that they would now depart without fuss. He'd have his video evidence to include a licence plate number and his bones intact.

There was a brief exchange between the men:

"Let's get inside."

"Can you climb in through the window?"

"No way, Carlos!"

*Carlos!*

The sound of the door being kicked in was noisy but no one, bar Roger and the two men, could be disturbed by it. Each blow to the door brought with it a slightly different sound, a blunt harmony changing tone as the lock began to yield. Then suddenly the music stopped as the wood of the door and metal of the lock adhered to the laws of physics.

There followed a period of silence outside. Roger could hardly describe it as tranquil, as he feared that his pounding heart sounded like a base drum. He was reluctant to look further, for when the men exited they would, for the first time, be looking directly at the van. He slid even deeper into the seat sliding like a flexible hose pipe into position, save that Rogers suppleness was severely challenged. After all, his private yoga sessions last year had lasted only a month, another fitness fad falling at an early hurdle.

The next sound that Roger heard petrified him. It was not that the sound itself that was inherently frightening, indeed, under different circumstances, it might have been quite endearing. However, the sound of an enthusiastically barking dog with front paws scratching at the side of his passenger door brought with it dread. Rogers's instinct was to sink even lower into the seat but he was already as low as physically possible. He had earlier dismissed the prospect of the men wanting to look into in the van as they were looking for people not objects, hence his choice of viewing gallery. But overt attention was being drawn to his hideout and he wished without malice that Bendi had bitten the intruders, as a good guard dog would have done, even if he had then suffered the ultimate penalty. The scratching didn't abate. *I can't exactly start the engine and drive off, can I?* The Motability scheme hadn't extended to trucks just yet. Nothing to do but try and slip even further into the seat well and pray that Bendi would take more interest in the intruders. The tapping on the car door window bore no resemblance to the earlier canine activity. It was human in form. Roger went rigid with his eyes squeezed tightly shut as though to throw an invisible blanket over himself. Roger felt paralysed in more ways than one as the passenger door flung open. *Why? Oh why hadn't I bothered to lock the cab doors?!*

Roger was disturbed from his catatonic state, by Bendi, as the dog scrambled up into the van and on to Roger's torso. *Man's best friend indeed.* Roger opened his eyes at the sound of laughter of the mocking kind. There was Carlos with pistol in hand. He said nothing at first but reached in and picked up Bendi with his spare hand. He was almost affectionate. Carlos was less caring with Roger, grabbing him by his collar and robustly extracting him from the cab and on to the ground.

"Get up," demanded Carlos waving his pistol.

"I can't," replied Roger, using his arm to straighten out his tangled legs.

"I said get up. Do it now or I'll shoot you in the leg and you won't be able to walk."

"Look in the truck. You'll see my wheelchair. I'm paralysed from the waist down."

Carlos looked at his colleague rather bewildered but gestured for him to explore the truck. Within seconds, his companion had plucked the frame together with a wheel and held them high. Both men laughed.

"They leave half a man to do a whole man's job," taunted Carlos. Roger had heard much worse and didn't react.

"Now I see why you are taking this lying down, my friend." It was the best that Carlos could muster but it was enough for his underling to guffaw approvingly.

"Sling the freak into the car."

"What about his chair?"

"He won't be needing that again…"

# CHAPTER THIRTY-NINE

This was not the first time that Roger had gained consciousness since he had been struck on the head by the butt of the pistol and bundled into the car. That said, he recalled little of the car journey thus far save that it was a bumpy, hot and uncomfortable one. He was unable to move in the rear of the car not because he was tied up but because the feet of one of the assailant's pressed heavily upon his torso and his head continued to spin. He felt dizzy and nauseous, in need of paracetamol.

Roger attempted to engage with his captives:

"What's the fuck's going on here? What do you want with me? I demand that you let me free." It wasn't quite *don't you know who I am?* But Roger thought that he sounded equally pathetic. His questions remained unanswered and his request for freedom unmet.

"Shut up!" was the height of engagement.

The captives did interact briefly with each other but only to provide directions. Nothing could be learnt about identity nor motive. The larger of the two captives temporarily released pressure on Roger's torso in order to better access his mobile phone from his rear pocket. This short respite enabled Roger to twist slightly catching a glimpse of his assailant – chubby cheeks with oily skin and a growth of stubble: Carlos. He was relieved to be able to free his nose from the dirty rubber foot mats in the seat well and take in not so much fresher air but a more tolerable stale version. Roger used the new found freedom to discreetly slide his hand to his back pocket to find his phone. *Might I be able to send a warning?* Nothing in the pocket. Roger fumbled around but could not find the phone. He turned his head and looked under the driver's car seat, hoping that he might be able to snatch a discarded petrol receipt or car park ticket, something to identify his captors when he was released. It is "when" and not "if," isn't it? Nothing of note to be seen bar a couple of cigarette butts, what looked like a condom wrapper and a polystyrene burger holder – *a classy date that must have been.*

"Take this left." Given the sudden braking and sharp turn, the instruction had clearly been given late. The centrifugal force squashed Roger's face further but Carlos' boot lifted from his back as he was propelled across the back seat.

"Cazzo!" cried Carlos, expressing his displeasure.

The road beneath them became uneven and the car bumped its way along. The driver, seemed not to have adjusted his speed to the conditions but it was Roger, not Carlos, who complained as he was buffeted in all directions.

"Is he trying to get us killed?"

Roger regretted his choice of words, which brought a laugh from Carlos followed by the return of his boot to the side of Roger's face.

With a sharp turn to the right and a gratuitous application of breaks the vehicle was at a halt.

"Wait here. Don't move – Ah I forgot; you can't."

Carlos nonetheless waved the pistol in front of Roger's face. Carlos slammed the door shut as he and the driver exited. Roger could not hear the conversation between them but it was short lived.

Within the minute the rear door opened and Roger saw a hand reach in and grab his shirt collar. It was Carlos, this time, without his gun. Carlos was intent in dragging Roger from the car and across the dusty mud drive. Given the effort involved, Carlos half wished that they had bothered to bring the wheelchair.

"Steady, steady," pleaded Roger, for although he had no feeling below the level at which his spinal cord was damaged, his skin was vulnerable. Pressure sores were a real risk and at their worse could cause septicaemia and prove to be fatal.

Roger took in his surroundings. In front of him was a wooden outhouse and a large shed. Its door was ajar and Roger could see a lock and chain swinging from it. He tried to reason with his captors as he was dragged towards the open door. He quickly glanced back over his shoulder, seeing nothing but the rough track over which they had travelled and dusty weed like plants, with the odd cluster of olive trees for as far as Roger could quickly take in. The shed adjoined an old run down farm house about twenty metres from the away. It was difficult to say if it was inhabited but there was no outward sign of life. *Where's the barking dog when you need it?*

Carlos tripped on the raised entrance to Roger's new home. He cussed.

*Spartan* was the best word to describe the outhouse. It clearly had been used as a storage area as each of the wooden sides were lined with shelving.

Carlos pulled up a wooden chair from the corner of the outhouse. The men took an arm each and lifted Roger without ceremony into the chair. Its feet were wonky and it wobbled under his weight. The thinner kidnapper reappeared, carrying a roll of gaffer tape.

"Don't suppose we need to bother with tying him up – he aint going anywhere fast." Roger thought that this may be his first break for he was remarkably agile even at floor level – no such luck.

"True but well follow instructions – tie him tight too."

First torso was first strapped to the back of the chair followed by his feet to the chair legs. *This is not the first time they had done this,* concluded Roger. Carlos' pal reappeared, holding a *Camel* drinks pouch, favoured by long distance runners, a fluid container with a straw. The unit was fitted across Roger's shoulders and he was encouraged to take a sip from the plastic straw. *Blackcurrant Lucozade* at a guess. *A nice touch.*

Having wet his lips Roger thought that it was time to interact further.

"Guys, tell me what you want! I will cooperate. There has been a big mistake here."

Roger was rewarded with a strip of tape across his mouth. It tasted foul, like sticky plastic. It was pulled off straight away by Carlos with vigour, stinging his mouth. It was his cue to shut up.

Roger could do nothing but wriggle and watch as Carlos made a telephone call. Roger could not hear the voice of the recipient but it was clear that the conversation was a pretty one-sided affair to the extent that the captive's contribution was modest and limited to, "Si" or "Si Signore."

The phone's speaker button was engaged and suddenly Roger was very much part of the conversation. A focal part.

"Kirtley, listen to me very carefully," came the crisp male voice over the speaker. The English was clear though but there was a discernible, albeit subtle overseas accent to the voice, European thought Roger. "I need your help, Kirtley, and *you unquestionably* need mine."

"You've got his phone?"

"Si," said Carlos as he reached again into his pockets to pull Roger's phone out.

*No wonder I couldn't find it!*

"What is the password, Roger?" came the echo from the phone speaker.

"Its fingerprint activated," said Roger, who rarely used the number-based access and was panicking that he might not be able to remember it in any event.

Roger was frightened enough as it was but his tense body jolted as the captive reached inside his brown leather jacket and pulled out what quickly became apparent was a flick knife. The sound of the blade springing into place made Roger shudder.

*They're going to cut my finger off.*

He closed his eyes and grimaced, his cry for mercy but a muffled gurgle. The first thing he felt was his tide hands being lifted and then, with relief and gratitude, he could hear the cutting of the tape. He opened his eyes to see his hands spring free. His mobile phone was thrust into them

"Open the phone now, Roger."

He could think of no good reason to disobey. There *was* no good reason given the unequal bargaining position between the two men.

"Open it and give the phone back."

Roger complied and handed the iPhone back to Carlos, who took it without gratitude.

"They are going to check your emails Roger. If you have sent one back to the office reporting developments and the whereabouts of your colleague, then I'm afraid that you will have become dispensable. Ironic that your efficiency would have been the cause of your demise, don't you think? "

Roger was grateful on this occasion for his poor administrative skills, not that he had had time to report to anyone.

Though Carlos could not understand the contents of Roger's emails and texts, given his poor command of English, he was able to see that no emails had been sent that afternoon and reported accordingly to his boss. He then proceeded to check the text message icon, where a red "2" showed up, indicating that texts messages had been received but not yet read. They were bound to be from Pina, thought Roger, who could just about make out the screen as it added further illumination to the surrounding gloom. The first message was indeed from Pina. Roger could only pray that it did not give away her location. He feared that she was likely to do so after all, she was efficient. The sound of Carlos' "Non Signor," sounded heavenly and Roger allowed himself a nano second of relaxation. The release of tension was short lived for the second entry denoted receipt of a voice message. Carlos pressed "121" as directed and the phone connected. This is it, thought Roger, *Good night Vienna*. Pina's inefficiencies surely couldn't last:

"You have one new message," reported the female, rather robotic voice. The tone was matter of fact given the level of the stakes.

"Message recorded at 2:30 PM on 16 June – *beep* – 'Roger, it's Pina. Where are you? I'm worried about you – call me straight away.' Her voice portrayed genuine concern and in more convivial times, Roger would have been touched. As it was, her concern was far from unmerited. The fact that this call had been made several hours earlier and had yet to be returned would only have significantly added to her angst.

"Return her call now, Roger. I need to know her whereabouts."

"But if she tells me, you've said that you will kill me…"

"I will certainly kill you if you don't," echoed the voice. Roger glanced at Carlos. He, Roger concluded, would need little encouragement.

"Roger, I was only jousting with you. I am a businessman not a monster. Now make that call and spare your life."

At that moment Carlos retracted his knife with its accompanying click. It was rather symbolic and Roger reached for the redial button.

"Don't try and be clever either, Roger. That would try my patience."

Pina, answered with gusto, "Roger! Thank God. Where the hell are you? Where have you been? I've been scared stupid for you."

Roger interrupted her. "Pina, I'm fine. It's okay. All is well my end."

"But where have you been all this time? I've called you several times."

"I know. I'm sorry, Pina, my phone ran out of battery and then I had to get a taxi back to see Mr antiques man. There are a couple of facts I wanted to verify with him. How are Beatrice and Luigi?"

"Do you mean Bella?" indeed, Roger didn't. It was his subtle attempt to alert Pina. Too subtle. He looked at Carlos nervously, even though he knew that he couldn't understand a word of what was being said. The man on the other end of the phone certainly could understand and he wasn't sure just how discrete he had been.

"Where are you Pina? Have you booked in to the Ritz in Pisa, as we agreed?" This was the final throw of the dice.

"No, not there but the Relais Hotel in the centre of town. Bella and Luigi have settled in very nicely I can tell you. Our credit card is getting a hammering. How long before you get here?"

"I should be there in just over the hour," said Roger, guessing, still not sure where his location actually *was*.

"Call me when you get to the hotel. The police have been less than useless. They can't see that any crime has actually been committed; they think that the painting issue is a civil, not criminal, matter." The words hardly comforted Roger but, he suspected, they had brought a smile to the face of the interloper at the end of the line.

"Did you see the men? What did they do?" Pina had so many questions to ask. If only he could provide the answers.

"No, they never showed up. It was a waste of time," said Roger, playing his role impeccably.

"Phew, well I'm pleased to hear that," said Pina.

"You're going to need a large drink when you arrive at the hotel bar for sure Roger"

"I will that and I'm going to buy us both a piña colada."

Pina laughed.

"Give me a call when you arrive in the foyer, Roger. See you then."

Roger gestured to Carlos that the call was at an end and he took control of the phone again. Little did they know that Pina didn't drink.

"Very good, Roger," came the echoed voice from the other phone. You've been sensible and you will be rewarded. As soon as I get my painting back you will be freed up to return home to your boring world of insurance. You will no doubt look forward to it."

Carlos deactivated the speaker phone and took further instructions.

The reappearance of the flick knife did nothing to reassure Roger that his senior abductor was being straight with him but as Carlos reached for a roll of gaffer tape resting on a nearby table, Roger felt more reassured. Within moments, his hands had been untied. The knife had been used to good effect to cut the tape and both men left turning off the lights on their way out. Roger could hear the turning of locks on the door, followed by the sound of feet on gravel. He heard the closing of car doors and the starting up of the engine. Roger listened to the car as it disappeared. It was the only sound he could hear and its departure plunged him into silence.

# CHAPTER FORTY

Luigi bounced contentedly on the bed. He was wearing just his large white Y front pants. With three crisp duck down pillows propped under his back, he was raised sufficiently to gain a good view of the wide screen television before him. In his left hand, he carefully nurtured the remote control for the television, flicking rapidly between news, entertainment and sports channels. He grew curious as to what was what he would discover if he pressed the tempting "pay to view adult movie section." In his right hand, he cradled his second bottle of chilled beer from the minibar. Meantime, Bella was taking a bath in her own luxury marble surround. She had never used so much water and toiletries. She had not heard of *Molton Brown* but now knew that their bubble bath was very effective, as the bubbles extended over the top of the bath. Bella shrieked with laughter when experimenting with the bath side controls. First, a television appeared from a cabinet at the foot of the bath and then she experienced intense vibration and movement of the water having pressed the Jacuzzi jet control. She reached out for her mini bottle on prosecco that Luigi had supplied earlier, sank further into the bubbling froth and smiled. *What, indeed would Mamma say?*

"Luigi, the water is alive," she called with joy.

There was no prospect of Luigi moving from his comfortable position. The Bellinis were enjoying their first taste of the good life. It would not be long before their first room service order. They were in no hurry to meet the art expert.

Luigi didn't move again until room service arrived: two club sandwiches, a jug of ice cold milk, fries and two bottles of Peroni– bliss. As Bella let her small, empty bottle of Prosecco bob up-and-down in the bath, she had no awareness of the potential danger faced by her and Luigi. Ignorance in this case was bliss.

Pina had been oblivious to the warning clues that Roger had tried to give her and she was expectantly awaiting his arrival at the foyer of Grand Hotel. She was mid flow preparing her report to head office when her phone pinged, announcing the arrival of a text. As anticipated it was from Roger.

*I've arrived.*

Pina too was unaware of the danger she faced. The lift arrived and she travelled with two other guests to the lobby. She adjusted her hair in the lift mirror, looking forward to seeing Roger and reprimanding him for causing her such worry. The foyer was busy, primarily with tourists either returning from their day trip to Pisa or checking in for their stay at this five star hotel.

It looked as though a coach load of Japanese tourists had arrived given the length of the queue and the number of guests wearing air-pollution masks.

Pina stood on tiptoes and surveyed the scene while standing alongside the concierge's desk.

The concierge offered to help. He was resplendently dressed in a maroon suit and with gold braid on the collar and cuffs.

"Grazie Signore. I am looking for my friend, he should be here any moment."

"If you need help just ask."

Likewise, as Pina searched for Roger so did Carlos and his pal seek out Pina. They were at a distinct disadvantage because they didn't know what she looked like.

Both searches were proving to be less than fruitful. Pina felt vibration from her mobile phone and looked down to see a further message from Roger's phone.

*Meet me at the lift*

Their eyes met at the same time but Pina reacted first. She instantly knew that she'd seen the face before. She summoned her memory bank. Her neurons quickly located the image. It was from the CCTV at the antique shop. He was the man accompanying Braithwaite. Having made the connection she was the first to make a move, but quickly followed by Carlos.

Pina looked for an escape route and saw one. Carlos was unperturbed, for he had seen the hunted run on many occasions. He was confident of apprehension.

Pina headed towards the lifts.

One of the three lift doors was closing. The other two were firmly shut, the lift being on higher floors.

*Was there sufficient time to get to the door*? Pina lengthened her stride. As she arrived, she could see that there was too little space to make it into the closing lift door and it was clear from the man with whom she made eye contact inside the lift, that there was no appetite for trying to reopen the door.

*Bastard.*

Pina banged the closed door.

She next turned sharply, sliding involuntarily on the marble floor before heading towards the fire exit stairs which were clearly marked. Pina had a head start on Carlos.

*I need to make the most of it.*

Carlos had closed the gap, but it increased again as he attempted to break through the queue of Japanese tourists. He tripped on a *North Face* bag and in reaching his hands out to break his fall he clutched a carry on, cabin-size suitcase that was on wheels. This simply extended his body and accentuated the fall. He hit the ground face first. The apologies from the dismayed tourist were lost on Carlos as he once again gathered momentum. Pina had to hope that Carlos had no idea of her room number or floor. She was on the second floor, room 218. If she could make it there in time, it would afford her a period and place of safety; the stairs became a lonely place. Pina kicked off her shoes and lifted her knee length skirt to the waist to enable her to take the stairs two at a time. She gripped the metal handrail to enable her to swivel around the corner with speed.

Carlos, though experienced in the art of entrapment, was much heavier than Pina and would have preferred the lift to the stairs. As Pina crashed through the door to the second floor, she glanced behind and although she could hear distant footsteps, Carlos was not visible. Carlos stooped instinctively and picked up one of Pina's shoes as he started the climb. He was certainly no Prince Charming. He was a killer. He killed to feed his family and pay the bills. He treated death as a way of life. He had first killed someone at the age of 15. To be fair to him, it was not his intention to kill, but wound, as part of a gang initiation ceremony. Unlike his colleague who was also on the hunt for Pina, he increasingly enjoyed killing. His methods became more sadistic over the years and there was nothing more frustrating for him as when the death had to look more like suicide than murder. He was well paid for his trade, so didn't need to kill very often, perhaps a couple of times a year. The perks of the job. The rest of the time he worked as a minder, a rough one who preferred to provoke trouble rather than try to quell it.

Pina turned onto the corridor and ran to room 218 trying to find her key card as she did so. She was alarmed to find it alongside her mobile phone, for she knew this could deactivate the card. Pina rushed the first attempt to open the door, pulling the card through the door's card reader with lightning speed. The all too familiar red light on the door lock flashed – no entry! She tried again with indecent haste – another red. Three strikes and she would be out, blocked from entry. As the stair door opened, Pina desperately tied to slow the third attempt, checking that the magnetic strip was the right way around. Success! The green light beamed up at her. She turned the handle forcibly, opening the door and slamming it behind her. The slamming was a mistake because Carlos, who at this stage was out of breath and making little ground, heard the door close as he entered the corridor. He could not be sure whether it was on the left or right-hand side but he knew it was at end of the corridor.

Pina was trying to gather her thoughts but she was panicking, her heart was racing; the air conditioning may have been set at eighteen degrees but she was beginning to sweat profusely.

Carlos slowed and walked down the corridor coughing whilst deciding how best to gain entry to the room:

*Which one is it? Which one should I try first?* Just kicking the doors down might be satisfying but would attract unwelcome attention.

Pina put her eye to the door spy hole. All it did was to exaggerate the size of Carlos in the small fish eye lens. She spied Carlos opposite her room. She placed an ear on the door. She could hear the knock on the room opposite. She backed away.

This time the knocking was on her door.

"Room service."

*Room service!*

Pina did not wait to see whether the door would open. She ran to the balcony and looked out. Normally, it would've been a beautiful view, an infinity swimming pool surrounded by manicured gardens with the River Arno running alongside.

*Think, Pina, think!*

She did not know whether Roger was safe or not. She feared the worse but maybe Roger had just been followed and he was waiting for her in the foyer.

*Maybe,*

She dialled Rogers's number. To her horror she heard the phone ring immediately outside her door. Her fears confirmed.

Pina grabbed the painting, which she had placed at the bottom of the bed. She had nothing to wrap it in and once again went to the balcony as she heard the first of several knocks on the door. She looked down. The drop to the balcony below on the first floor was about four metres. If she hung from the lower rail of the balcony this probably reduced the drop to about two metres. For Pina the climb was an easy one, not so much the suburban climbing wall so detested by her ex, more a playground monkey bar. The balcony below was empty, bar two chairs both with wet towels on them. Pina dropped the painting first and it fell onto the balcony noisily. She straddled the balcony and clambered elegantly down, releasing her grip. She yielded upon impact with the floor and despite having nothing on her feet, it was a pain free drop. The glass door to the bedroom apartment was partially open but no one came to investigate. Again she peered over the balcony to see the below. Regrettably, this time the balcony was occupied by a young couple sitting enjoying a glass of wine, preparing to watch the sunset. With eloquent charm Pina sought their assistance:

"Forgive me. Can you give me a hand? I've locked myself out."

The couple were initially startled but the young man stood up and smiled back at Pina.

"No worry – What room number are you? 118 I guess? I'll call housekeeping for you."

"No time for that I'm afraid." Pina did not wait for a reply. "Here, catch this."

Pina dropped the painting into the hands of the bemused Englishman whose sundowner had been interrupted.

With the ease of an accomplished climber, she again clung to the lower rail where she felt the hands of her helper upon her thin hips lowering her gently to the ground floor.

Pina immediately thanked the couple for their help and took back her prized possession. The ground floor balcony lead directly on to the hotel garden via a latched gate. Nothing to climb.

The garden area lead down to the pool terrace and she took the nearest path. As she did so Pina looked up and saw Carlos reaching for his phone as he stared at her from the edge of her balcony. He may be a killer but he certainly lacked agility and had a fear of heights. Pina was safe. She made her way past the pool where a few guests sat drinking an aperitif from the poolside bar which was preparing to close for the evening. When Pina looked back, Carlos had disappeared and was no doubt making his way down by a more conventional route. She had too big a head start on him to be caught.

Pina made her way through the wrought iron exit gate lead from the garden steps to the cobbled walkway adjoining the river. As she opened the gate leading to the Arno, she spotted him – taller than Carlos though similarly dressed in jeans and leather jacket. Someone overdressed and out sync with the hotel guests. He was coming down the stairs two at a time in athletic fashion with a mobile phone pinned to his ear.

*Run, Pina, run.*

Pina closed the gate behind her. It would not cause her pursuer delay. The walkway itself was busy which hindered her progress. The painting knocked into several strolling couples walking hand-in-hand, enjoying the cool of the early evening. She took one further look over her shoulder; he was gaining and gaining fast. Unlike Carlos, he was fit and as determined. He was now less than twenty metres away.

Pina looked to her left where the tidal waters of the Arno flowed down to the Ligurian Sea 10 miles away. The small colourful lights that hung from the overhead rail, stretched reflections out into the water. Pina paused. Twenty metres was down to ten – *He'll catch me.* Pina, still with the painting in hand, swung her right leg up on to the top of the ornate stone wall; her left tucked in behind it in sequence. Her weight had barely settled on the plinth when yes felt a tug on the painting's frame.

Pina leapt into the river. Her weight and momentum enabled the artwork to come with her. She had no idea how deep the water would be as her feet entered first. The tide was in and her head descended under the water. The cold temperature shocked her. She swallowed two large bacteria filled mouthfuls of water; the taste was vile. The impact with the water had caused her to release the painting from her grip. The tide was gentle but persistent and the painting was now floating five metres away. It shimmered as it caught the side wall lights. She took her eyes off it for a moment to check if she was being followed into the Arno. Her pursuer was perched on top of the wall but unknown to Pina, swimming lessons had not formed part of his limited education. Pina swam towards the painting, more concerned with function than style. There was no way she would be putting her head voluntarily under the water. Pina reached out and grabbed the Cezanne with both hands. She managed to pull it under her chin and it acted as a makeshift floatation aid. She knew that the painting might be damaged but survival was her priority; her sole focus. Pina kicked her legs vigorously to create further momentum with the tide and direct herself further away from watching eyes and into the centre of the river.

As one immediate danger abated for Pina so another loomed on the horizon – literally. As darkness began to set over Pisa, she was but an insignificant piece of flotsam in a fast flowing, active river. During the day, the river accommodated industrial barges destined for ports further down the Arno but during the evening the river cruise boats dominated the area. With bright lights and blaring music, the *Pisa Express* was bearing down on Pina rapidly. It was full of tourists enjoying the views and it would seem, the drink, given the boisterous nature of the noise coming from the main deck. The visibility for the helmsman at the wheel was limited in any event. This would not have been helped by his consumption of grappa since the boat left dock an hour earlier. Pina tried to calculate in her own mind whether to move left, right or simply stay still and let the current shoot her past the vessel. The bow of the boat Towered above her, closing deceptively fast, rising and falling gently on the opposing tide. The combined impact speed of the boat moving fifteen knots in one direction and the tide five in another would surely be enough to kill Pina out right, as the steel hull yielded for little. Pina decided to go with the tide and then kicked vigorously behind her. The splashes would not be seen by the helmsman but she was able to gain momentum and by turning the painting to the left she attempted to steer to the starboard side of the oncoming boat.

Her challenge was added to by the fact that the boat was travelling at a slight angle towards the mooring on the hotel side of the river. This cross angle was impossible to calculate from Pina' precarious position in the water.

The boat was now within metres and impact look certain.

*This is it.*

Illogically, she just gripped harder on to the frame, kicking again, desperately trying to clear the bow. Pina shut eyes and waited for the impact. It came. Pina screamed. She felt the steel hull hit her right leg. Rather than crush her it had the effect of pushing her aside. The top right-hand corner of the painting came into contact with the side of the boat and was knocked again from her grasp. She opened her eyes, swallowed some more liquid bacteria and managed to put in four strokes to clear the rear of the boat and catch hold again of the floating painting.

Pina could see as the boat advanced away from her that it was full of diners, dancers and drinkers, many of whom were leaning on the starboard rails, taking in the romantically lit shore line. For all that, she remained unnoticed.

Pina despaired as she saw ahead of her an even larger entertainment boat. She began to shiver not through fear but cold. The water temperature at 11° had been an initial shock to her body and she had now been in the water for what seemed like an eternity. Her teeth chattered. She looked again at the boat ahead of her. It did not appear to have moved. She however was floating closer to it. It was difficult to see with precision because as night-time fell so the west winds had picked up counter opposing the current and thereby creating choppier waters. As Pina floated even closer to the boat she saw that it was alongside a wooden jetty set in mid river. It appeared that the boat was moored up. She dipped the left-hand corner of the painting, kicked again and began heading towards the boat, jetty side. She misjudged the speed of current and crashed into the pillars of the jetty. She managed to twist the painting to avoid any serious damage to it but instead smashed her wrist painfully against a wooden pillar.

She was being dragged away from the jetty so wrapped her legs around it to get better traction. She could feel the slimy green jetty weed; gunky and very slippery, challenging her grip. She could not reach the mooring ropes which secured the boat as they were too high up. She was frightened of being trapped between the sides of the boat and the jetty structure. Rubber fenders squeaked as the boat crushed them against the wooden sides. They would protect the boat but they would do little to assist Pina. It was then she heard the cry:

"Man overboard! Man overboard!" This was very much a woman over board but the sentiment was accurate. She had been spotted not by crew but a passenger taking a smoke break from the more formal three course meals being undertaken on board. Very quickly a crew member, dressed in white with immaculately starched trousers and short sleeve shirt, jumped down onto the jetty and stretched out a hand to her.

"Take this first," pleaded Pina, as she offered up the painting, as best she could. The sailor obliged and then first took her right and then her left hand to drag her onto the ridged jetty floor. She lay there exhausted and unable to move or talk for few seconds until lifted to her knees by the sailor. She had been joined by other crew members, one of whom was carrying a tartan wool blanket which was swiftly wrapped around her goose pimpled shoulders. Within minutes, she was on board and inside the staff quarters which were basic but warm and comfortable.

Her pursuers were anxiously scanning the water from the bridge but fifty metres away from where Pina rested. Their immediate conclusion was that she had drowned but the primary concern was finding the painting, which would still be floating. They could see the moored boat but had taken little notice of it given it was so far away from with Pina entered the water. As Pina's boat set off downriver to its next port of call the terrible twins gave up their hunt and prepared for what was going to be a difficult and painful call to their boss. They knew that his displeasure was to be avoided and he treated failure with distain and often punishment.

After a few minutes, Pina's thoughts of survival had nothing to do with her stalkers. Having survived without drowning she was able to re-focus on the primary dangers.

Pina was delighted that her mobile phone had not fallen from her dress pocket in the escapade but it was completely water logged and dead – the screen failing to offer even a flicker of enthusiasm as she pressed the side power button in quick succession, more out of habit than optimism.

At least the company credit card inside the phone's wallet was intact, less so her paper identity card and the soaking euro notes.

She had not wanted to come on deck earlier for fear of being spotted by her trackers and was content to travel inside the cabin area for the four kilometres or so down river towards Florence, where final embarkation would begin. She waited for passengers to start their short journey down the creaking walkway that extended out from mid ship, checking to ensure it was safe to get off the *Pisa Express*. She could see no one of concern port side and joined the passengers heading off having expressed heartfelt gratitude to the crew members who had looked after her. They remained intrigued as to how she *had fallen from another boat* clutching a painting but were delighted to have a come to her rescue. A beautiful woman in distress, who could resist. They were disappointed that she would not accept the suggestion of a medical check-up as they had offered to travel with her to hospital, given their journey was at an end. Pina waved and headed down ship to shore creaking walkway, still draped in the tartan blanket but having changed into a spare set of the crew's white uniform. It was loose fitting but her other clothes were in the dust bin, stained and sodden. Finding shoes had proved to be more of a problem and Pina felt more as though she was wearing flippers than the oversized deck shoes that had been sourced for her.

# CHAPTER FORTY-ONE

Pina inspected the canvas again. It had reacted with the water and begun to bubble in places but the oil paint had repelled the water. Pina had been able to remove the excess water and silt and the canvas was already beginning to dry out. Pina's secured the Cezanne under her arm. Her first port of call was to stop at the small telecoms shop on the corner of Via San Martino. She noted that it would stay open till 10 pm that evening, offering an array of phones, together with an overwhelming number of supporting tariffs. The accessories were prominently displayed—phone protectors and Bluetooth ear pieces in different shapes and colours to satisfy all tastes.

Pina felt disproportionate excitement that her credit card was accepted and having made it quite clear to the overly helpful assistant that she was short on time and tolerance, Pina reappeared onto the main thoroughfare with a new phone in hard and old SIM card expertly inserted within it, thereby preserving her mobile number. Though the Samsung was not completely charged it was full of life and the familiar

Vodafone jingle singled that the tool was ready use. *Who shall I call first?*

The decision was taken out of her hands as the phone vibrated. The movement was unexpected and caused her to jerk, dropping the phone to the pavement. It continued to vibrate and as Pina retrieved it she noticed that the screen was already cracked.

*I told her to take out the insurance* thought the sales assistant as he watched from behind his counter. Pina swore but noticed no diminution in the phones energy level.

"Hello," she answered almost casually.

"Ah, Pina, at last. This is a friend of Roger's."

*Who needs enemies?*

For a moment Pina was naive enough to believe the caller but quickly realised that, right now, *she* was Rogers only friend.

"Who is this?" enquired Pina assertively.

"As I say, Roger's friend, just like you, Pina. You have something of value to me, Pina and I have something of value to you. The solution is obvious, is it not?"

"So, you want to trade now rather than rely on your gorillas?" Pina felt angry and was not feeling as intimidated as she should have been. She was an insurer and he a killers' paymaster.

"It is the painting, not you that they wanted."

"They could have asked politely," said Pina growing in confidence.

"In that case, let me ask you politely, Pina. Please may I have my painting back…and in return I will spare Roger his life." His cold, taunting repost jolted Pina. This was not a situation under her control.

It was impossible for Pina to think straight. How could she possibly devise a plan in such challenging circumstances, mind twirling at speed, unable to focus, unable to rationalise. The idea of returning to the hotel to affect an exchange, even to her befuddled mind seemed a nonsense, far too dangerous. She was hindered by the fact that she did not know Pisa well, only having previously been there on a school trip many years ago.

"I will give you the painting at the Tower itself. Get your thugs to be there at 10 pm and they will get the painting."

"I warn you, Pina, that if you contact the police or there is any sign of police presence, this deal is over and so is Roger's life. You understand that clearly?"

"And you understand that you need to stick to your part of the bargain too."

"Pina, I keep telling you I have no interest in Roger. My interest is in the painting. 10 pm at the Tower."

She knew that she should ring head office straight away and call for help. She also knew that the company's strict protocol was to involve the police straight away – use the professionals. But all of PNP had been shocked last year at the murder of one of their vice presidents in a failed kidnap rescue. That though was in Argentina not Italy, Pina trusted the Caribinieri but she didn't trust Roger's friend.

Pina knew at least that today was the feast of San Ranieri The patron saint of Pisa. The celebratory firework display would provide a distraction but also protection, for the area around the cathedral and Tower would be full of revellers.

Pina looked at her Apple watch, which to be fair to the manufacturers claims had proven to be water resistant to five metres. Pina remained grateful that it had been tested to a greater depth. She would be able to use it to good effect.

The 'Find My Phone' facility *might, just might* lead her to Roger or a least to where the captors were based. It was, she thought, *worth a try,* as she unstrapped the watch and turned her attention to the frame of the painting.

She had about forty-five minutes to make it to the famous leaning Tower, which she calculated was two to three miles away. She could not risk collecting the car from hotel car park as the key remained in room 218. She was not going back there in a hurry.

She picked up the painting and made her way back to the nearest taxi rank. There was a queue. The clock was ticking. Having finally been picked up by the licenced taxi, she made her way to the Tower checking the time on the taxi clock frantically. She was short of time. Pina needed to get there earlier than her pursuers as an extra precaution. The idea of handing over the painting in person brought a trade. But what else could she do. She had at least managed to change out of her sailor's costume and acquired a less than perfectly fitting dress at one of the many stores adjoining the river walkway. The dress was dour but she figured it was better than ill-fitting jeans and a *I love Pisa* T-shirt.

As they drove along, Pina looked down at the painting, which was resting alongside her on the back seat. She had managed to persuade the clothing shop owner to let her use some bubble wrap that she had spotted in their storage area. There was insufficient to fully enclose the frame. She tried to stretch the plastic but only succeeded producing a familiar "pop" as one of the bubbles burst. This only served to cause the taxi driver to jolt the steering wheel and swerve, much to the annoyance of the oncoming vehicle which sounded its horn aggressively.

He looked in his mirror and realising what that happened, smiled rather than the reprimanded her.

"Sorry," apologised Pina, as yet another bubble bust under her grip. She noticed the hanging rosary from his interior mirror. Though baptised and confirmed in the Catholic Church, she had not been to Mass since leaving school. It did not stop her quickly summoning up a silent prayer in support.

As the taxi finally turned turn left off the main road, the Tower itself came into view. It was lit up for the celebrations. Pina had visited it many years ago but she couldn't help but be impressed. This was due partly to its architectural beauty but primarily the fact that the lean of the Tower was much greater than she had recalled. Yes, she had seen those endless selfie photographs of tourists *propping up* the Tower but the 4.6 metre lean at the top was eye-catching. How it actually stayed up was a mystery to her and thousands of visitors. However, now was not the time to pull out the tourist guide nor to study architectural and mathematical theorem. It was clear that the taxi driver was heading towards the designated parking spot but she asked him to pull over. She handed over a generous cluster of Euro obtained earlier from the cash point, and joined the throngs.

She was anxious to avoid being spotted. Most visitors were carrying a camera or a rucksack – the painting rather stood out.

The queue for the Tower was long. It was rarely open in the evenings and building works designed to ensure the safety and longevity of the Tower were scheduled to begin the following week. The maintenance, which involved a reinforcement of the foundation as well as the replacement of the lower tier masonry were due to take 18 months during which this famous icon would be closed. Knowing the pace of Italian builders, that time could be doubled and feared the Council of Pisa, who were funding the restoration, so could the budget.

Both locals and tourists from afar were taking the chance to visit before the scaffolding arrived

All of those queueing had pre-booked their tickets and there were no purchases on the day. Pina surveyed the queue, which extended at least a hundred metres towards the main entrance to the cathedral. The visitors stood broadly in line within the metal barriers that had been erected for the occasion. Patience would be rewarded later, for the views at night were spectacular and for those who timed their visit to the belfry to coincide with the planned fire work display would be especially graced. Staff with walkie talkies and dressed in white shirts with a district green leaning Tower logo on the breast pocket, checked tickets and gently disappointed visitors expecting to be able to purchase admission. Pina concluded that the staff would see themselves more as Tower and Cathedral Guides' than security guards. Depending on how matters developed this could be a benefit but may prove to be detrimental if some protective muscle was required.

Pina checked her phone and noted that she was now two minutes late. That gave her no time to assess where best to position herself and she felt exposed. *I bet they're watching me already.*

She weaved in and out of tourists, most intent on taking clichéd photos of themselves holding up the Tower, whether by hand foot or butt. A great shot for the family album even if very low on the scale of originality. Pina tried to use them as cover, hoping that, as before in the hotel, she and not the gorillas would make the first sighting. Pina made her way to a point some fifty metres from the Tower, where the metal barriers enclosing the lucky ticket holders turned at 90 degrees to signify the final transition zone to the Tower entrance. The queue moved slowly but Pina could see visitors being ushered through the arched entrance doorway whilst other exited the same entrance having descended the eight flights of stairs from the belfry.

# CHAPTER FORTY-TWO

Carlos had the advantage of cover and surprise. He closed in, using tourists as a shield. He had already opened the flick knife and held it at his side in readiness. It would be quick and silent. Unlike Pina, he knew that a busy venue at night offered less chance of being caught; everyone was focussing on their own pathway, no one wants to help and it's easy to disappear in a crowd. Just then, Pina was startled, as a sparkler was lit up two metres to her left by an enthusiastic visitor with firework in one hand and a bottle of beer in the other. It caught her attention and for an instant it lit up the night. She saw him appearing from the shadow off the student's right shoulder. Their eyes met. Carlos pushed the sparkler aside and reached out to grab Pina. She thrust the painting at Carlos. It stopped him briefing in his tracks. He gripped the frame to stop it falling and Pina watched as he turned and passed the painting to his accomplice who was behind him. Yes, they had the painting but now he wanted her. Pina turned, gripped the top of the railing bar with her left hand and straddled it in one movement barely touching the bar with her legs as she did so. The Tower Guide witnessed her manoeuvre but was far too slow and too far away to intercept Pina, who was now running at full pace towards the Tower entrance. The guide to the entrance itself was positioned inside the stone facade and had not seen her climb the barrier, being more preoccupied with cajoling the visitors not to push but nonetheless to keep moving. Pina slowed to a walking pace a couple of metres from the opening and stepped into the entrance without pausing. The Tower guide may not have been sure as to Pina's provenance but those tourists waiting in line were unequivocal and vocal in protest.

"No wait! Hey, you!"

Pina extended open palms nodding her head;

"Forgive me – I don't understand."

She smiled as best she could at the guide who was already receiving a walkie-talkie report of Pina's dash to the Tower. Pina approached the guide calmly and then at the last moment darted to her right, pushing away two tourists blocking the access route to the small hallway that lead to the Tower steps. The steps extended clockwise up to the Tower. There was a four-metre run to the bottom of the steps and Pina could see that on each of the steps there was a visitor moving slowly upwards. When the stairs were first built, no doubt there was room for two people on the steps but this was now unrealistic given the size of the average visitor embarking on the journey. There were perhaps seven steps before the initial spiral turn began. Everyone on those steps turned to see what the fuss was about in the hallway. Pina by this stage had made it to the bottom of the stairs and angling her body sideways began to climb herself. She could only take one step at a time due to the congestion.

Her rolling apology met with little acceptance. As she made the initial turn a large Italian tourist deliberately blocked her path putting his hand up.

"Stop – there's a queue – wait your turn like everyone else."

Without hesitation, Pina stuck out a right fist. The target area was large and found the stomach area readily. The surprised and winded Italian immediately yielded way for her and she continued on her bumpy journey. As she made the initial turn she looked back for the first time but saw no one in pursuit. She was comforted by the fact that if she was struggling to make this journey, given her petite stature, then there was no hope for Carlos. She pushed on for a further three flights of the eight before pausing to gain breath and joined the more orderly queue of visitors.

There was no one chasing her. Pina was relieved to reach the top of the bell Tower. Had she not been focused on survival, she would've been able to enjoy the magnificent view afforded the other guests.

*What now?*

She had received no call from the paymaster since handing over the painting and this rather reinforced her view that this was a one-way bargain. Instinctively, she checked her phone again to make sure there were no missed messages. Nothing.

All previous calls to her were from an unknown number so all she could do wait for the call. *It would surely come.*

Pina had to assume that Carlos or his friend were waiting for her at the bottom. There was only one way in and one way out. Would they really be so bold as to try and capture her in such a public forum? Was she prepared to take that risk? It was the shouting from further down the stairwell that heralded the imminent arrival of Carlos. How he had bulldozed his way up the narrow stairway remained a mystery but Pina could tell from the disgruntlement of those being knocked aside that Carlos was closing in. The exit stairs ahead of her were not only full but presumably lead straight into the arms of the other unwanted suitor.

Pina looked through the turret closest to her then hurried to the opposite side of the Tower and stretched out with her right hand to take hold of the protective wire that have been fitted outside of the turret to stop thrill-seeking BASE jumpers and those more intent on jumping without a parachute. Suicide attempts had been common. She could, ironically, use the wire to assist in crawling to the ledge of masonry that extended out from the turret. The gap between turrets was narrow even for her but Pina was able to squeeze through and as she did so she was able to look down on the angled Tower beneath her feet – all fifty-seven metres. It certainly was not called the leaning Tower for nothing and the 5-degree incline would be Pina's key to survival. In technical terms, she thought the climb down was relatively easy even though she was hardly dressed for the occasion and did not have the benefit of robe and crampons. The lean of the Tower afforded her significant friction, defying the natural pull of gravity. She took a half step to the left onto a stone pillar which extended down to the seventh floor. Pina was able to wrap her feet comfortably around its 25 centimetres diameter before stretching out with her right hand on releasing her grip from the wire, to be fully suspended on the pillar its self. The rough texture of the column assisted with the resistance and to her surprise rather than having to use her feet to break a slide, she needed to use her hands to encourage her body to start to move down along the pillar. The difficult part was then moving from the base of the column to the next floor, but again she was aided by another "Suicide wire." Hanging comfortably from the wire with both hands, Pina again adopted a position with her feet on the pillar which then lead to the sixth floor. She was moving far quicker than anyone else in the Tower. From 7 to 6 to 5 to 4… Her knees and ankles were being scuffed by the pillars but her hands coped easily with the textured stone as it was kinder than much of the rock she had encountered in the lower reaches of the Alps and Dolomites.

She was what is known as a grade 4a climber, capable of climbs, which were sheer provided she had a sufficient number foot and hand holds. To that end the 5° lean of the Tower proved to be remarkably comfortable descent. Putting that in perspective though, she knew that if she fell from this height death would be pretty much guaranteed.

Infuriatingly, the most technically challenging part of the climb was from the first floor to ground level because the otherwise symmetrical layout of the Tower changed. Pina judged that the drop from this gallery to the floor was too great to jump without sustaining injury. An ugly gargoyle stood between Pina and safety. The gargoyle with large ears, pointed face and extended tongue was fixed to the structure immediately below her, such that for the first meter at least, Pina would be climbing blind. She held the gargoyles ears with both hands, before extending her arms and lowering her body until the creature was taking her full weight. As a gesture of defiance, she kissed it on the nose whilst sliding down, before swinging her legs, trying to make contact with whatever structure lay beneath her. As she had hoped, the familiar feel of a pillar came into play and she was able to hug her feet around it, lowering her body with a hand grip upon the gargoyle's face. Pina gradually released the grip of her feet and she slid the final five meters to the raised base plinth and then jumped clear the ground. Pina's position at the Tower base was such that she was now at the furthest point away from the entrance and exit, free from Carlos' friend, who would not have had a view of her landing site. Pina moved swiftly to the corner of the adjoining building, which cast her in shadow and therefore relative safety.

# CHAPTER FORTY-THREE

Roger had time to think, too much time. As he sat in the comparative darkness and increasing heat of his new home, he tried to piece together both the events of today and those leading up to his capture. Initially, he posed himself more questions than he produced answers. It was clearly highly significant that for someone, be it an individual or an organisation that this, the Gauguin, had come to light. Roger couldn't be certain that the other painting found at Luigi and Bella's house was an original, but it looked as though it was. The one thing he was sure of was that it wasn't a cheap copy that Luigi could have bought at the local hyper market. This was either an original or a fine copy of the masterpiece. His money was on it being genuine.

Given the lengths that someone had gone, to track both the painting and he and Pina down and the fact that he was now incarcerated in the middle of God only knows where in Tuscany, meant that this just had to be an original painting. *But so what?* As soon as one concluded that the Cezanne was genuine then the other pieces of the jigsaw fell more easily into place. If the Cezanne was the real deal, then the Gauguin, stolen from the antiques shop *just had to be too.* This meant that the artwork on display and then stolen at the gallery was a fake. That then might explain the audacious and very public theft, which seemed, at first blush, to involve far too much risk for seasoned professional thieves. A theft not so much in broad daylight but definitely in the glare of the spotlights. Why such a public display? It only made sense if they had no option but to seek to steal the painting then. A time-critical raid?

Roger ran through the timeline in his head. The antiques burglary had taken place the day before the gallery raid. Why the rush? Why not just steal the newly discovered painting and then hide or destroy it – no one would be any the wiser – that didn't make sense.

Peter Brinsden had of course been the wiser, reflected Roger. *Some suicide.*

*And what of Braithwaite – what was he doing carrying out a burglary?*

Something else dawned on Roger at that moment and it brought no comfort to him. It was obvious, it had been so from the moment he was captured but this environment was not conducive to straight thinking. *I know too much to be kept alive.*

He was of value only to extent of being able to assist in the recovery of the Cezanne and the entrapment of Pina and her fate was also clearly mapped out.

Optimism, hope or perhaps sheer naivety had lead Roger to believe that his captor would honour his word and free him – *a business man not a monster*, his very words. It now looked text book business strategy to get rid Roger and Pina.

*I must have a pee.*

The dehydration Roger was experiencing as a result of the very hot temperature of the room and his earlier exertions, had helped to abate the call of nature. The problem was that, for Roger, nature was rather cruel; he was not in control of his bodily functions. Bladder management itself had become an art form. Today, Roger had gone too long without use of a catheter. His supply was neatly packed away in the small rucksack that hung off the back of his chair and went everywhere with him, save when he was kidnapped, perhaps. Roger had slipped from his camel drink devise intermittently, not knowing how full the container had been nor how long he was going to be detained; that said he had not passed water for the better part of four hours. If he was unable to relieve himself he could suffer from a condition called autonomic dysreflexia, a form of acute high blood pressure; one that can kill – just for not having a pee. Roger considered himself lucky in the spinal cord injury community for he had some sense at least when his bladder was full and with movement of his body could normally induce flow. Though Roger couldn't feel the hot liquid running down his leg, he could enjoy the pleasure of the release – it felt empowering – control over at least one element of life. His headache eased almost instantly and if he hadn't been in a dire state of emergency he would have afforded himself a smile. This liberation was very short lived for he soon felt miserable. He welled up inside and was unable to wipe away the tears that rolled down his cheek. Tears of despair, tears even of shame and guilt; after all, he had been the one who had chosen Pina to help. *Poor Pina.*

He realised that wallowing in self-pity would do him no good.

*Get a grip, man.*

However, his escape options looked to be decidedly limited. Roger was bound by extra strong gaffer tape, which did not appear to yield in the slightest. He tried nonetheless.

Roger attempted to look around his cell but it was getting darker as the sun set. He wondered if he would be able to shuffle around the room while strapped in his chair. He tried to move his seat by somehow by gently rocking in order to create movement. The task was a forlorn one. What if he tipped the chair over whilst secured to it? Roger couldn't see what he would fall onto but remembered when entering the shed that the area immediately around him was pretty clear. Roger engaged his neck and shoulder muscles and began to rock the chair side to side, gently at first and then with greater rhythm. Gravity and the law of physics took over.

"Ahhhh."

The chair crashed to the ground.

"Fuck!"

There was also a squelch as the *Camel* drinks bottle was squashed between the floor and the chair. A jet stream of sticky fluid ejected from the plastic mouthpiece onto Roger's face. The drenching was unexpected and unwelcome.

Even though he had braced himself for the fall, it was painful as his left arm was trapped between the floor and the chair rest. His head impacted on what he could feel was a wooden floor; a head that was still aching having been knocked out earlier. The impact left his entire brain throbbing. Roger began to cough and splutter as the disturbed dust floated in the darkness.

*What now?* Roger tried to shuffle forward but was unable to do so given that his legs provided no assistance. He needed somehow to be able to roll onto his front so as to utilise his fingers and wished now he had been brave enough to have simply fallen forwards; after all he had fallen out of the chair this way on many occasions in the past. This may have led to a more significant bump on the head but given the aching he was now experiencing, it could hardly have been much worse.

The laws of gravity were not so kind to him this time. His first attempts to wriggle the chair through the initial 90°were feeble. He needed to utilise all that was left of his limited core muscles. The success of the manoeuvre required coordination and as Roger was realising, a good deal of luck. He tried unsuccessfully again and conceded that it wasn't going to work. Next, Roger contemplated shuffling forward. It was possible to do so by adopting a coordinated whiplash movement initiated by the head, followed by a tightening movement through the shoulders. Progress was painstakingly slow. In the darkness he tried to recollect the position of the lamp. He estimated that was two metres to his right. He continued his slow and by now exhausting shuffle. His path took him through a puddle of liquid – a mixture of urine and spillage from his drinks pouch. Although this was unpleasant to say the least, equally it affirmed that he was moving in the right direction. Roger heard his right foot finally knock against something solid. He wasn't sure at first if it was just the side wall. He jolted again as best he could and heard the noise of an object sliding slightly on the wooden floor; it was a leg of the cabinet table. His plan, in theory, couldn't be faulted and was straightforward; dislodge the table and the lamp would fall. Where it would fall and whether the bulb would break in the process remained issues of real concern. Assuming there even was a bulb.

*Push! Push!* Roger grunted with effort as he shuffled further along until his foot this time came into contact with what he calculated was another cabinet leg. He tried, unsuccessfully, to create enough momentum to unbalance the lamp from its resting position. He could get the cabinet to move a centimetre or so with his foot but that was insufficient to rock the cabinet as required. He desperately need to get his hands in contact with the leg of the cabinet. This now required a 180° anti-clockwise manoeuvre – synchronised swimming practice on dry land. There was a good reason why the event didn't feature in the Paralympics. Though his hands were tied tightly, Roger was grateful to Carlos who in re-taping his hands had not secured his fingers as he had done earlier.

Roger's technique was improving, even if his stamina was sapping. Slowly, ever so slowly, he began to gyrate anti-clockwise towards what he hoped was the cabinet. His nose was the first part of his body to strike the cabinet leg. He sniffed it. The contact hurt but at least helped him to get his bearings. He needed to shuffle backwards and take a tight right turn. He did so and this time his upper torso impacted with the leg. He was then able to use this leg for leverage and shuffle his aching body such that the tip of his left index finger felt the target. He was both excited and galvanised by his success and within seconds, he had both hands on what he calculated was the left front of the cabinet. Roger began to shake the table, trying to dislodge the lamp. The aim was for the lamp to fall on to him so as to enable easy access and avoid damage to the lamp's bulb. He clearly needed a big effort to complete the task rather than the subtler movements he had been adopting. *Do it, Roger!* He paused briefly gathering his draining strength. His fingers had cramped due to the restricted blood supply caused by the tethers. Having wiggled the blood back into his digits he gripped the table leg once again with his fingers and jerked the table towards him. Suddenly, the centre of gravity was overcome and the balance of the table disturbed. Roger released his grip, however too late to stop the table falling on top of him followed by the crash of the lamp onto the floor. Its base and stem must have been made of metal given the clatter it made. Roger waited for the sound of breaking glass – that fragile bulb – nothing – the ill-fitting lampshade may have dislodged but it had served the purpose in softening the fall.

*Where's the switch?!*

It was likely to be up towards the bulb itself. Roger turned his body to try and access the lamp shade. The table slipped off Roger's chest to the ground with a further thump. Roger heard the sound of small object hitting the floor, *coins perhaps?* He ventured, as he listened to something roll across the wooden floor boards and settle. Roger reached forward and caught hold of what he guessed was the lamp's electric cable running from its base to the plug. He would use that to guide him. As he edged along the textured surface he came to the end of it sooner than had been anticipated. It was not the power cable after all but a shorter lead, connected to the switch mechanism. The first bit of luck Roger had incurred in a while. Again, he paused briefly, closed his eyes and flicked the switch. Even with his eyes closed he realised that he been successful, for the lamp bulb, which was less than a third of a meter away from his face, shone brightly in the darkness. Roger open his eyes, dazzled at first by the brightness.

"Get in!"

Roger looked away from the bulb taking in the view, as best he could, given his constraints. The room looked less attractive than it did in the darkness with urine extending across the floorboards. Fortunately, most was being soaked up rapidly given the dryness of the floor boards. Roger, was elated by his success. He lay on his side adjusting to the light. His effort had been monumental. *But now what?* If the perpetrators returned it would all be for nothing. He looked once more around the room looking for a tool or object to help free him from his bindings. This may have been a workshop in its day but it seemed to have been cleared of all utensils. Roger couldn't see what was on the higher shelving but would be unable to reach it in any event.

It was simply too much to hope that within the lamp table drawer there would be keys to the locked door. In a way that would be more frustrating because he would have the means to escape but not the ability to access it. Total frustration.

Roger made a mental note of the items in the room:

*One lamp with broken lamp shade;*
*One oak lamp table with dislodged draw;*
*One rusty wood burning stove;*
*Two piles of old magazines and newspapers;*
*Cobwebs galore;*
*Two or three small coins, presumed to be Lira;*
*One trust up and wretched insurer.*

Not much to work with.

Roger, screamed out in frustration for he had again moved from the ecstasy of the working lamp to the despair of capture in but a minute. These were fast track mood swings.

The cabinet draw which had partially opened as the table

fell now rested on the floor half in, half out. Roger twisted himself towards the end of the draw and was slowly able to fully extract it from the table. He stretched his neck to look inside. More Lira, an old box of matches and an empty key ring. No 'get of jail free card anywhere'

He got an idea. It was ridiculous— no, dangerous and ridiculous in equal measures.

"Don't go there, Roger," he whispered.

Roger could hear the sound of a car approaching in the distance. The return of his captors…He stopped breathing and raised his head up from the floor to aid his hearing. Definitely a car, one getting closer. His adrenaline raced once again, he gasped for air, having forgotten to breath.

*This is it.*

Roger awaited the arrival of the vehicle rumbling up the drive to his prison. It never came. The sound rescinded and then dispersed leaving a screaming silence. Roger could hear his heavy breathing and smell more urine.

Roger felt that he had faced death and he didn't like it. He would take control now and at least die at his own hands trying to escape…

The adrenaline had not dissipated. This enabled him to move relatively quickly to the first pile of newspapers. It was not the time to read but he noticed that they were not as old as their faded facades made them look. The date of the top paper was 30 July 1979. He managed to grip the top sheet and slide it off.

He was able to screw this sheet of paper into a loose ball applying a limited degree of dexterity with his tapered hands. The second sheet followed and then a third. He needed to strike a balance between having sufficient flame from the paper to be able to burn through his ties yet at the same time not risk setting fire to the room itself or serious burn his hands. It was clear from the way that his urine soaked into the floorboards that they were very dry and therefore amenable to the spread of flame. Perhaps four sheets was too much, he contemplated and removed one from the pile by knocking it sideways. Next, he picked up the small box of matches resting in the corner of the table draw. There were two loose matches that had from that had spilled from the pack and he picked them up also. He could tell from by shaking them as best he could that the box was at least half full. With his index finger, he pressed the inner shelf of the *Matrix* matches. As the door opened however Roger was distraught to see that all of the matches had already been used, their blackened charcoal remains having been neatly re-packed. It was an irritating habit of a compulsive obsessive. *Damn them!*

He tipped out the box contents onto the floor and was able to retrieve another unlit match. *Five in total.* That should be sufficient for his purpose, concluded Roger.

He wasn't much point in trying to burn off the ties to his feet first. If anything they provided greater stability in there chair for now.

Roger picked up the first match in between his thumb, index and first finger and positioned it as though about to casually light up a cigarette. The gripping of the box with its ruffled long side for striking up was easy enough to do but bringing point A to point B to affect ignition, was not straight forward. He could just about make contact but with insufficient speed or vigour to create the much-needed flame. In attempting to readjust the box, he dropped the match and had to start on over again. The matches themselves were small, which hindered leverage but looked dry and intact. Roger decided to change from a more conventional technique to one where he flicked the match across the abrasive side of the box which he cradled tighter in the palm of his left hand – instant success save that the lit match flicked beyond the fingertips which were extended to catch it. Roger watched as the flame extinguished quickly and fell between floor boards.

This time Roger moved the newspaper itself to form a catch and contain area for the match to settle if it projected further than hoped.

Gaining confidence with his technique, he flicked, once again with success and the lit match landed perfectly in the centre of his paper cradle. As the crumpled paper nurtured the burning sticks, the dry paper began to smoke as small plumes of grey rose. Roger attempted to blow gently on the matches to encourage them. Through over exuberance the matches went out and more importantly the smoke did not turn to flame.

"Nooooo!"

Roger was now three matches down and nervous. He looked again around his prison. Although the paper was dry it needed further kindling. Roger shuffled once again and secured strands of what appeared to be packaging straw. He sprinkled the content onto the final two sheets of crumpled newspaper. He couldn't risk using both matches so took hold of the penultimate life line and flicked it across the matchbox. As though in slow motion Roger watched the ignited stick somersault into a crevice of the newspaper which was preloaded with kindle. The effect was instant. Not only a flame but a sustainable one.

"Yes, Kirtley, you've done it!"

Roger briefly offered the flame support by whistling onto it but as the flame took hold Roger knew that he had to move swiftly to utilise it. He raised his tight hands above the flame and then immediately withdrew them, as instinctively his body reacted to the heat.

There was no way he would be able to do this pain-free. He bit his teeth together and grimaced ready for the pain.

"Do it! Just do it!"

By placing his wrist directly over the flame he burned off the tape. It was difficult for him to see the accuracy of the burn but he could smell the plastic melting. Regrettably, he could also see smoke rising from his buttoned shirt cuff.

"Ahhh…fuck!"

The melting tape fell onto his bare wrist, blistering it instantly.

The pain intensified. Roger attempted to pull his wrists apart. The tape resisted his pull but suddenly gave way as the flame spiked beneath him.

Roger's euphoria was tempered by the pain from his burnt wrist. The melted plastic stuck to his blistered skin. He peeled it off, grimacing. It was a relatively easy task to move the chair from the floor to its upright position. Roger simply gripped the wooden struts that supported the out building and levered himself up. His tethered feet did indeed aid the process, as predicted.

*God, that feels good.* He opened his arms wide, stretching out the stiffness in his shoulders and neck. He brought his hands up to his face to wipe away the sweat, grime and remnants of the sticky drink. He bent forward trying to find the end of the binding around his feet but was unable to do so. Roger tugged at the tape but it was impossible to pull off without being able to unwind it. Time to use the final match. At least this time Roger had easy access to it and was able to prepare an additional sheet of paper in preparation. Holding the flaming sheet Roger was easily able to direct the flames between his feet and watched as the plastic readily melted and divided in two.

Carlos had conveniently concluded the taping of his body in Roger's central torso and with a bit of a wiggle it was loosened.

Roger enjoyed his new found freedom and stretched upwards like a Yogi.

His satisfaction was cut short as he saw smoke coming up through the floorboards.

"What the…?"

Roger was confused as the smoke was not close to where he had been striking the matches. Within seconds more smoke appeared directly beneath where his first match had dropped. Smoke turned to flame mid-way down the shed where there was a crack the size of a two Euro coin. Roger did not know what was beneath the floorboards but it was clear that whatever was there had been there for a long time and was very dry and combustible. He reached for his drinks supply. Grabbing the feeding nozzle, he pointed it directly over the hole where the flame was flickering. It was growing in size and intensity. The container produced a squirt of water which Roger directed into the hole. It quenched the flame but it was insufficient to put it out and it was quickly rekindled. Shaking the *Camel* casing upside down and shaking it produced but a further few drops which were futile in the circumstances. The smoke began to bellow a little and flame appeared from the far corner of the shed. Roger was sitting on an uncontrollable underfloor heating system.

He stretched forwards picking up a loose section of shelving support wood from the floor and proceeded to break both the nearest panes of glass.

The windows were too small for him to climb through but as the smoke began to rise he would at least be able to try and breathe in fresher air. He was not sure whether the opening up of the window was a good idea because a breeze was able to flow through the cabin and Roger feared that this would only further oxygenate the fire. He levered himself up, put his face to the widow frame and breathed deeply.

Whilst he knew that the door was securely bolted on the outside he wondered as to its overall strength, given that, after all, it was but an old wooded cabin and this was not a thick oak framed door. He nudged at the door with his shoulder to see whether there was any given in it. He rocked to the side and impacted it with greater power. The shoulder yielded more than the door.

"Grrrrr." He grimaced in pain. He heard the lock rattle upon impact but there was no other movement. He then tried to slam the shelf supports into the frame. They may have been effective with the glass but less so on wood. He aimed at the lower half of the door in order to get maximum impact. Again, the locks rattled but there was no sign of the door giving way. Not even a crack in the panel. Roger took his handkerchief from his pocket and covered his mouth in order to try and gain further protection from the toxic carbon monoxide. Smoke was now streaming out of both windows.

*Help me Lord, please help me.*

*Fight fire with fire.*

Roger slid from the chair to the floor and shuffled over to the pile of newspapers and then spread some across the base of the door before stacking them pyramid style against the door

Taking a couple of sheets from the pile, Roger placed them in the flame lapping up from the floorboard. He set fire to the pile of newspapers propped against the door. He would burn the door down or enough at least to weaken it. He returned to the window coughing; this time he didn't try and return to the chair but just held on to the window's narrow inner ledge and hauled himself up until his chest was able to take the weight. He sucked in the air. Visibility was reducing. He could just about see that the wooden frame was beginning to catch light but the smoke was beginning to take hold. Crouching down under the plume he could see smoke hovering in the rafters of the cabin roof. The heat was intensifying and Roger was beginning to feel lightheaded. He knew that this was a very dangerous sign. *Stay awake*

"Help!" he cried through the window but there was nothing but darkness. He was sure that the fire would be seen by anyone nearby but assumed that his nearest neighbours were miles away.

Through the smoke, Roger could just about discern the orange glow surrounding the door frame. Had it weakened the frame sufficiently for him to be able to break out? He readied his wooded ram. He put the full force of his body behind the point of impact. There was a crunching sound as the wood broke through the door panel. But one small hole did not grant freedom. The door and the locks remained defiant. Roger sighted what appeared to be a rusty metal rod

on the corner of the cabin. *Do I have time to try and get it?*
He set off on all fours but as he did so his mind floated, his
eyes closed and he fell with the chair to the floor overcome by
smoke fumes. There was no out of body experience. His life
did not flash before him. He was about to die, but it would
be painless.

# CHAPTER FORTY-FOUR

Even the terrific noise made as the hire vehicle crashed through the front of the wooden structure didn't disturb Roger from his smoke-filled slumber. The locks to the shed door remained intact but the door to which they were attached now stretched across the bonnet of the Fiat. Fire quickly lapped around the vehicle, as the rush of oxygen from the evening air fuelled the flames temporarily. Pina instinctively covered her face as the fire wall engulfed the car windscreen. She put the vehicle in reverse, backing up five metres. She tried to apply full beam to gain greater visibility but only one bulb of the four was now working, the others having shattered on impact. She quickly opened the car door, looking unsuccessfully as she did so, for something to cover her nose and mouth. Before slamming the car into the locked door, she had seen Roger lying unconscious on the floor, having looked through one of the windows at the side of the cabin. She was confident that she would not run him over but less so whether she could reach him in time.

"Roger, wake up. Roger! Roger!"

There was no safe route through the fire. She took a deep breath and strode into the blaze. She jumped over the first flame which was half a metre high. To her surprise she felt no pain, no heat around her legs but a burning sensation to her face as she encountered a falling section of flame damaged roof; ducking under it, she could make out Roger's silhouette and she stretched to reach him, immediately withdrawing her hand as it passed into another flame rising beside him. Taking a half step to her right she stretched out once more and managed to grab hold of Rogers's shirt and shook him.

"Roger!"

She quickly felt her way up to his collar with one hand followed by the other and attempted to drag him. She was shouting for him to wake up, but her efforts were in vain. Roger was slumped against the rear cabin wall and as Pina pulled, he readily fell into a horizontal position. The problem for Pina was that although she was prided herself on her strength, an 80 kg dead weight was not easily shifted. Pina crouched as though she was about to carry out a squat down her gym and then thrust backwards, overcoming Rogers inertia. Once moving the weight felt lighter and she was able to shuffle backwards pulling Roger across the flames as she did so. Within seconds, she had pulled him through the open front onto the gravelled area outside. Two more thrusts and he was pulled safely from the flames. Pina's dress caught fire as had at Rogers's hair. She leant across Rogers head smothering it and the flame as she did so. She then used Roger's torso to extinguish her own flames. She was exhausted, breathless still panicking. She turned her attention to Roger's breathing. She felt for a pulse by the side of his neck and was overwhelmed with relief to find one. She wasn't sure what to do next. He may be unconscious but he hadn't stopped breathing. *Should she start mouth-to-mouth resuscitation?* She saw no downside in doing so though she now wished that she had attended the first-aid course that had been offered at work recently.

As she straddled Rogers's chest, she heard the sound of feet on gravel to her left. Her hearing was more effective than her sight in the darkness but it afforded Pina no opportunity to take avoiding action as a boot in the gloom found its way onto her shoulder projecting her off the motionless Roger and on to the ground. As her attacker moved around to where she had fallen, the light from the damaged but still functioning headlight threw light literally and metaphorically upon her attacker – Carlos! A grinning, knife bearing Carlos. He had his prey at last and seemed to be enjoying the moment. He looked to be alone this time.

"You bitch."

He once again put his boot to productive use and pressed its sole against her chest forcing her down to the ground. For the first time she could recall Pina was not bemoaning her lack of bosom. She was now securely pinned to the floor. Carlos reached for his phone and made his second call of the night. The message was the same;

"I have the painting…yes, I'm sure this time." Pina would have smiled if she could have breathed.

"I have the bitch." Carlos withdrew the phone from his ear and focussed on Pina.

"Where's the fucking painting, bitch?"

"Didn't you like the one I gave you, big boy?" Pina was not really in a position to take satisfaction from the fact that she had duped Carlos earlier at the Tower by switching the original painting for a cheap one purchased from a local artist selling his wares at the side of the river Arno. She had figured correctly that by swapping the frame, the gorillas would not know one landscape from another. She had also been able to dip it in water and rub in silt from the riverbank to further disguise the true nature of painting which depicted a Tuscany hillside three hundred miles from the scene of Cezanne's painting and produced over a century earlier.

Roger's captors had not spotted the watch between the frame and the canvas creating the makeshift tracker. All she needed to do was log into her iPhone and follow the trail. Her plan had gone well up until the time the "painting" appeared to take a U-turn and work its way back to Pisa. Pina had traced the route. As she had approached the point at which the tracker had paused before turning back, Pina saw the burning workshop containing Roger. She had cautiously driven up the driveway but seeing that there was no vehicle present and no lights on in the adjoining house she simply assumed that both men had returned to the city to continue their pursuit.

Carlos had been made to look a fool and was in no mood to enjoy her teasing. His boot pressure increased and moved from Pina's chest to her neck.

She was unable to speak let alone continue hostilities.

Pina reluctantly pointed as best she could to the car. Carlos leant down and grabbed Pina by her hair and dress and dragged her to the vehicle. Though *she* had struggled to drag Roger, this task presented no problem for a man of Carlos' strength, even with a phone tucked under his ear.

The driver's door was still agape and Carlos was able to look inside using the light from his mobile phone. There on the back seat was the object of his boss's desire – the Cezanne and this time the real thing.

Upon the request of his paymaster, he took a photograph of it with a view to texting it to him for verification.

"Let me run the bitch through boss." As he made his request he removed his boot, lifted her up by her hair and fumbled in his pocket for the knife that he had hope to use on her earlier. Pina could not hear the reply but Carlos let go of her and she slumped back to the ground hitting the base of the skull as she did so. Carlos left her lying there and walked towards the lifeless body of Roger. Pina felt helpless. Carlos, with both hands under Rogers's armpits dragged him back towards the burning cabin. With a big heave, he humped him back through what was once the doorway. Pina pulled herself to her knees and then shakily to her feet before running towards Carlos simultaneously pleading with him, "No! No! No!"

Carlos turned back from Roger's lifeless body and easily resisted her verbal and physical pleas. He grabbed her by the arms. Spinning her around, he placed one arm up her back and escorted her away from the burning pyre to the adjoining house which was twenty metres away.

"Roger, Roger…" Pina sobbed openly. She'd not cried with such venom since the unexpected death of her father seven years before. Not even when her lover, Jamie, said goodbye, setting off to fulfil his mountaineering dreams did she feel so desperate and miserable. Carlos showed no compassion. She felt he was trying to punish her.

The door of the farmhouse was open. Carlos fumbled for a light switch inside the doorway. Suddenly there was light. From what Pina could see, the property had not been lived in for many years. It was devoid of furniture. In the dim light Pina could just about pick out the hanging cobwebs from the ceiling which were old and plentiful. She was dragged into what would've been the kitchen area. Where once the kitchen table would have been positioned there were two modern chairs and a table, better suited to a camping trip than farmhouse life. They looked new and Pina presumed they were Carlos's idea of comfort. He pushed her back into the aluminium chair and because it was so light it afforded no stability and she fell straight back onto the tiled floor, again striking her head. Carlos, far from being sympathetic, was irritated at her instability and pulled her up once again. As he did so Pina tried to land a critical blow with her foot to the groin but was hopelessly off balance and lacking the power to do so. Carlos blocked the kick with his knee and reminding her of the imbalance of power, slapped her around the face and placed the six-inch blade to her neck. She could feel it pressing into her skin and expected it to have drawn blood. She froze.

Backing away to the area above the sink, Carlos collected the binding tape which, ultimately, had proved to be ineffective in securing Roger, albeit the fire that he had created to free himself could hardly be viewed a success. Pina's pleas for leniency turned more hostile.

"You fat murdering bastard! Your mother would be disgusted with you! You fucking rotten pig!" She spat at him, something she had never done before. Her technique was poor but the point had been well made.

By way of penalty she had her mouth taped as well. Pina, to her credit, tried to bite Carlos' hand as he applied the tape and she managed to nick the end of his index finger, causing him to wince. He slapped her, hard, and she tried to let him see how it hurt. He did not bother to secure her to the chair, for he needed her to be mobile straight away. Her hands were strapped to her sides and her feet tied just far enough apart to afford a shuffle but not a bid to escape.

As Pina was escorted to the car she looked despairingly towards the burning cabin. It was unrecognisable from its former self. The front had been smashed in and one side and the roof had collapsed in on itself. There was more flame then smoke and Pina let out muffled cry from the beneath the securing tape. Her tears had dried up but she felt rage and anger. She was thrust onto the backseat of her car and the door was closed behind her. She lay across the seat, helpless.

Having safely secured Pina, Carlos picked up the painting, which he had propped up against the front wheel arch of the vehicle. He reached inside the driver's door, pressing the button to release the lock on the boot at the rear of the Fiat. It gave a familiar click upon release. As he opened the boot, he was struck powerfully in the face by the car jack. Roger had dug deep within himself in order to summon up the strength and courage to launch the attack. He had regained consciousness as the flame burnt his exposed flesh. Dragging his body to the boot was painful but took little time to achieve. Pina would have been impressed with his climbing skills to access the boot. The small dim light inside the boot had afforded little illumination but the silhouette of Carlos stood out and enabled him to aim straight at his face. Carlos had no time to react and although the blow did not knock him out as Roger had hoped, he stumbled and rather than fall backwards and out of reach, he clung to the boot for support. Roger struck again; a cleaner strike this time given that Carlos was nearer and stationary. Roger dropped to the jack for an instant so as to hold onto Carlo's shirt; keep him within striking zone. The third blow to the back of the head made Roger wince; metal on bone but this was no time for sympathy. There was no need to hang on to Carlos this time for although he fell away from the open boot, he was not going to rally anytime soon. Roger exited the boot effectively without grace and used Carlos' amble frame as a landing cushion. Carlos didn't stir.

Roger patted down Carlos' leather jacket and quickly located the lump he had sought. Reaching inside his pocket, he secured the flick knife and then, as a precaution, opened it. On this occasion, the click accompanying the appearance of the sharp blade was a satisfying one. There was no prospect of dragging Carlos closer to the vehicle so that he could keep an eye on him. Roger knew that the safest course of events was simply to run the knife through Carlos' heart without pondering his state of consciousness. It would be easy enough to disguise it as classic case of self-defence; nobody would bother to investigate carefully whether or not his captor was conscious or not. Roger lay across Carlos' abdomen. He held the knife in his right hand and placed it just under Carlos' rib cage. He then carried out a practice run; an upward thrusting movement that would miss the ribs but would cut deep into flesh and organ. He pulled the knife back again and prepared to lunge. He paused at the top of his stroke and took a deep breath… *No, I can't.* He just couldn't bring himself to complete the movement. *This isn't right.* He was an insurance rep not a cold-blooded murderer. He could not do it instinctively, let alone with time to think. It came as no surprise to him killing was a difficult thing to do even when your life may depend on it.

Instead Roger retracted the blade and put the knife away into his rear trouser pocket. Instead wacked him again a final time with the jack for good measure. This too may yet kill him but it felt a more humanitarian pathway.

Roger could hear the guttural noises that Pina was making from inside the car, her cries muffled by the tight tape. She did not know what was happening outside save that she had heard Carlos' cries of pain as the attack ensued. Roger was the last person she expected to see. In fact as he just managed to open the door she couldn't see him at all as leaned in at ground level. She looked down and spotted him. There were tears in her eyes and her pupils were dilated, partly due to the surrounding darkness, partly out of sheer exhilaration.

Roger put the knife to more effective use, this time to cut Pina free rather thrusting it up to its hilt into Carlos' torso. She assisted by laying forward to enable Roger to delicately cutaway the tape from her mouth, sliding a finger beneath the tape in order to avoid cutting her face. He noticed as he did so that her hair was matted with blood and having partially released her, he cradled her in silence for a moment to his face before beginning to cut her arms free. She then took the knife to free up her feet. They collapsed together on the ground, oblivious to its lack of comfort.

Pina tried to recover her breath and although she had many questions to ask, was on able to speak coherently.

"Shh. Calm, Pina, calm. Take a deep breath…"

The prospect of dragging Carlos back into the house was a daunting one given his size and given the concern that he may come to at any time. Safety first, thought Roger.

Pina told Roger that the gaffer tape was in the house and she went to collect the roll. Roger took no chances to the extent he leaned against Carlos' chest and held the knife securely to his throat. He was in no doubt that if Carlos awoke and was agitated, Roger *would* use the damn thing this time to finish him off.

Pina returned and they began the trussing up process. They had learnt from their own experience what was effective and disarming. They started with his hands before moving down to secure his feet tightly. For the moment anyway, they didn't want to hear anything from Carlos and taped his mouth too. Pina didn't even want to see his eyes and took the tape from Roger cutting off a short strip to place it to over them.

If Pina Had struggled to drag a lifeless Roger from the burning outhouse, moving the trussed up Carlos back into the farmhouse presented an even more daunting task. They decided to roll him in the end. His rotund frame assisting the task. A final heave by Pina and Carlos was in the kitchen where he could be left him lying on the floor. Pina paused breathless before helping Roger up on to a makeshift kitchen bench along a dirty kitchen table.

The idea of torturing Carlos to get information from him appealed far more to Pina then it did Roger. Indeed, Pina seemed content to extract revenge without confession.

"Let me have a go at the bastard," Pina said.

Roger looked at Pina with concern, for she actually sounded serious.

"No, Pina! No, we can't; we just can't," retorted Roger, his voice trailing off as though to emphasise *his* more rational thought. "In any event, he is a hardened pro, who wouldn't tell us anything. If he did he probably wouldn't live long afterwards."

"Yes, but it would be such fun to try," interrupted Pina, eagerly.

Pina, this time, to Roger's relief, had the faintest of smiles across her face. "We wouldn't even know where to start."

"I would, Roger – trust me. His testicles for starters." This time the smile extended more readily across her face.

As though subconsciously unsettled by the prospect of castration, Carlos made his first movement and noise. The latter was indecipherable but a sign of life nonetheless. A bit of Roger was disappointed.

"I think I'll take hold of the knife for now, Pina," said Roger stretching out to receive the weapon, smiling himself this time.

"We need to use Carlos, the painting and the pair of us as bait, Roger. If the paymaster is prepared to kill to get the painting, then he'll be prepared to come out of hiding for it. If he thinks he can get us both into the bargain, then so much the better."

"Speak for yourself, Pina," said Roger, sounding alarmed again.

"I've seen what it's like dangling on the end of a fish hook and it's no fun."

"We need to reassess our priorities, Roger. I don't give a toss about the painting any more. I don't care what its worth but I do care about getting the bastard who's behind it all. He can have the painting if we can find just find out who he is. Job done, Roger. We have the Cezanne, we have that baddie or at least one of them and we for now are safe – it's time to get out of here and get help."

And Roger couldn't agree more.

"I will certainly drink to that!"

"I might even join you for once," came the reply of the stressed teetotaller.

"We probably won't be able to get anyone at the office until the morning but the police can now take over."

Pina returned to her mobile phone and dialled 121.

"Polizia grazi…"

"I would like to report a murder and attempted murder, a kidnapping, arson and theft…"

*Quite a list,* thought Roger. He was that less comfortable with the reference to arson given that he had started the fire himself but realised Pina was keen to make an impact.

He was unable to overhear all of the conversation but it was clear that the operator was seeking further details.

"Si, Pina, Pina Venti and Roger Kirtley. Yes, we are in need of urgent assistance. The immediate danger has passed but we fear another attack. I'm not sure of our exact whereabouts, about an hour west of Pisa. Can you check it on the phone?

"No, we don't need medical services," she replied looking down at Carlos who was beginning to groan. Actually, an ambulance maybe of some use upon reflection.

"I cannot explain all over the phone. I work for PNP insurance and we have recovered a missing painting by Cezanne…C-e-z-a-n-n-e.

We are detaining one suspect. He is very dangerous though – a killer. We need immediate back up." She paused. "How long? That's too long to wait. We will need to move from here. We will head back to Pisa."

Pina put the phone into her pocket.

"They going to take up to an hour to get to here, Roger.

We should wait but I'm not sure it's safe. Let's take the painting and run."

"Yes, Carlos' pal is bound to be on route. But if we leave Carlos here he will be freed by his pal and they could both escape before the police arrive."

"You're right. Let's drag him into the darkness of the back garden and reinforce the tape around his mouth that way he won't be seen or heard." With that she turned the key the back door. Roger could only watch as she yanked the door open. It scraped noisily along the floor.

"Pina, you drag him outside if you can and I'll go and turn some more of these lights on. That way the house will be easier to find by the police."

"Will do," replied Pina less confident than Roger that she would be able to move him far enough on his own. Roger slid from the bench into a seated position, shuffled to his left to secure a worn out broom, whose bristles were matted but the handle would serve well as light switch flickers. He began to work his way backwards out of the kitchen. He could hear Pina's grunts of exertion from the garden as he saw Carlos' feet disappear into the darkness. There was a central corridor that facilitated access to other areas of the bungalow. Almost to Roger's surprise the, first of the light switches worked a treat and threw light on the rest of the property. The first room on Roger's left sprang to life as the broom stick did its job. Not a pretty sight; a small unmade bed with sheets perhaps never changed this century. The next was far more interesting; *Wow look at that,* thought Roger as he pulled on the bedsheets to get a better view.

"Pina! Pina, come quickly! She was still in the garden with Carlos and didn't hear Roger's initial calls. She did the second time but was worried at Roger's seemingly anxious tone. She put in a short sharp sprint across the kitchen and down the corridor.

"What is it? What is it Roger?"

Pina stood at the entrance to the second bedroom. She looked at Roger and then looked down on the floor around him.

"No way!"

"Hard to believe, isn't it Pina?"

They're lying on top of the torn and dirty bed quilt that Roger had pulled from the bed were two nude paintings – identical save that one was an original Gauguin and worth £35 million more than the other. They both looked at each other but said nothing for the moment, just taking in the scene. They were both excited.

"Two masterpieces in one day."

"Just an average day in the office, Pina."

She picked up each painting in turn and placed them side by side against the wall for a clearer view. Roger accepted a hand to help him up on to the bed.

"Good job the frames are different, Pina, otherwise we could mix the original with the fake."

The frames were decidedly different but in the relatively gloomy light proffered by cob web ridden bulb, the paintings looked to be identical.

"I couldn't tell the difference. Could you, Pina?"

Roger was keen to get away as soon as possible but was still drawn to inspecting the paintings in greater detail. Roger, invited Pina to hold each painting in front of him so that he could inspect the finer detail. There were some differences in tone and if anything, one was more was more vibrant than the other.

"Which is which then, Pina?" asked Roger teasingly.

"If pressed, I would say that looks a better piece of work," said Pina pointing at the fake.

A loud noise from the kitchen made them both jump.

"What's that?" Pina gripped Roger's arm.

"Shhhh." Roger placed his finger over his lips.

Their eyes met briefly. Pina looked afraid. They both listened intently. Had gorilla number two returned? They froze as though any movement now might alert as to their whereabouts, forgetting the untold noise that they had been making in their excitement. . The silence was broken by the sound of Carlos moaning. A further ten seconds passed and, again, they heard nothing but Carlos. Their immediate fears began to subside. Roger looked around the bedroom and pointed to a water jug by the side of the bed mimicking for it to be used as a weapon. Pina understood. Roger fumbled in his back pocket and once again took out the flick knife. The noise made by the extending blade seemed to echo around the silence. Roger indicated that he would take the lead as he slid off the bed; to be fair, with his wheelchair he could be as effective as anyone. He had even had a few sessions of wheelchair karate last year. Pina however saw that without the chair, the odds were unfavourably stacked. This was not a time for political correctness and she therefore brazenly just stepped over him and entered the corridor. Roger briefly tugged at her trouser leg but was not about to give a lecture on disability equality. Adrenalin had obviously surged in Pina for rather than creep down the corridor, she ran at full pelt screaming out. She did not feel brave but for a moment her battle cry provided her with courage.

Any trouble was to be found in the kitchen. Pina burst

in. Because the house had been stripped there would be no place to hide. The door to the garden was open; a gust of wind caught it and it banged against the side wall. The same sound that they had heard a minute earlier. No one had come in for there was nowhere to go without them being seen, could they? That didn't stop her tip towing towards the flapping door. She peered into the darkness. For once Carlos, trussed up like a turkey was a welcome sight. *Nothing, sweet nothing but Carlos.* Her relief was immense. She came back inside and kicked the door shut.

"Its fine, Roger, its fine."

Roger took a moment to blow out his cheeks and looked up to the heavens in relief. He shook his head, smiling to himself just as Pina's smiling face reappeared at the bedroom door.

"There's no one else but a squirming, Carlos."

"Here, give me the jug."

Pina looked down, surprised she was still holding it. She smiled and handed it to him. Roger placed the jug on the floor. Pina knelt and they embraced out of sheer relief.

"Shall we go now, Roger?

"Too right! I've been trying to you out for the last twenty minutes. Grab his feet," directed Roger as she then proceeded to shuffle the dead weight into the overgrown back garden. Roger could offer little assistance. Pina needed to get him far enough away from the door so as not to be visible. Pina dropped him.

"Shuffle him up a few more metres. He will be hidden then."

Pina looked at Roger in exasperation but gripped then grunted recognising the value of the extra effort.

"He's going nowhere but we should drive somewhere in the car and hide nearby," said Roger.

Pina was in the agreement, even if the police were on their way they were too exposed.

The groans from Carlos were increasing and he was beginning to roll his buttocks, clearly in a state of agitation.

"Carlos, it's time for *you* to shut up. The boot's on the other foot." As if to emphasise the literal role reversal, Pina pressed her foot down on the wriggling chest. Without hesitation she the lifted her foot but then she returned it, boring down heavily on Carlos' neck – causing a gurgling sound. Such was his state of agitation that Roger leant in to check that his bindings were secure. He was satisfied that as angry as he was Carlos, there was no immediate threat.

"Leave him Pina – it's time to go. Can you get the car a bit closer for me and grab get the paintings."

"I will but don't take this in the wrong way, Roger, but you stink. I noticed a spare shirt and trousers in the bedroom. Not exactly haute couture, but just look at you!"

Roger looked down at himself and joined in her laughter. Dust, charcoal, blood, dirt and urine. He would change quickly, or as quickly as he could, given that it could sometimes take over an hour to wash and dress in the morning.

The decrepit farmhouse was at the end of a road just under a kilometre long. Curiously, only the first twenty metres had tarmac on it. The rest of the road was rutted and uneven. Pina had driven cautiously up it, when seeking Roger, guided as much by the flames from the fire as the headlight beam on the road ahead of her.

They were now keen to escape as fast as possible but the road surface prevented a quick exit and with no fire to use as a direction beacon, Pina needed to rely on the broken headlights. She rather wished that she had reversed into Roger's burning prison even if this would have exposed the fuel tank to the flames. *Perhaps not.*

Out of habit more than caution, both Pina and Roger plugged in their seat belts. The radio came on automatically but this was not a time for melody. The irony of the tune, *surfing USA* by *The Beach Boys*, was lost in the moment.

The start of the journey did not go well, as Pina clipped the wing mirror on the side of the wooden gate that demarcated the end of the road and the beginning of the property's plot. The damage was on the passenger side and upon hearing the impact Roger immediately leaned towards the Pina.

"Steady Pina!"

Pina had yet to consider what Hertz would make of the damage to vehicle.

She gave up apologising for the bumpy ride after less than 100 metres. She leaned forward towards the windscreen, trying to get a better view from the partially lit road that was only illuminated by the remaining offside headlight bulb.

Pina's headlight now contrasted sharply with the beam of light appearing out of nowhere in the immediate distance.

"Shit," cried Roger, who noticed it first. Then Pina looked up from her focus on the road immediately in front of her. "Shit!" They both realised that it could be only one thing: the second gorilla returning.

It was difficult to be precise but given that the other vehicle had just turned into the access road, it had to be at least 500 metres away. The roadway curved in an elongated S shape which made judging distance even harder.

"Quick! Off with the lights!"

Pina was still unfamiliar with the vehicle and only managed to switch on the windscreen wipers, which scraped horribly across the dry screen. In her fluster, rather than turning them off, she simply moved them into faster mode.

"Other side!" shouted Roger, who lent over and turned the control switch to turn out the lights. The isolated headlight was obviously giving off more illumination then Pina had given it credit, because they were suddenly thrown into complete darkness. The only light was coming from the approaching vehicle. Fortunately, given the state of the road there was no prospect of the oncoming vehicle descending upon them at speed.

"Now what?" Roger cried, more for his own benefit than Pina's.

"Drive off the road, Pina. It's our only chance."

Pina did not seek further guidance, she gripped the steering wheel tightly and turned it 45° to her left. Their initial journey was, if anything, smoother than before. The experience was short lived because without warning the Fiat met the edge of a sharp drop of two to three metres before the ground levelled out again. They both screamed. The vehicle was probably only in freefall for a second or so but they experienced it in slow motion, uncertain as to their fate. The front bumper struck the ground first and was partially dislodged on impact. The noise of metal nuts being torn away from their fittings was a far from harmonious sound. The noise reverberated through the vehicle and Pina felt sure that the impact would have been heard by the oncoming driver. Pina had hit the break when in freefall and had not taken her foot off the pedal. This only enhanced the impact.

Pina released the break and the vehicle started to roll forward once again. She quickly reapplied the foot break and this time lifted the handbrake in order to apply extra grip.

"Kill the engine, Pina."

She turned the ignition key to off as requested and they waited in the dark silence, barely daring to breathe. Had their headlight been spotted? Could they be seen even in the darkness? Would the driver have heard the crash?

For a moment, there was no sign of the oncoming headlights, yet they knew that the vehicle couldn't have passed. And, then, there it was ahead of them, probably fifty metres away to their right. For an instant, the oncoming headlight beam seemed to be pointing straight at them, lighting up the car interior. Roger and Pina tensed. A second later the direction of the light changed, as the vehicle straightened up on the bend.

"What should we do now?" asked Pina, reaching for the door. If the other car stopped they would be in real trouble but somehow their car afforded them a protective box of steel. Roger reached over and put his hand on her arm. "Lock the door."

No sooner had the four doors engaged in lock mode then the noise of the vehicle passing alongside them could be heard. Within seconds they could see that the car had passed their marooned vehicle. Their means of escape may have been scuppered but it would be impossible to find them in this dark wilderness.

"Fuck! He's not seen us, Roger."

Roger flung his head back in relief.

# CHAPTER FORTY-FIVE

If the beam from the oncoming car had temporarily dazzled them, then the spotlight that swooped in from above was overwhelming. So was the noise. The downdraught from the helicopter blades caused the vehicle to vibrate and then rock from side to side accentuating its precarious position. The spotlight fixed upon them briefly and the vehicle was lit up as though it was daylight. Roger covered his eyes and Pina her head, to avoid the glare. The spotlight was transient as had been the earlier headlight.

"It's the paymaster, Roger. We need to try and hide. The police must be at least twenty-five minutes away yet."

"You're right, Pina. We can't risk it. We will have to leave the paintings. If they find them they may leave us alone. I won't get far but its dark out there and I can hide behind a rock or in a bush even. You must run, Pina; run for your life."

"No! I can't leave you; won't leave you"

"Pina, don't you see? If you get away, then you can save us *both*."

With that, Roger opened his passenger door and sliding to his left extended both feet out and into mid-air... He may not have feeling in his legs but he knew the pull of gravity when he felt it. He had been holding lightly onto the vehicle frame to guide his exit but now gripped it tightly. His life might depend on it.

Roger shouted to Pina, who was herself half way out of the vehicle. Though she could not actually see his predicament, it was clear from the tone of his voice that he was in real difficulty.

"Quickly, Pina! Take my hand. Pull me back!" Roger took the calculated risk of releasing one hand from his life support panel. Pina grabbed his arm with both her hands. She hauled him back into the vehicle with her knees on the driver's seat. She used the steering wheel to get extra leverage.

By now the spotlight from the sky was firmly fixed on the farmhouse. A voice from an amplified voice boomed out from the helicopter overriding the noise of the blades and engine.

"This is the police. We are armed. Come out with your hands above your head. I repeat. This is the police. We are armed. Come out with your hands above your head." Within the crowded confines of the Fiat, Roger and Pina hugged for the second time in short succession, out of relief.

They watched as the helicopter circled once again above the farmhouse and gave out another clear and assertive message.

The flying machine then backed away from the building still maintaining a clear spot light upon it.

From their view behind the helicopter, Pina and Roger could just about see in the shadows two or three figures being lowered to the ground by way of what Roger assumed was some form of rope and harness system attached to the cockpit. He had no doubt that they were armed police. Whilst the initial temptation was for the couple to work their way back to the house, given the state of high alert and the fact that the armed police were likely to be expecting the worst, it seemed sensible for Pina and Roger to stay where they were in the car. Roger checked in the glove compartment in the hope that there might be a torch, even if only for night-time map reading. No such luck in the modern world of satellite navigation. Given Rogers' recent near miss, it was another good reason for not moving anywhere. They had gained the impression that the vehicle had been spotted by the police search team but they would not be a priority until Carlos and his pal had been safely detained. Given the apparent manpower, this was something that was likely to be achieved quickly, even if Carlos had been freed by his compatriot. Carlos' knife rested firmly in Rogers back pocket too. Even if his ally was armed, and there was every chance that there would be, the extent of the police fire power as compared with a hand pistol would make for an unfair contest.

"Keep your hands on your head. I repeat keep your arms on your head. This is the police. We are armed. Now kneel down on the ground. Kneel on the ground. Do not move. Do not move!"

From their position at the bottom of the ditch they could not see whether one or two of the villains had been apprehended but it was clear that the dangerous part of the operation was at an end.

"They've got the bastards, Pina."

"Yes, and we have the paintings in case you'd forgotten."

"That we do – I feel a bonus coming."

"You better share it with me, Mr. Big Shot."

"I'll think about it…"

They figured that it was time for them to be rescued. They had little time to wait before the helicopter swivelled and returned to their hiding place. The intensity of the searchlight was reduced in order for a wider search beam to be utilised, speeding up the location process. Their vehicle soon came into focus and became the centrepiece for the lights. Roger climbed across the passenger seat pulling his legs up and over the central console and joined Pina who was standing by the driver's door waving with both arms as though about to be rescued following a spell as a shipwrecked sailor on a desert island. She had been expecting a warmer welcome.

"This is the police. We are armed. This is the police. We are armed. Get out of the vehicle and put your hands on your head. Get out of the vehicle and put your hands on your head."

"Hey," shouted Pina. "It's us!"

"Pina, stop waving and put your hands on your head as instructed."

Roger exited the same door, bottom first, unable at first to comply with the request to put his hands on his head. He leant against the car door and then complied.

"Now take two paces forward and kneel on the ground. Keep your hands on your head at all times. Take two paces forward; kneel on the ground and keep your hands on your head at all times."

No sooner had Pina stepped forward as instructed, when a torchlight appeared from her rear, accompanied by the sound of fast moving boots.

"Do not look round. Keep your hands on your head – armed police." Pina couldn't help but try and glance over her shoulder. She was reprimanded for the movement but was able to confirm, providing some comfort, that the escorts were indeed either police or military personnel, to the extent that she could make out that the two men were wearing uniforms. She saw that at least one was armed with what appeared to be an automatic weapon of sorts and this had unnervingly been pointed in her direction.

"Eyes to the front – I repeat – eyes to the front only."

Roger offered a quarter turn of his head to try and make eye contact with Pina but having seen the guns, she was obeying commands to the letter, for once.

First Pina and then Roger had their hands tied behind their back. Seemingly not in conventional metal handcuffs but in tight fitting rather sharp plastic fasteners: quick, effective and bit painful for the recipient. To be tied up twice in twenty-four hours was, in Oscar Wilde's terms, *careless* concluded Roger to himself.

A body search of Pina produced little but her battery drained IPhone whilst the recovery of a flick knife from Roger was a more interesting find and kept the policeman on high alert.

They were both told to stand up. In the heat of the exchange it was difficult for Roger to explain that he wasn't being awkward, he really couldn't walk.

"Are you injured?" bellowed the armed officer, sceptical at Roger's non-cooperation. Pina his time broke ranks and turned around.

"He's paralysed. He's paralysed"

"Has he been shot? enquired the armed and irritated officer as he peered down looking for a wound. Roger took up the mantel, speaking with the full glare of a torchlight in his face.

"I'm fine – just a paraplegic without his chair – I need help."

The policeman diverted the torch on to Roger's legs. He could see that Roger's thighs were disproportionately small when compared with his well tone upper body. Without warning, let alone request, the policeman reached forward and actually clenched Roger's thigh to reinforce his visual assessment. Satisfied, he called out to a colleague and again without warning or request, Roger was unceremoniously hoisted up onto the broad shoulders of another armed policeman who seemed to barely notice the load.

In order to get back onto the pathway leading to the farm house they had to scramble up a relatively steep incline adjacent to, though less extreme in ascent, the precipice that had caused them to plunge in the first place. For Pina, this climb was not easy to achieve with hands tied behind her back but a guiding thrust from an escort into the small of Pina's back and the task was completed. The assistance was more impressive given that it came from the guard with Roger on his back. *These were not traffic cops*, thought Pina.

The intense noise and down draught of the helicopter had subsided suddenly. It had landed on a relatively flat stretch of land adjacent to the house. The engines had been switched off and the blades slowed to a halt. The search lights were still directed onto the house, throwing an abundance of light upon it and the immediate surrounds. There lying on the ground were their two pursuers – Carlos, still strapped in tape but now with the additional plastic hand fastening and his partner, also tied and lying face down. Standing beside them and now clearly visible in the light were two armed officers, dressed in blue and black combat outfits. Big boots, bullet-proof jackets with contrasting lightweight baseball cap. It was difficult to tell whether the offices were police or army save for the yellow 'Policia' letters across the top of their cap.

"Take them inside," directed the third officer who was clearly older than the others; he was dressed similarly save for the fact that he was not wearing a cap and not had not bothered to do up his flat jacket. His non-compliance was indicative of his seniority.

Pina and Roger, who was still suspended shoulder high, were escorted into the familiar surrounds of the farmhouse kitchen. The door to the garden was ajar again but afforded no cause for concern this time.

The officer in charge turned to face them and looked bemused at Rogers's predicament. The weight bearing officer briefly explained the position and proceeded to seat Roger on the kitchen bench. Unable to support his core he simply fell backwards before being caught again before striking his head on the solid floor. Resting now against the table itself, Roger was secure. The senior officer looked down at the screen on the phone he was holding in his left hand and swiped it left and right looking up at his prisoners as he did so. It was obvious to Pina and Roger that he was carrying out facial recognition – more simply put, looking at their photos for a match. Satisfied, he nodded to one of the offices whose attention had not strayed for a moment from them and as the officer walked behind in order to free their hands, the senior officer's frame of mind changed spontaneously.

"Pina, Roger, forgive the formalities. It's protocol, you

understand. I am Inspector Paulo Lottie from the Policia di Stato, assigned to Interpol," he informed them, reaching for and displaying his metallic badge encased within its black leather wallet. He waited for both to be untied and offered his hand, as much by way of an apology as an introduction. Roger noticed him taking a second look at his ill-fitting and only slightly fresher clothing.

"Don't ask, inspector."

Paulo sat himself down on top of the kitchen table alongside Roger and invited Pina to join them. With his feet swinging, Inspector Lottie invited a more relaxed atmosphere. The officer who had previously been guarding them had released his grip on his weapon and placed the couple's property, still inside transparent "evidence bags" on the table alongside his superior officer.

"Sorry, Signora, you can't have the phone back yet. We need to check to see whether any calls can be traced, which I'm afraid to say is very unlikely. In addition, we don't want to give away your location when we move back to HQ. How long ago did the phone die?"

"Probably an hour or so," said Pina looking at her Apple watch. Inspector Lottie noticed with curiosity that she was wearing two watches but said nothing.

"That's good, then, because your last phone signal location will be here. If anyone else is sent we can then be waiting for them. It's an ideal hideout location for the criminals, yes, but for us as well."

"Yes, sorry about the phone, inspector. You don't remember to pack the charger when someone is trying to kill you," Pina reflected, as she picked up the phone. Inspector

Lottie then held up the flick knife from the table and opened it with a discrete press of the release button.

"Standard insurance issue, Roger?"

All three smiled.

"As the Boy Scouts say, always be prepared, inspector."

"I think I better take this for safekeeping nonetheless," he said, retracting the blade and handing it to his junior colleague.

"By the way, you made it to us quickly. We were told that we may have to wait an hour for you to arrive."

"Ah, well, that's the advantage of Interpol— different agency, more resources. The regular police are still on their way. Details of your call were intercepted and forwarded to us at Interpol. Although part of Italian police, we are a seconded to Interpol. Our Umbrian base is in Florence where there's a helicopter. We can have it the air in less than seven minutes – you were just fifteen minutes flight time away."

"What do you mean of call was intercepted?" enquirer the intrigued Pina.

"Oh, it's a very sophisticated system based on computer algorithms more than human intervention. References to parties or places of interest, possible terrorists, rogue states, wanted criminals, the bad and the mad. The computers detects references, written and oral, through a wide range of networks and will send warning alerts depending on the strength of the algorithm correlation. A web site reference will be low grade perhaps, a phone call from a terrorist suspect a higher priority."

"What? And Pina was on the most wanted list?" goaded Roger.

"No, you'll be pleased to know, it was not Pina but

reference to the Cezanne painting that created the alert at HQ."

"I'm surprised the painting attracts much attention. It's hardly the stuff of international terrorism," observed Roger.

"You say that, but the trigger was not the Cezanne, exactly, but two parties connected to it that are, shall we say, of interest to us. I cannot say anything further at the moment until we get back to HQ where we will need to carry out an obligatory debriefing of you both and we can then talk further."

"What of those two pigs?" asked Pina, pointing in the direction of Carlos and his pal.

"Leave them to us. The local police will be here soon and will take them back by secure van. Ever been in a helicopter?" asked Inspector Lottie, enjoying the opportunity of offering patronage. It was clear that Pina was more excited at the prospect than Roger, who had previously declined opportunities to do so. Roger, I'm sorry but even Interpol don't carry a spare wheelchair.

"Come, let's go. Florence looks fantastic at night from the air." Roger had obviously acquired a new status, for the officer politely asked this time asked if Roger minded the shoulder lift and was far more delicate in its performance.

As the group exited the house and walked towards the waiting helicopter, they passed within metres of Pina's *pigs*. From his prone position Carlos angled his head slightly and saw them approaching.

"You bitch," spurted out Carlos. "I will cut you to pieces."

Roger reached out from his great height to try and touch her shoulder and comfort her but she pushed it away and before the Inspector could intervene, she had stepped forward and planted a swinging foot into Carlos's side, impacting his right kidney.

"… Bitch…" Carlos just about managed to repeat, though it was virtually inaudible due to the acute pain. Pina turned, cathartically satiated and walked towards the helicopter, looking forward to her first flight.

# CHAPTER FORTY-SIX

As Inspector Lottie had advised, following the excitement of the helicopter ride, they arrived at Interpol for their debriefing. Lottie had called ahead and there was a wheelchair waiting to greet Roger as the doors of the chopper opened. It was a remnant from the store room; it was old and heavy with one of the tyres partly deflated. For Roger it was like sitting on a regal throne given his recent depravation and his aching body yielded readily to the cushioned support. He would need to be pushed rather than self-propel but he was beyond worrying about his dignity.

Interpol had no separate facilities as such. Indeed, as an organisation, although it had worldwide governance, Interpol was essentially made up of national and regional police forces, joining together to share information and resources. Whilst there were several ongoing projects involving police officers from several countries under the command of a senior Interpol officer, most activity was carried out within a clearly defined national jurisdiction. There was, for example, no Interpol uniform, no branded logo. All central funds had to be vigorously fought for each year and with global austerity becoming an increasing feature, budgets had decreased and not kept pace with inflation. Inevitably, this led to a less effective force, at a time when crime itself was becoming less regionalised and more international. The debrief was carried out in separate interview rooms by individual officers. Although these were the same rooms in which suspects would be interviewed on a daily basis before being charged, the mood was far friendlier. There was no need to advise Pina and Roger of their rights, as they were specifically told that they were not suspects in any crime and certainly there was no need for legal support. Food and drink was supplied for them both. Pina in particular had started to feel dehydrated and realise that she had been several hours without drink and many hours since she ate some food, back on the boat.

Pina and Roger both freely consented to their debrief session being recorded. There would not have been an issue if they had preferred for them not to be. They gave their respective stories with clarity, accuracy and felt no temptation to embellish at all or gratuitously elaborate on what, for them, had been an extraordinary 24 hours. This was a tale that did not require enhancement. As professionals, they were used to working with outside agencies, though, particularly during their early careers, they were more used to being the ones taking the statement, as opposed to giving it.

Pina relayed her Pisa exploits. Though she underplayed the agility and strength required, the interviewing officer, Detective Alberto Costello, was incredibly impressed. He put down his pen and smiled at her.

"Magnifico, quite magnifico."

She reported her despair at thinking Roger initially, had been killed by smoke fumes and then worst of all, left to burn to death by Carlos. She could feel herself welling up with emotion as she told Detective Costello of Rogers rescue

Roger's tale was perhaps less heroic up until the time he was able to overcome Carlos when his feats became centre stage. He relayed with enthusiasm the amazement of discovering the two Gauguins.

The individual sessions took less than an hour. The interviewing officers thanked them for their time and cooperation, arranging for further sustenance.

Before they'd had an opportunity to start eating the rather unedifying supplies from the police canteen, they were politely escorted upstairs, where, just along the corridor was an office with a sliding nameplate; inserted in the holder ‹Inspector Lottie.'

The escorting officer firmly knocked twice on the door. The swift reply of "come," echoed from within. The officer opened the door and with his left hand and gestured with his right that they should enter. As the officer closed the door behind him, Inspector Lottie got up from his desk and once again shook their hands. For the second time that day, he offered them a seat but on this occasion, he was least able to take up position behind his own desk; a desk that was remarkably free from paperwork, one that was dominated by a computer with a flat screen attached to a flexible arm that enabled him to move it out the way so that he could have clear visibility across his desk. Inspector Lottie began where he had left off earlier, by praising Roger and Pina for their efforts and thanking them for their cooperation. He checked to make sure that they had been looked after but did not offer to supply tea or coffee. Despite his display of courtesy, it was apparent that he was a man with something on his mind.

Lottie leaned forward, placing his elbows upon the desk, clasping his hands together.

"You were right earlier, Pina, when you said that you was surprised that your name or indeed a painting should trigger such a response from Interpol. I accept that it is probably an indictment of our police force or realistically the resources available, that the kidnapping and attempted murder you reported didn't merit a SWAT response unit. It is just the changing world in which we live in. What I'm going to tell you needs to be in absolute confidence. It can be discussed with no one, not even senior members at PNP. Can I take talk off the record and candidly?"

Pina readily nodded.

"Inspector, you should know that we will do all we can to help," Roger said. "That is a given. You do place us in a rather difficult situation because obviously, at the moment we don't have a clue what you're going to tell us. This may put us at odds with the duty that we owe to PNP for example." Roger looked at Pina and she acknowledged, thinking about the matter further that there could be a potential issue. Inspector Lottie unclasped his hands and leant back in his spring backed chair. It strained noisily. He pause briefly before continuing.

"Roger, you are of course quite right. I put you in an invidious situation, I understand that. For reasons that will become apparent, your guarantee of confidentiality is required. I know that, ultimately, without getting you to sign the Official Secrets Act there is nothing I can do to prevent you discussing the issue more widely. I do know however that in the insurance market the slogan for many years has been, my word is my bond. That word would be good enough for me."

Roger nodded.

"Reference to the painting, *Col de Galibier, did* trigger an algorithmic linkup sufficient to cause our notification. The painting brings together two people very much of interest to Interpol. With your agreement, I will tell you who they are and why they are of interest to us."

Roger and Pina looked at each other. Pina lent across and tapped Roger's knee with her hand playfully, indicating that they should in her terms "go for it."

"It is to deal, Inspector – Err...let's go for it," Roger contributed. Pina patted him on the knee again.

"The two men in question are Harold Reidler an attorney based in Geneva and Pavlov Stets, a Ukrainian billionaire who lives in London." Roger could barely contain himself and lent forward encroaching across the desk.

"Don't tell me that Stets owns both the Cezanne and the Gauguin! I met Stets only this week. I went to his home!"

"Yes, too much of a coincidence, isn't it? The archives show that the Cezanne was exhibited last year, having been loaned out to a galley in Paris by none other than Stets himself. Roger, as for your visit, we know you did, to be fair. The algorithms would have noted you too, Roger. I promise we weren't snooping on you but it just forms part of an ongoing operation." Roger sat back in his chair rather deflated that his contribution was old news.

"Art is what links Reidler and Stets together. We believe that Reidler is a significant part of a money laundering enterprise using art as his medium. Reidler, either through his own significant wealth or the wealth of his often unscrupulous clients, cleans money by purchasing works of art from around the world. These are not pieces of art that you will see coming up for auction but involve private transactions with a substantial exchange of cash. From the stories you have both given, it is clear that someone has been desperate to recover the Cézanne and Gauguin paintings. We don't know why, but we do think that Reidler is involved along the line somewhere, indirectly or if we are very lucky, directly."

He glanced at Pina and then Roger.

"As you say, it is simply too much of a coincidence that Stets is the owner of both paintings. There just must be a correlation between the two and maybe, just maybe, this could be our chance to nail Reidler. There have been suspicions surrounding both men, particularly Reidler. But it has been impossible to put together a case that would even justify a prosecution, let alone a successful conviction. We've explored all areas: fraud, tax evasion, exploitation, blackmail, money laundering and even murder, but nothing sticks. He is incredible well-resourced and, we fear, well-connected. He was detained last month by the FBI at JFK airport for a couple of hours but it was nothing but a cursory interview. It was more of a, *we are watching you* meeting, than an investigative one."

"I could trade the paintings for money. That might flush him out? Pretend that I was going to pocket say ten million dollars in return." Pina looked at Roger and Inspector Lottie expectantly. The men smiled at each other. Pina was irritated by their patronising behaviour.

"What's so funny about that?"

The Inspector tried to diffuse her annoyance.

"Reidler is never going to believe that you have turned tables and come onto the dark side. He will know it's a set up."

"Yes, he's right. You don't drink, smoke or gamble and yet here you are offering a ten million dollar fraud. A bit like Mother Teresa robbing a bank – not credible." Roger thought for a moment. "I've an idea, inspector – Pina, hear me out on this one – what if the reward for the painting is me not money. Does Reidler know I've escaped? What if he thinks I'm still being held captive? Now Pina, that *is* credible – me for the paintings!"

"Huh, you think I'd prefer you to ten million dollars? In your dreams." Pina rolled her eyes.

"I see, Roger. It may not be Pina's preference, but Reidler wouldn't know that."

"Exactly."

Pina mused;

"But we don't know what that pig Carlos had told his boss."

"True enough but we can check phone records – the problem is Carlos will need to cooperate. That is a big problem I'd say. He will be crying out for his lawyer any minute now – he knows the form."

"And as soon as his lawyer knows, Reidler knows, I suppose?" Pina asked.

"You've got it. I could though hold him under the Terrorism Act. That allows us thirty-six hours without access to legal representation provided we get a court order – they are controversial and difficult to get but maybe, just maybe we can link an international money laundering operation to terrorism."

"What about the murder of Peter Brinsden?" chipped in Roger.

"We are looking again at the post-mortem but the likely conclusion still remains suicide – likely on the evidence available. That's always the way with him thus far. Everything is circumstantial. Even if we overcome the evidential burdens, there is still no direct link to Reidler. My files are full of such," said a clearly frustrated Lottie, gesturing to the red lever arch files that decorated his surrounding shelving.

"We need something direct and unambiguous. We need to find out just how desperate he really is to get the painting back." Just as Lottie finished his assessment there was a short rap on the office door. Without waiting for a formal invite a police officer, dressed in civilian shirt and tie, leant his head around the door.

"Pardon," he proffered to the inspector's guests, before giving his boss the thumbs up. "It's a goer, inspector." The inspector took this as his cue to elaborate further to Roger and Pina, his proposed strategy.

"Right, guys, we're good to go. Roger, you wait here a minute whilst a take Pina through to the briefing room. When I return I want to talk to you about those other criminals, Mr and Mrs Bellini."

# CHAPTER FORTY-SEVEN

Pina felt nervous. She sat inside a police car parked in the HQ compound, in the backseat alongside the detective who had earlier escorted them into Inspector Lottie's office. Lottie himself sat in the front seat. He gestured to Pina, giving her the cue and she pressed down the power button of the iPhone. It was now fully charged and responded quickly. She applied her thumb to the finger recognition login but because her hands were sweating with apprehension the phone did not recognise the finger print and she was forced to type in her backup password. She could feel her heart pounding as she pressed the "recent calls" logo and there, top of the list was him. Reidler? She wondered. Pina pressed "call" and waited. It rang three times.

"Wait one moment, wait a second," came the reply from the familiar voice. It appeared to Pina that he had taken the call, perhaps in the middle of a meeting, which he was now exiting quickly. She could hear talking in the background, though could not make out the words. She sensed a degree of urgency in his voice but perhaps this was wishful thinking.

"Ah, Pina, Pina Venti, I thought I'd lost you." There was a

pause as Pina took in the fact that he now knew who she was. It was an unfair advantage. Pina's pause was telling. "Dear Pina, it did not take any rocket science to track you down. I could only find three prominent female members of staff on the PNP website. Yours was the only one with an out of office email reply. Your efficiency does you proud."

Pina visibly winced. Inspector Lottie turned again to face her and shook his head, as though to indicate that it was not a problem. He gestured with his right hand for her to continue the flow.

"Listen to me Reidler it didn't take me long to track you down either! "

It was now Inspector Lottie's turn to wince. Pina had in a sentence blown the agreed plan apart. Prior to the call, she had been the focus of a detailed briefing, none of which involved mentioning Reidler whatsoever. In fact, the whole point was for Reidler to be completely unaware that he had been identified. That, the team concluded, was the only way of being able to flush out into the open. Anonymity appealed to him and gave them a chance. Inspector Lottie and Detective Costello were sure that the plan had just imploded. From Pina's perspective, she had been taken aback by the fact that he knew who she was and simply couldn't bear for him to think that he had one up on her. She acknowledged her mistake in deviating from the plan by mouthing "sorry" to Lottie and Bellini.

"All I want is Roger back alive…"

There was a moment's hesitation. *He's recalibrating* thought Pina. Reidler appeared to gather his thoughts again.

"Roger is safe and well. I repeat; I wish him no harm. I just want my property back Pina.

"I want to meet you eye ball to eye ball, Reidler. I don't trust you for one minute let alone your bully boy cronies."

Reidler was non-committal but he did not disengage, nor hang up.

"I am listening Pina, still listening. Tell me where you are now and I can arrange a collection."

"Because of you I am stuck in a car in the back end of Tuscany avoiding the police who somehow think I'm responsible for killing three people."

"That must be very inconvenient, Pina. I understand that. Why don't we meet somewhere quiet just you and me. That way we can both be safe."

Inspector Lottie held up two fingers to Pina indicating that she should opt for plan B as discussed earlier. She nodded, acknowledging the instruction

"No way am I meeting you anywhere quiet. It needs to be a public place, so public that neither of us will be recognised but somewhere where you will be caught if you try anything untoward."

"Don't tell me, you've got somewhere in mind, haven't you?"

"I certainly do. It is quite appropriate too I think. Meet me in Florence tomorrow at 12 00 pm in the queue for the Uffizi Museum. Given the increased terrorist threat they have doubled security. Enough armed guards to carry out a coup de state let alone make sure that you play by the rules, Reidler. You get the paintings in exchange for Roger."

"It's a deal. As soon as you hand over my property I will give you the address of Roger's safe keeping. He will be freed and unharmed."

Pina looked to Lottie for guidance albeit they had already discussed how best to deal with the hand over. If she insisted on actually *seeing* Roger before the handover it was clear that Reidler could not of course deliver Roger and therefore wouldn't turn up himself. If she rolled over too quickly he would be suspicious.

"No way, Reidler. I may be new to this but I'm not stupid. You stand with me until I see Roger in the square, then and *only then,* do you get the goody bag."

The pause was disconcerting. This *was* the moment.

"It strikes me that you have little choice young lady. You want Roger alive more than I want the paintings. I care not for him. Happy for him to live; happy for him to die. No, that is not true. I would prefer him to live but if he doesn't, at least I will know that this will be on your conscience not mine."

Lottie gave her the thumbs up.

"I can see that I have no choice but to trust you. I will be there.

"Will I recognise you from the lovely photograph on the website, Pina?"

"I will be carrying a large red vinyl sports holder that will hold the paintings. I will wear sunglasses and a red baseball hat with *I love Pisa* on it. That should make me pretty easy to spot. If there is even a hint of you not being alone, I am going straight to the police.

Inspector Lottie gave the cut throat sign, indicating to Pina that it was time to close out the call. She did so without hesitation.

"Noon tomorrow in the queue. Now fuck off, Reidler!"

Pina checked twice that the call had in indeed been

ended before exhaling a large sigh of relief. She sank back into the seat and lent her head against the head rest.

Inspector Lottie and detective Costello congratulated her on a job well done.

"Great stuff, Pina. It is not over to the fat lady sings, as they say but he must be pretty desperate to get those paintings back."

"I've been thinking about getting a police officer to stand in for you. With sunglasses and hat on it might be possible to get one to look just like you."

"No, inspector! We cannot take the slightest chance that he won't cooperate. My photograph on the website is a fairly recent one. Were he to carry out a wider Google search there will be other photographs that would help to identify me. Why take a chance? We are going to be right in the public eye. I'm sure that he won't be stupid enough to try anything. Just a straight exchange of goods. The paintings for Roger."

"I understand your point and I certainly don't want him spooked. Let me think about it further and see who else we've got at HQ who might be able to help us. At the minute we should work on the basis it's going to be you. I want to work through with you what you're going to say and what you might ask him in the event that them you can get him to engage in a conversation."

"Also we want to discuss contingency plans with you as well, in case something goes wrong," Detective Costello chipped in. "We will have armed eyes on you but you need to master the drills just in case something does happen. Your safety is paramount."

"We have a safe house at the ready for you. It is under a

mile's walk to the Uffizi which is perfect for us. I will arrange for the paintings to be delivered to you this evening, in a red vinyl bag. I take it from what you said you already have your *I love Pisa* hat?" teased Inspector Lottie.

Second in command, Costello, continued.

"We will have you wired up in the morning. Anything he says could be vital evidence and we need to record it."

Roger was keen to accompany Pina to this place of safety. Lottie consented but only on the basis that Pina revealed nothing of the details they had discussed. This was good practice in the sense of "need to know" limitation but it avoided Roger seeking to scupper the operation. The *safe house* was not only secure but comfortable. It was a two-bedroom flat on the third floor of a three-story block. It was modern and anonymous. There were two entrances front and rear operated by an entry pad system and there was a small lift which avoided the necessity of using the multiple flights of stairs. On each floor, there were only four flats. The kitchen was well-equipped, though. Pina wondered how often it was actually used. The television was a large flat 42-inch affair which was tuned into a news channel upon her arrival. The pair were accompanied by Officer Teresa Fellanie from the *Guardia di Finanza*, a military corp of the Italian police. She would operate the first of the two-shift watch system. Roger was still confined to his distinctly public sector wheelchair and so Pina pushed him into her bedroom for the night, complete with en suite bathroom. The chair was so wide it marked the door frame paintwork and narrowly missed trapping Roger's fingers.

"Almost as good as the Intercontinental," she enthused as she parked Roger peeked behind the lowered blinds.

"No mini bar though."

"Yes, even I could be tempted tonight," said the teetotaller.

"It has been quite a day for sure." As Roger reflected on their extraordinary adventure, he saw for the first time Pina's vulnerability; she looked as though she had a tear in her eye. She wanted to share with him the full details of tomorrow's plan to capture Reidler; her concerns and fears.

He leaned forward and met her hug square on. He yielded slightly with a view to kissing her on the cheek but as their lips met and lingered, neither was in a hurry to return to the operation in hand. Their quiet moment of privacy was disturbed by the pending arrival of the police officer whose steps resonated on the tile floor. Pina and Roger broke off the embrace quickly and recovered their professional persona.

"Time for me to leave you to it, I fear. You could do with an early night," he said, checking his watch but noting that it was nearing midnight. He corrected himself, "well some sleep anyway."

"Yes Pina," said the officer, "and I want to run through the plan again before you settle down for the night. Roger, Officer Logis will take you to a local hotel for the night"

All three left the bedroom and Roger and Officer Logis headed for the door. The officer insisted on opening it and checking that the outside corridor was clear before entering.

Roger patted Pina on the back and as he withdrew, their hands touched ever so lightly, but touched nonetheless.

"Be careful Pina, promise me."

Briefing over Pina attempted to settle down for the night. She looked for a book that might distract her from the task ahead. The lounge shelving contained an array of books. Pina thought that they made for an interesting review. The library seemed to cover a diverse range of subjects; fiction, non-fiction, classic literature, trash and a range of biographies – political, media and historical. No one having the misfortune to have to use the safe house could complain that they were without a book to read. This was the last thing Pina felt like doing. She knew that she ought to try and get some rest but though she lay on her bed, she found it impossible to sleep. Pina played over again and again in her mind the role she had to play tomorrow and how she would deal with any evolving situation. This did not aid drowsiness. She had desperately want to call Roger but this was on the inspector's forbidden list. *No outside contact* he had exclaimed. No one outside of the small team were to know the details of the operation *and that includes Roger.* Had Roger been aware that Pina was being used directly as bait he would have objected vehemently. As far as he was concerned all contact with Reidler would be by telephone and the exchange of goods would be at a distance; a long one at that.

# CHAPTER FORTY-EIGHT

Although Roger was not involved in planned entrapment of Reidler, he was not free from responsibility. When Pina had departed the inspector's office for her first briefing yesterday evening, there had followed a more heated discussion between Roger and Inspector Lottie regarding how best to deal with Luigi who had somehow got the paintings in his possession in the first place. No one knew how he had done so, though the odds, as expressed vehemently by Inspector Lottie, of it being by legitimate means, were long. Inspector Lottie wanted to arrest Luigi and Bella with a view to putting pressure on them to find out where the paintings came from. He accepted that they had information may be of value. Roger advocated a more lenient policy towards them because, from the outset, they had been both charming and cooperative. They were, said Roger, without in any way seeking to patronise them, *simple people, with simple tastes.*

"Leave them to me. They trust me and I can get them to talk."

"And those simple tastes run to owning a Cézanne or two I guess," chipped in Inspector Lottie sarcastically. In the end Inspector was persuaded to accept Rogers's course of action. He did so as much to appease Pina and keep her engaged and cooperative. He knew that she would be supportive of Roger's approach. Lottie knew that there would be only a limited number of opportunities to catch Reidler and the prospect, albeit still small, of a successful prosecution, far outweighed the showing of leniency to an Artisan in the Tuscan hills. It was a simple trade-off. Inspector Lottie said that he did not have the authority to grant immunity from prosecution but he would them seek it with a supporting recommendation.

Although Pina had satisfied Roger and the police that the Bellinis were safe at the Grand Pisa Hotel, he felt less comfortable going there. Inspector Lottie agreed that the place may still be under surveillance given that Pina remained checked in and her hire car was still parked up in the car park. Although the police could offer both Roger and the Bellinis protection, given that he was now meant to be kidnapped, his presence will be unhelpful. They therefore selected a neutral venue for the meeting between Roger and the Bellinis.

The Intercontinental Hotel at Pisa was far enough away from *the Grand* to avoid detection, yet afforded an excellent business centre where Roger was able to spend a restless night before booking meeting room facilities that morning. The local police had even collected his abandoned chair and it had been delivered to his room before breakfast. It would make life so much easier.

The Bellinis were able to stroll along the narrow tow path, the one that caused so much drama for Pina and cross the adjoining bridge to the entrance to the hotel. The business Centre receptionist advised Roger that the Bellinis were on their way up to the seventh floor and Roger waited in reception to meet them. As the lift door opened, Luigi forgot his manners for a moment and burst out through the lift doors ahead of Bella, smiling cheerfully. Roger extended his hand for shaking but instead was met with both of Luigi's hands on the top of his shoulder greeting him with far more enthusiasm than Roger had anticipated. It was clear that they were enjoying the change of scenery from the arid Tuscan hills.

"Bella, Luigi, I'm so sorry we haven't been in contact sooner. Things have been very busy back at some head office. I hope your stay is been a comfortable one?"

"Signor Roger," said Bella with an even bigger smile than Luigi on her face. It is amazing; thank you it has been quite wonderful."

Roger escorted them into the functional, sparsely decorated but nonetheless comfortable meeting room.

He duly offered them coffee from the espresso machine.

"We have one of those machines in our room," said Luigi, "but we don't know how to work it. Take a close look Bella." With coffees on the tables Roger tried to get down to business, but Luigi was more interested in talking about the hotel.

"The foods is super; they even bring it to your room," he said with enthusiasm.

Bella sensed Rogers's impatience and interrupted in timely fashion.

"Luigi, Signor Roger does not want to know what you're been eating. He perhaps has some good news to tell us about your paintings?"

"News? Yes, I do have news but it's a mixed package, I'm afraid." Bella and Luigi looked at each other, clearly disappointed.

"The good news is on the one hand we do think that the paintings is an original a masterpieces worth a lot of money, Luigi." Roger deliberately focused on Luigi, because he sensed that it was he and not Bella who would have any useful information.

"Luigi, as insurers of the painting, Roger rather embellished, we are obviously interested in where it came from but, regrettably, so are the police."

Reference to the police caused Bella to panic. She squeezed Luigi's arm with both hands firmly, shaking him.

"You told me you bought them at the market," Bella added.

Luigi couldn't bring himself to look at Bella and this raised her concern.

"Luigi, what's going on?" Luigi kept his head and said nothing.

"Luigi, Luigi, what have you done? Tell Signor Roger the truth."

Luigi was looking down at his half empty coffee cup. He could not bring himself to make eye contact with either Roger or Bella. He clasped his hands between his knees.

"Listen to me," said Roger, more softly spoken this time. "It may not be as bad as it all seems. I am working with the police and they are prepared, at the moment, to leave it to me, as the insurer, to resolve this with you privately. We have a short opportunity to tie up any loose pieces between ourselves. If we cannot, then we will have no choice but to leave it to the police to investigate. That is not what I want, Bella." He glanced at the woman.

There was a period of silence. Roger lent back in his chair as if to throw open the forum to Luigi. Although Bella held on to Luigi's arm she loosened her grip.

"Tell me Signore, that I will not go to prison," Luigi pleaded.

"Luigi, I assure you, if you tell me the truth today here and now the matter is at an end. You have my word."

"About three weeks ago I worked on a job clearing an old warehouse following the death of the owner. It was a messy job and the warehouse was full of rubbish. Absolutely nothing of value. There in the warehouse I found this couple of the paintings covered under an old rotting carpet."

Not having been reprimanded thus far by either Roger or Bella, Luigi felt confident enough to lift his head to speak further.

"I thought they were worthless. I took them home to show Bella. I thought she might like them and I was sure they were going to be thrown in the rubbish skip by Signor Portelli."

"Signor Portelli?" probed Roger.

"Ah, sorry, yes, Signor Portelli. He is a local attorney who commissioned us to do the job. He acts for a lot of elderly in the town and when they die, he often pays us to carry out the house clearances for him.

"Us?"

"Yes, me and the boys: Alex, Mike and me. We often work together."

"Do they know you have the paintings?"

"Yes. They thought they were rubbish too."

"Sorry, Luigi, I interrupted you. Carry on."

"There's not too much else to tell. I took one of the paintings into Lucca and tried to flog it in the flea market.

Nobody wanted it, which again made me think it was rubbish. It was then that I bumped into Alberto's shop and he seemed to take quite an interest in the painting. Next I know, you and the Signora are visiting us and we are rushed off to be put up in a five-star hotel. Per favour Signore, per favour, believe me I didn't mean to do any harm. Bella, I took them for you. I wasn't stealing. I thought they were just rubbish."

Bella was unimpressed.

"Don't you bring me into this! You are a fool. What will Mamma say – I cannot imagine. You have bought shame on us."

# CHAPTER FORTY-NINE

Signor Portelli did not have a receptionist nor secretary. He found that he was able to cope by mastering Dragon Dictate as well as outsourcing more significant documents. Roger had called the office number that he found online on the Florence Attorney Association's website. He called the number and was advised that this call was being transferred, no doubt to Portelli's mobile phone, thought Roger.

Signor Portelli duly answered the call and sounded professional from the outset.

"Signor Portelli, how may help you?"

"Good morning to you. My name is Roger Kirtley, from PNP insurance. Do you have a few moments to speak?"

Roger could hear in his voice that Claudio Portelli had a distrust of insurance companies. Roger wondered if insurers had cost him cases and clients.

"Signor Kirtley, per favore, continue I'm all yours," he said, sounding guarded.

"It would seem, Signore that we have a client of mutual interest or rather did up until a few weeks ago."

"We do?" Portelli sounded more interested than surprised.

"Yes, Andreas Bartelli."

"Ah, yes, Andreas Bartelli, now deceased, as you imply."

Roger was reluctant to discuss the position in much detail over the phone and was pleased that Portelli, the attorney, was able to confirm a mid-afternoon appointment at his office, which was just over an hour's drive from the *Intercontinental* in Pisa where Roger continued to work following his meeting with Bella and Luigi. As ever Roger had to enquire as to whether or not there was disabled access. He had lost count of the number of aborted meeting because he couldn't even get into a building due to the stepped access.

Roger's had been caught up in traffic and his taxi driver was reluctant to make up time as his clock continued to tick. Wheelchair passengers were considered a nightmare by taxi drivers because they took so long to load up – that time was off the clock. For that reason, Roger had, on a number of occasions, been left waiting on a pavement hailing taxis that pretended not to have seen him. He was dropped off close to the main square, as the town operated a pedestrianised zone in to which the attorney's office fell. He proceeded following the map that he had printed off and rested on his lap. Coming to a halt Roger checked another piece of paper upon which he had written Portelli's details and was surprised to see that the office address, 27 Via Delle Tagliatelle, was a lady's fashion store. However, by the side of the main entrance was a small plaque confirming he was at the right address: – *Signor C Portelli attorney at law* Roger looked up above the shop and could see that there were further two floors.

He assumed that Portelli had rented space in one of them. He could not be sure of which floor because the second more prominent plaque said, *Michele Bartrom BSC MD – chiropractor.*

Roger folded away the details and placed them in the side pocket of his ruck sack which, down the years, had been the home to countless insurance forms and folders. Pressing the button marked *Attorney at Law,* Roger was not left waiting long.

Portelli himself answered, as before in a professional manner.

"Claudio Portelli."

"Signor Portelli? Hello, it's Roger Kirtley from PNP. Sorry I'm late."

"No worry at all – come on up – first floor – the lift is straight in front of you. It's a bit temperamental so be patient." The electronic lock on the door buzzed and Roger entered, skilfully manoeuvring his chair through the narrow doorway.

Roger reiterated his thanks to Signor Portelli for agreeing to the meeting at short notice. Following the initial exchange of pleasantries Roger handed over his business card. Signor Portelli patted his trouser pockets as though trying to find a card to reciprocate, but Roger got the impression, looking from the modest surroundings, that he might not have a card to spare.

Roger put him out of his misery. "No worry, Signore. It was more important that you saw my credentials." The lawyer thoughtfully removed a chair to enable easier access. The men sat at a large mahogany table which was covered in part by a green leather baize and included a good old-fashioned inkwell. The well, Roger could see, was used to store pens pencils and an old-fashioned envelope opener.

"Do continue to expand upon the reason for his visit. You only provided limited details." There was no hint of impatience.

"As explained briefly on the telephone, PNP are major insurers of art and antiques around the world. We act for most of the major galleries but also small outlets as well. The scale of the business allows us to be competitive for small and large alike. PNP insure a local antiques dealer here in Tuscany. His shop was burgled a week or so ago and during that raid he lost a number of items."

"I understand, but how exactly this involve Mr Bartelli?"

Roger was unsure as to what his professional association, the ABI would make of his explanation, given that it was part fact but more fiction. He couldn't mention Luigi.

"Forgive me for being slow in coming to the point. It would seem that about ten days prior to his death, Signor Bartelli had visited the dealer to see whether he was interested in buying a painting. The owner was indeed interested and thought that the painting itself could be of good quality. Before agreeing a price, it was agreed that the dealer would hold onto the painting for couple of weeks whilst he did some further research."

"Oh, I see," said Portelli, quickly grasping the point. "And this painting was one of the items stolen in the burglary – I understand then our mutual interest."

"Signore, you have it in one!" said Roger, acknowledging the attorney's prowess. "The matter however gets more intriguing because it does appear that the painting may indeed be valuable; this has to be verified yet but all the early signs are very positive."

"Just how valuable?" asked Portelli trying not to sound too enthusiastic.

"I can't say precisely but put it this way, the painting is thought to be an original Gauguin..." Portelli tried to look calm yet his face told a different story.

"The question we both need answering is," began Roger before offering Portelli the chance to jump in.

"How on earth did Andreas Bartelli, deceased, come to own a Gauguin?"

"A mystery that may well be worth solving," Roger said. "I know that we both have professional duties of confidentiality but I think that in these circumstances we are able to share information to the mutual benefit of our respective clients."

"No problem. I agree entirely."

"Who actually is your client, Claudio?" enquired Roger in more informal terms, "given that Signor Bartelli is dead."

"That Roger, is a very good question. I officially act in behalf of Andreas' Estate but in reality, my role is to ensure that if there are any beneficiaries, they receive the proceeds of the estate, after all taxes and legal fees are paid. It was only at that moment that Portelli realised that, given his fee was based on a percentage of the net value of the estate, the fact that a Gauguin may now form part of the portfolio was rather significant.

"Signor Bartelli had come to my office about a year ago saying that he wanted me to prepare a will. I remember him telling me that he was unwell but he didn't go into any details. It was a pretty straightforward transaction. Whilst we should all really settle a will by the time we are 40, in truth, people tend to leave it until they are staring death in the face. Many leave it too late, leaving their family to suffer the taxation consequences."

"Yes, that does rather remind me that I need to put my house in order," Roger said and laughed.

"Attached to the will was the schedule of property – basically a list of items owned. At the time, I paid the list little interest. A small flat in Lucca, a lock up in Lunata – ten miles south of here. Certainly no hint of wealth. He left everything to an Anna Cohen or those that survived her."

"Anna Cohen?"

"Yes, I know as much as you really. I have only just started to try and trace her. I assumed at first that she was either his partner or close friend living in the town. That isn't the case. When I collected papers from his flat I took the opportunity to speak with a couple of neighbours, who describe him as being very introverted and isolated. As far as they were aware, he never had any visitors. They knew of no family. Certainly there was no partner or spouse on the scene. One neighbour told me that he frequented a local bar perhaps too often than was good for him, as he used to arrive home late and seemed to struggle noisily on the wooden stairs to his first floor flat. I even popped to Bar L'auroa myself and spoke to the owner. Similarly, as the neighbours had told me, Andreas was a loner.

"He would visit to the tavern most nights and although he would say hello and occasionally talk about the weather or watch the football if it was on television, he kept himself to himself. The owner couldn't say that he had any friends as such. He would stay most nights until closing time but was never any trouble and was always then ready to leave when the bar was closing. He might even occasionally have a bowl of pasta at the bar for supper but normally stuck to his routine small glasses of beer and a chaser of Pastis."

"So, no sign of her at all? Could she just be a fantasy? Perhaps he just drunk himself into oblivion and made her up?"

"The thought did cross my mind and I have had early dementia clients where this has occurred – leaving everything to a non-existent child – very sad. However, Andreas was very concise and articulate when I met him. He was able to answer all of my questions clearly. I thought that he may have a shy personality but there was no doubt in my mind that he had the ability to understand what he was doing – testamentary capacity, as we call it."

"What of income? How did he manage to live?"

"All the bar owner knew was that he was or at least had been an artist. As he said it was difficult to talk freely with him but he did say that he had from time to time sold a painting and this kept him going. An area of his apartment was cluttered brushes and dried up paint tubes. There were a couple of unfinished oil colours of local scenery and there was an ongoing still life watercolour. I must say that thought the quality was excellent."

"Any clues in the paperwork?"

"That's my next port of call," said Portelli standing up and picking up a cardboard box full to overflowing. As he placed it on the table a couple of folders fell on two the desk. Roger picked one up and opened it nothing but a couple of energy bills, years old but neatly hole punched and in chronological order.

"Do you mind if I take a rummage, Claudio?"

"Be my guest – feel free to stay here and do it – I ought to keep the documents in my possession, I suppose. I have a meeting in ten minutes in town but be my guest;

make yourself at home." Portelli did not like to say that the appointment to which he referred was with his barber.

"What next with the Gauguin, Roger?"

"We expect the authentication process to take a couple of weeks yet." Can we meet up again later in the week?"

"For sure – I will be flexible," replied Portelli, whose diary of engagements for the week was limited, hairdresser aside.

"The door is self-locking and there's no alarm to set," reported Portelli. If you find anything of interest just leave it to one side and I will get it copied for you.

"You have my number if anything important crops up. See you later in the week. It has been a pleasure to meet you."

Roger rolled with the lawyer the few steps to the door, shaking hands and steadying the door with his chair wheel to avoid it slamming shut.

Before settling himself down to plough through the box, Roger fixed himself a further espresso from the office machine which had a healthy supply of coffee capsules in an adjoining dish. He took off his jacket and placed it on the back of Signor Portelli's chair and then transferred into it from his chair for the review. Rather than taking each document one at the time from box, Roger angled it, allowing half of its contents to spill across the desktop. A pattern quickly emerged. The thin black A4 folders, of which there were several, contained bills of one sort or another. As previously noted each was carefully filed in date order. There were two leather bound diaries but with no entries in either. There second half of the box contents looked equally uninspiring save for a cluster of eight or nine envelopes tied together by a length of green ribbon.

Roger pulled the bow and the ribbon fell away, freeing the envelopes which, bar two, were vanilla coloured and thick. It was clear to Roger that they each contained a letter. He stopped point was to look at the front of the envelopes. Each was hand written and addressed to Andreas at the same address in Vienna:

Flat 14
Wien Buildings
Neuhaus District
Vienna

Each had been posted and there was a postal cancellation mark across the Austrian stamp. Not all of the date stamps were clear but Roger could see that the spread of letters was broadly between December 1937 and April 1938.

Roger turned to the first envelope and pulled out from it to sheets of paper that matched the envelope.

At the top centre of each page was a printed address namely:

Ville de Wiener
Fist District
Vienna
Austria

The letter was dated 12 December 1937 and began:

"*Dear Andreas,*
   *I ache for you.*
   *Every part of my body yearns to be with you....*"

It was quickly apparent to Roger that these were love letters. Rather than read on, he immediately turned to the writing at the end of the second page and there, as he had hoped, more than expected, was the sign off:

> *Love always*
> *Anna*
> *Xxx*

Hallelujah – Anna, our Anna it just must be....

Roger telephoned Portelli straightaway to tell him of his find.

"Get back here now, Claudio – drop whatever you are doing."

Portelli complied with the request and Roger noted the shorter hair but said nothing for fear of embarrassing him.

Roger placed some of the envelopes back down on the desk. Each of the letters was now extending for easier access.

"Have a look at these Claudio," said Roger. He gently tossed three more envelopes across the letters had bright pink fluorescent tags upon them.

"I have marked them at the top, one, two and three, work in that order."

Portelli said nothing but reached out quickly for the first of the envelopes and then sat down, pushing his coffee to one side.

"You can forget the salacious bits for now. I've marked the most important entries."

As Claudio pulled the letter from the first envelope there was a further tag, this time bright yellow, at the top of the second page of the letter.

Portelli immediately saw the name of the author and recipient.

"Andreas and Anna!" He stood still reading the letter.

"Read on Claudio – it gets better."

Portelli looked up to Roger again inquisitively. He squinted his eyes and shook his head as he did so.

"I'm not sure I get it, Roger."

"Read that and then go on to the second letter."

Portelli did as he was instructed. The second letter also had a yellow tag.

Portelli read the extracts, not once, not twice but three times. He then looked up at Roger.

"They tried to con the Nazis," said Portelli, stating his conclusion more in disbelief than fact.

"And you know what's even better, Claudio? I think they bloody well pulled it off."

The pair shook hands across the table as though they had just solved the Enigma code.

# CHAPTER FIFTY

Inspector Lottie had arrived early at the safe house, in an unmarked police car. He brought with him the paintings, which were already nestled in the large red sports holder. He had also brought along with him a younger officer who he had arranged to be seconded from the traffic division, PC Michelle Fianta. She didn't know that she was a possible stand in for a major criminal sting but was pleased to be away from directing rush-hour Florence traffic for the morning. Upon arrival at the flat, other officers were already present, ready to fit out either Pina or Michelle with the voice surveillance equipment. Pina realised straightway the purpose of Michelle's visit. Inspector Lottie formally introduced her.

"Pina, before you say anything, let's just look at the options. At the end of the day it is my decision and not yours."

This was the first time the Inspector Lottie had spoken so forcibly to Pina and with it he reinforced the fact that it was he, not her, who was in charge; this was a police, not an insurance investigation.

The two women stood side-by-side. Both were similarly dressed in jeans and a shirt. Both had been instructed to wear running shoes in order to provide the operation with greater flexibility if they had to move quickly. Pina was a dress size slimmer than Michelle and Michelle's hair was shorter than Pina's.

"Let's have a look with the baseball caps on."

Pina had her red 'Pisa' hat at the ready and the other officer handed Michelle a baseball hat that had been brought along for the exercise. As instructed they both put on sunglasses. The two looked pretty similar, not identical twins but enough to fool Reidler?

"Say a few words, Michelle. Tell us about the weather today in Florence."

The voice was unquestionably different. Michelle had been born in Northern Italy, Where the dialect is different; faster in pace, a tad more staccato than further south.

Pina, who had been remarkably patient up to now, finally voiced her objections.

"Reidler is going to be on high alert. He is taking a major risk in meeting in public. If I can engage him in conversation this could really help the case. Who knows what he might be prepared to say. We've spoken on the phone already. With respect to Michelle, he will know that she is not me."

Inspector Lottie said nothing and stood observing the two options. He called over Detective Costello and they left the central television room and moved into the kitchen.

They closed the door behind them.

"Boss I'd go with Michelle. It's too risky using an amateur. One who seems unable to follow orders too."

"Yeah, I get that but they do look different and sound different. We can't spook him. This could be our one chance to get this bastard."

"You will be a hero boss but if it goes wrong forget that promotion I'm telling you."

Lottie put his hand on Detective Costello's shoulder, not in the slightest offended at his junior's candid analysis – it was spot on.

"Let's keep our options open for the moment at least."

Their deliberations took just over a minute. Inspector Lottie came back through the Door.

"Right, guys. Wire up them both up for now."

Pina allowed herself a brief smile but that soon turned to a grimace of concern as the small microphone, disguised as a rather attractive lady bird brooch, was attached to Pina's blouse.

It was time to focus on the job ahead.

"Should I give Reidler a call just to confirm the details or something like that?" asked Pina.

"No. Let's maintain radio silence and not give him any opportunity to change the plan. We have boots on the ground in the square ready to affect an arrest if needs be. Let's not risk that position unnecessarily. The more important issue is to protect you. We still think it unlikely that Reidler will come alone and we cannot risk members of the public being injured let alone in a shootout in one of the most famous squares in the world. They will be briefing the Carabinieri too about now to ensure that they are on increased alert. Specialist plainclothes officers will also be in the square and in the queue ahead of you. There is certainly no need for you to know they are. Pina, you just stick to the plan; no going off piste like last time."

Pina had no time to formally respond as one of the officers intervened.

"Pina, can you say a few words for us. Speak at the normal conversational level." Pina, took Michelle's lead and spoke briefly about the weather in Florence that morning. The audio technician was then content and there would now follow the longest hour's wait in Pina's history.

Inspector Lottie used the time to reiterate the timings.

"Let's allow fifteen minutes for the walk to the Uffizi. I have checked and at this time of day the queue will be at least sixty metres long. On a busy day, it could be up to a hundred metres but it makes no difference to us. You simply arrive and join the queue. Even if you get there say at ten to ten just join the queue. It moves slowly and there is no prospect of you getting inside the building before the 10 am deadline."

# CHAPTER FIFTY-ONE

Everyone in the room jumped when Pina's mobile phone rang. It was resting on the glass coffee table and reverberated loudly. Pina felt instantly nauseous as she stretched out to pick the phone up. Inspector Lottie reached out to hold her arm preventing her from answering the call until it had been vetted.

"It's okay," said Pina, relieved. "It's Roger."

"I specifically told Roger not to call."

"Roger, hi. I'm meant to be keeping the airways free remember... Yes, he's here with me now. I will try but the timing isn't good."

"Inspector, Roger wants to speak with you."

"Tell him to call me later but not now. I will come back to him later on today. Get him off the line as soon as possible."

Pina returned to the call.

"Roger, oh, you heard did you? Yes. He said he'd definitely come back to you later today.... I will try Roger but your timing is horrible..." She glanced up. "Inspector, he absolutely insists. He need to speak to you for 30 seconds."

"Give him here. He's got 20 seconds..."

Inspector Lottie took the call. The 20 allotted seconds turned into a couple of minutes.

*

It was 9.45 am and time to go. There were no locker room speeches to be made. No final words of encouragement were required. It was time for action. *I love Pisa* hat on. Red hold-all on shoulder. Sunglasses at the ready. This was it. As the lift doors closed, Pina gave the thumbs up sign and Michelle reciprocated. Following a struggle to get through the front door due to the holdall knocking against the framework, the walk to the Uffizi awaited. She repositioned the bag on her right shoulder put on the sun glasses, checked her watch once again and set off down the four shallow access steps that led to Via Lambertesca.

It all happened quickly. In an instant. The two motorbikes descended on her like hornets. Noisy and nasty. Both motorbikes bumped the curb and trapped her in a pincer movement. All she could see was the reflections from the four black helmets which now enclosed her. The noise from the 125 cc Honda engines was as distinct as the pungent smell of petrol fumes. She didn't even see the pistol that was to kill her. Regrettably, she had heard the first of the shots, for the off balance pillion driver had missed from close quarters in his rush to complete the kill.

It was though quick and simple. Within seconds, the bag was gone and the lifeless body lay on the Florentine side street.

*

The CCTV footage from the entrance to the flats would show from start to finish the robbery and shooting had taken less than ten seconds. Inspector Lottie had, via the Ladybird brooch, heard the noise of the motorbike engines, a scream and two very distinct rounds being fired into her head. He could do nothing to assist.

There had been an unmarked police car parked on the opposite side of the road, barely 20 m from the scene. Yes, they gave pursuit but the chase was a pathetic one because the motorcyclists were able to almost immediately turn left down an alleyway barely wide enough for the bikes let alone the Fiat. That getaway route took them away from Uffizi square, where the bulk of the police resource awaited.

Inspector Lottie was the first on the scene, cradling Michelle's head, before the air was soon filled, not this time with the sound of motorbike engines, but of emergency response vehicles. Sirens from every direction. The scene was an embarrassing mess for Inspector Lottie.

Pina had insisted in coming out of the safe house, defying Lottie's orders. She rushed over to where Michelle lay dead. The horror of that sight would remain with her. Pina covered her face. Lottie looked up at her but said nothing. Words were of no significance at that moment. Pina felt an illogical pang of guilt: *that should be me.*

A description of the motorcyclists was quickly dispatched. Easy to describe; black bikes, black leathers, black helmet, black pistol and one red bag. The number plate of one of the bikes at least had been picked up by the pursuing officer. The plate would obviously be false but might assist in the subsequent review of the city's CCTV system. Lottie knew that in such a well-planned operation the bikes and the bag would, very quickly, disappear. His betting was that the bikes would drive up ramps into the rear of a waiting van within half a mile from the attack.

Inspector Lottie was incandescent with rage.

That anger partly stemmed from the fact that the plan had gone disastrously wrong but primarily because this was clearly an inside job. The safe house and its surrounding zone was, ironically perhaps, the least protected area. It was the weak link in the chain and somehow Reidler knew of it. In such circumstances, no one could be above suspicion. There was a sense of quiet, not calm, as the realisation became apparent that there had been a leak of information within their own ranks. Almost certainly this leak would have been a deliberate one and that significantly compounded the heightened sense of anxiety.

*What a fuck up*, thought Lottie.

Had Lottie been in charge of an operation where a member of the public had been shot during an undercover operation, his career would have been at an end. Especially if that person had been recruited to help at the expense of a trained police officer. It would have mattered not that Michelle was 'Traffic' and not 'Counter Terrorism.' His decision to swap Pina for Michelle was made late on, but nonetheless saved him from immediate suspension and an inevitable sacking. He may still yet need to seek 'early retirement' but for the moment the operation was still very active and he was responsible for salvaging something from what Lottie's boss, Chief Inspector Mennea, had accurately described as a 'wretched situation.'

The fact that Mennea had not completely gone berserk in the immediate aftermath of Michelle's assassination simply reinforced how serious the position was for Lottie – a twenty-year career at real risk of degenerating overnight.

It was the call from Roger in the immediate run up to the shooting that had led to the change of personnel. Roger had told Lottie about the content of the letters and the obvious conclusions that he and Portelli had drawn. In many ways, the finding hadn't altered the position dramatically but it had lead Lottie to reassess risk. He did not foresee the assassination but he did think that there could be added danger for Pina. Before then, the assessments had been made on speculation but given Reidler's well documented history of involvement with Nazi art, the odds had shifted, the danger enhanced. It was a good call. If anyone said that to Lottie he would punch them.

# CHAPTER FIFTY-TWO

It was now Roger's turn to be wired up. Fortunately for him, the surveillance recording would not be through a Ladybird brooch but a stylish ink pen clipped to his front jacket pocket. It would also digitally record the meeting. Both Lottie and Roger had been surprised how easy it had been to arrange the meeting and this meant, they concluded, two things:

Braithwaite had no idea that Roger was supposed to be kidnapped and therefore as a consequence, secondly that Reidler and Braithwaite were not close confidants. Both conclusions were seen to be positive.

Braithwaite had agreed to meet at PNP's Florence office. It had been the most natural venue, one that would not cause Braithwaite suspicion. He would enjoy the business class flights and limousine service and could even review a modern art exhibition at the Uffizi. Roger had met with him at the office before even if most of their get-togethers were in London. The last meeting took place only about four months ago when Braithwaite assisted PNP in verifying and valuing a collection of Renaissance drawings held by a private collector in France. Though he was paid a modest fee for his valuation services for the purpose of setting a premium, PNP would look to retain him in the event of a dispute arising over the valuation of a lost piece of art and to that end the valuation work was seen more as a prudent loss leader. These cases often led to him being a litigation expert where the rewards were far more substantial and led to his standing and therefore profile within the art well-being raised.

Roger greeted Dr Braithwaite in the PNP reception area. The visitor had seated himself as requested by the receptionist and was casually reading a copy of that day's Times. As Roger entered the reception area his guest folded the paper in half, threw it casually on the coffee table in front of him and stood up.

"Roger, good to see you, old boy. How are you?" He looked relaxed and cheerful as he slapped Roger on the shoulder. It was clear to Roger that was no hint at all that Roger was somehow involved in the Gauguin investigation, let alone that Reidler had ordered his capture. Braithwaite was rather flamboyantly dressed, as had become his trademark media image. He wore a blue maroon and white striped blazer complete with white silk handkerchief spilling from the breast pocket. His maroon chinos perfectly matched the blazer stripe and his suede loafers were in keeping with the look; it was a confident one.

From the reception area on the second floor of the twenty-two story office block they took the lift to the twentieth floor where the company meeting rooms were based. From here the views of the city were spectacular and couldn't fail to impress. Braithwaite, as with many before him, paused in front of the window forming part of the atrium in order to take in the scene.

The men chatted amiably in the lift. Roger had not gone into any detail save to say that assistance was required with a valuation that was proving to be problematic.

Roger led the way into the meeting room. It would normally be set up for a meeting of up to twelve people complete with chairs table and coffee making facilities. On this occasion however, all extraneous items had been removed in order to achieve greater impact. The only features were two easels with the two Gauguin nudes resting upon them – one original, the other fake.

It would be difficult to over exaggerate the transformation in Braithwaite's demeanour as he entered the room. He looked at Roger almost in a state of panic. Roger pretended not to notice as, without even referring to the paintings, he rolled his chair straight to the coffee machine.

"Black or white, Simon?"

He received no reply. Braithwaite's eyes were fixated on the two seemingly identical paintings before him.

"You may read that Gauguin's *Tahitian Princess* was stolen at the Milan Post-Impressionist exhibition. We then receive a tipoff and low and behold we find two of the buggers." Roger's jocularity received no response from Braithwaite who moved closer to the paintings which were mounted on flipchart holders, normally used for recording blue sky thinking initiatives.

"The problem for us at PNP is that we don't know which one to return to the owner. We assume that one is a forgery – a bloody good one at that and the other one is worth upwards of US$30 million. You can see our dilemma. I thought you were just the man for the job. It is right up your street, isn't it Simon?"

"Yes," mumbled Braithwaite, "right up my street..."

Braithwaite was suddenly on guard and very wary;

"What is all this?" he then said in an aggressive fashion. This was going to be a critical part of the meeting and Braithwaite needed to be man managed correctly. If an EEC monitor could have been attached to Braithwaite's head, it would have been very active. He knew which one was the original. There were certain tell-tale signs, some of which could only be picked up by closer inspection by an expert. The vibrancy of colour was also different. Brushstrokes were slightly longer in the fake than the original. The palette of colours differed slightly. If observed at close quarter even the signature differed slightly and Braithwaite had recalled that at the time he authenticated the fake this was his main area of reservation. He had no idea still that the meeting had been staged. He was however beginning to sweat and began to bide his time in inspecting both paintings even though within seconds, he knew which was which.

"Obviously the stolen one is the original and the other one is a forgery," said Braithwaite, trying to look as if he was stating the obvious but probing for further information.

Braithwaite had to think quickly on his feet. If he identified the original as a fake then this could be the perfect solution. Stets would get back a masterpiece instead of the fake; the one that he had falsely authenticated two years ago.

"Yes and that's why we need you, Simon. You can tell us which is which."

That was bliss to Braithwaite's ears.

"This is the original," said Braithwaite being accurate for once and pointing to the masterpiece. The quality of the work stands out. Gauguin at his best. There are clear differences between the two. A decent enough copy though," concluded Braithwaite as he examined the fake, the very one he had authenticated for Reidler. You can return the Gauguin to its rightful owner with confidence."

"Oh, yes, Simon, we will certainly do that."

On cue, there was a knock on the door followed by the entry of a plainclothes detective in the guise of a PNP insurance executive. He introduced himself but Braithwaite was in rather a defensive mode.

"Good news, Charles. Dr Braithwaite has been able to confirm which is the copy and which is the fake – that makes our life much easier. I said to Simon that I couldn't tell which one was from the gallery."

"Ah, but I can, Roger. When the paintings were first recovered they were in their respective frames. The gallery were able to identify theirs. I've marked the gallery painting in pencil on the back."

This revelation caused Braithwaite to panic.

"Let me take another look. I may have been hasty in my conclusions. The light isn't perfect in this room after all. Roger and Charles looked at each other as the sunlight streamed through.

Braithwaite laboured over both works, appearing to inspect intently.

"Umm, so sorry, Roger. I gave you the wrong one. This is the original Gauguin. I shouldn't have rushed. Yes, yes, this is it and the other is a fake." Braithwaite had made a complete U-turn.

This was exactly the change of heart that the investigators had been waiting for and they descended on meeting room

12 from meeting room 8 opposite from where they had been based watching the charade unfold.

Inspector Lottie was the first through the door followed by two other officers. Lottie was extending his Interpol badge.

Braithwaite looked bemused and fearful. He looked to Roger for assurance but received none.

"Simon Braithwaite, I am arresting you on suspicion of fraud, conspiracy to deceive and tax evasion." The tax evasion charge had only sprung to Lottie's mind that morning. Presumably, figured Lottie, Braithwaite had been well paid for the false authentication yet hadn't been able to run the money through his books. No doubt a lucrative offshore account had been the solution. For the first time in the week Lottie felt a hint of satisfaction.

Within fifteen minutes, Braithwaite was at the Police's Florence HQ, sitting in one of the identical rooms used for Pina and Roger's debrief.

Braithwaite was trying to fight back.

"You lack one vital ingredient, officer. An important one in both our fields – evidence," he said. "I accept that I may have made a mistake when looking at the two paintings just now – easily done – the forgery or should we just call it a copy, is of excellent quality. But remember this, I am the expert not you. What I say goes. That's the whole point of being an expert."

"Well, Peter Brinsden won't be able to question your judgement that we do know."

"What of Peter?" Braithwaite asked with genuine surprise.

"Murdered – hadn't you heard?"

It was clear that he hadn't. Any growing confidence instantly evaporated.

He struggled to ask a coherent question.

"But Peter…"

"Yes, you spoke to him only last week. We know. You also wrote his death sentence. Did I not mention the accessory to murder charge?"

At that, Inspector Lottie flicked his head towards the door indicating to his colleague that it was time for Braithwaite to reflect on his position.

The investigating officers were able to watch Braithwaite via the CCTV system. He was restless. He stood up, paced the room before sitting down again and putting his head into his hands gripping his hair tightly before resting his head and hands on the table.

"What do you make of him, boss?"

"A man with some big decisions to make. Grass up a psychopath? Upset a power mad belarusian or just serve ten years in the slammer? Take your pick. I suppose that he might get to run some art classes after five years inside."

"Could we carve him a deal?"

"Immunity?"

"Yeah, with witness protection."

"His ego is so big. I think he'd rather do time than be anonymous."

Both men laughed.

"What next?"

"Set him free…No charges."

"Boss?"

"At the moment, he is our link to Reidler," Lottie explained. "Let's set him free, tail him 24/7 and wait for Reidler to make contact."

"How will Reidler know that Braithwaite has been pulled by us? *He* won't let on you can rest assured."

"Reidler will know alright. Put in a call to the media team and get the story out there. *Celebrity assisting the police with their enquiries over reclaimed Nazis artwork.* Something like that should do. I'll go and give him the good news. It will be interesting to see how he responds."

Upon hearing the news of his release without charge, Braithwaite stayed motionless refusing to move from his chair.

"Is this a wind up?"

"You are free to walk the safe streets of Florence," said Lottie opening the interview room door wide as if to emphasise the point.

"Safe for anyone with nothing to worry about anyway." Lottie's words echoed Braithwaite's thoughts.

"As you say we need evidence…"

"And I need protection."

"Really? From whom?"

"Fuck off!" came the reply as Braithwaite realised his dilemma.

"At this stage, we usually say don't leave the country but in your case…"

"Screw you."

As Braithwaite exited to freedom his literacy repertoire seemed to be stunted as were his options, thought Lottie. He turned to detective Costello, who had enjoyed seeing the petrified look on Braithwaite's face.

"See him of the premises then tail him to the airport whilst I get authority on high to track him out of the country if necessary."

"I'll need back up. Can I pull in some of the airport undercover team?"

"Sure, but say that he's dangerous. That way it's their budget not ours"

*

Inspector Lottie glanced at his phone and noted that Detective Costello was ringing. He had been dispatched to tail Braithwaite to the airport. Lottie listened in disbelief. It can't be true. Braithwaite never checked in for the

13:40 Alitalia flight from Florence to London. He was found hanged in the gent's toilet by a distressed janitor. *Another suicide…*

"But we were there; all over him."

*Found hung in the airport toilet.* Those words crushed Lottie. At that very moment, he felt not for Braithwaite but himself; just how can things go so wrong, so often, on my watch. I'm fucked. Selfish but honest.

Lottie clung on to the telephone update – *Cut down by a janitor and still breathing* – A life line. Hope.

By the time that Lottie had arrived at Florence Central Infirmary, Braithwaite was dead.

*

The inspector informed Roger of Braithwaite's death by telephone, his tone was monotone. Roger was unable to offer any positive spin on the position.

Lottie had been suspended and attempts to trap Reidler with the paintings had been closed down forthwith.

"Did he say anything before he died?

"Nothing that made sense."

"Meaning?"

"In the ambulance before he lost consciousness he apparently repeated the same phrase.*chair and window.chair and window*...less than hopeless.

"Did he, indeed?"

# CHAPTER FIFTY-THREE

Bella even beat her mutt to Roger's taxi before it had time to park in her driveway. She waited impatiently for him, as the driver removed Roger's wheelchair from his boot.

Bella opened the rear passenger door and Bendi jumped up to greet Roger. It brought back very bad memories and was grateful for Bella's forceful removal. With Bendi out of the way, she handed him up each quick fit wheel in turn and Roger swivelled out of the car into his chair. The taxi driver reversed out of the drive agreeing to be back in an hour. The sixteen-degree taxi air con contrasted with the thirty-degree ambient temperature. Roger's smile was lost on Bella. Her hormones were clearly engaged as Roger endured what smelt like a combination of rose water and stale beer. There were no pleasantries;

"Tell me, Mr Roger, is Luigi going to prison?" She gripped his shirt at both elbows as she pleaded for an answer.

"Bella!" he said, more assertively than he had intended.

His tone was effective in that she released him straight away realising her apparent rudeness.

"Do forgive me, I've been worried sick. Come, come. How was your journey? Luigi is waiting and the coffee is freshly boiled."

Even Bendi the dog sensed that the household was stressed and stayed outside as Roger entered.

Luigi had made a special effort for Roger's visit. No vest or braces in sight.

Bella had put out her best China on the kitchen table. She couldn't recall whether or not it had ever been used. The milk jug certainly hadn't.

"I come only with good news. Let me put you out of your misery."

Before Roger was able to provide any details, Bella began to sob loudly. He paused. Bella wiped away tears with her hand before turning her attention to Luigi, whose smile disappeared as quickly as it had appeared on hearing that the visit brought good news.

"You fool Luigi! Your complete fool! How could you do this to us?" She wanted to say more but the cathartic release of emotion took over and she sobbed further.

As a distraction, Luigi was happy to pour the coffee for them, another first.

Roger felt no need to deal with the catalogue of violence and death which had inadvertently surrounded Luigi's discovery. It would unsettle Bella and they were no longer in danger.

"The police have confirmed that no further action will be taken against you in light of your cooperation and they will write to you in those terms in the next few days."

Bella rose from her seat and smothered Roger in her ample bosom, complete with the fragrant rose beer aroma.

Roger freed himself politely and readjusted his dishevelled fringe. He was not used to such client gratitude.

"I do though have some more good news for you. As you know, my company, PNP, insured the stolen painting. At the time of its theft we put up a reward for information leading to its recovery. You provided that link. Without you, we wouldn't have got it back." Roger knew as well that without them the thing wouldn't have been stolen in the first place but left that unsaid. He couldn't dare tell them that they were masterpieces just yet. They would panic.

"The reward then is yours."

Bella looked grateful but confused.

"It can't be much as the paintings are copies, aren't they?"

"They are Bella, but fortunately for you, we didn't know that at the time. So, the €250,000 is all yours. Tax free as well…"

It was now Luigi's turn to hug Roger. Same intensity, but unfortunately for Roger, the aroma lacked the rose water scent.

As the details of the funds transfer were discussed Roger declined to join them in a celebratory carafe of wine, but promised to visit again when he was in the area.

# CHAPTER FIFTY-FOUR

Roger decided to where his exoskeleton suit today without a hint of hesitation. There was no wedding or funeral to attend but there was a very important meeting on the agenda. On this occasion too, he was pleased to accept the offer of a helicopter ride from Pavlov Stets. The small private air strip was but a short limousine ride from London's City airport. It would save a tortuous journey across the city before the open suburban roads of Surrey down to Stets' palatial mansion, Goring House. Roger was, this time, keen to arrive in style.

The manufacturer of his electronic standing frame specifically prohibited driving in the suit but not for the first time convenience trumped caution. As his car approached the heliport terminal in docklands, there, waiting for him, was the familiar blue and white blazer of a Stets staff member. No trousers but a skirt this time, accompanied by blond hair, unruffled by the gentle breeze and cosmetically enhanced white teeth, showcasing a gratuitously big smile.

The big smile faded briefly as Roger exited the vehicle looking like something from a sci-fi movie, but she quickly and professionally regained her composure. A firm hand shake announced her as 'Christie' and she would see to his needs before the flight. Roger could see the Robinson helicopter on the landing mark with blades ambling in anticipation.

Christie's offer of champagne was tempting but he declined it.

"Maybe upon your return?" she ventured with seamless smile.

Taking his briefing seriously, Roger ducked his head as he approached the helicopter in order to avoid contact with the blades on the down draught. The pilot acknowledged Roger's arrival and didn't need to prompt him to clip on his safety harness and fit the accompanying headphones that were essential given the increasing noise intensity of the engine and rotas. He was asked to switch off the electronics to his suit for the flight to avoid interference with the flight instruments. Once seated that was not a problem and he settled into position. His second helicopter ride in a week and this time he didn't need to be carried in on someone's shoulders. It was time to go. The blades were whirring now, a blur.

With radio link up in place, the pilot was able to introduce himself, advise him not to open the door in flight, as if and where the floatation aid was, in the unlikely event…

They were soon in the air, turning west and following the meander of the Thames past The Dome, Tower Bridge and the Houses of Parliament.

The views were spectacular at such close proximity and the commentary informative. Famous building were soon replaced with famous patches of open green space;

Richmond Park, Wimbledon Common and the grounds of Hampton Court.

The journey time was ridiculously quick and future trips by taxi would always be second best.

The pilot confirmed that he was at Roger's disposal and would be waiting for him after his meeting had finished.

As if by magic, another blazer greeted him in the grounds of Goring House, just after touch down on the manicured lawn at the rear of the house. The Exo suit had been tested on many terrains but Roger was still rather nervous of walking on the gravel drive, with each foot step crunching the pebbles. He was escorted patiently to the entrance where the suit impressively climbed the stairs; slowly yes but perfectly balanced. The relay baton was handed over to an immaculately turned out chap that reminded Roger of an Oxford Boat Race crew member, tall and muscular with a rather plummy accent. Polite to the point of sarcasm.

Roger, was lead into the same orange themed anti room as before. From a standing position the room looked even bigger. Little had changed since last time, save that the flowers were fresh and the brandy decanter was full.

The coffee pot was already on the silver tray anticipating Roger's arrival. He wouldn't waste any battery in sitting down and would stand for effect.

Roger could hear Stet's voice, but couldn't see him. He assumed that he was on the phone. Indeed he was, for seconds later, he entered the room with the device held to his ear. He was ringing off and the tone was cordial. The sight of Roger standing tall in front of him stopped him in his tracks.

"Well look at you, Roger. I've seen photos of the kit but never seen it in action – very impressive. A good spin in the chopper, I trust. There was no need for you to make the effort to come and see me but I appreciate the gesture – it is respectful and I value that attention"

"Thank you. Yes, it was a real treat to see my home city from such a different angle."

Stets indicated with his hands that it was nothing. "No problem."

Stets diverted to the drinks trolley.

"Still too early for you, I suppose."

"Let's live dangerously. It is a Friday after all."

"Good man. Remy Louis X111"

"Perfect."

The generously filled cognac glasses arrived. They each swilled the brandy out of respect for its vintage, raised their glasses, avoiding the ceremonial 'chink' given the quality, and for that matter, expense of the Irish crystal ware.

"So, you found the bugger. A pity really." Stets laughed loudly but Roger was less responsive.

"I could do with cash, No?" He gestured around the room as if to display his wealth.

"I have had the interim payment wired back to PNP yesterday."

"Yes, we are grateful for the return of the funds." Stets continued enthusiastically;

"I've asked that the painting itself be returned to the exhibition as there is still another month to run on it."

"So, I understand. It's for that reason that I've asked see you."

"What do you mean? What has it got to do with you?" The joviality in his voice slipped slightly.

Roger tightened the grip on his glass and edged backward two half steps. He felt unexpectedly nervous.

"It's a delicate matter." He paused, gathering himself.

"We did recover the paining but in doing so discovered that it was… a copy not the original."

"Fake?"

"A deliberate forgery, we fear."

This time there was no pause as Stets slammed his brandy down on to the glass coffee table. The force was such that the expensive golden fluid spilt over the glass edge in a wave effect.

"What is this bullshit?"

"I'm sorry but…"

"No, you will be sorry. This is bullshit."

Stets stepped forward. His sizeable figure partially blocked the flow of sunlight and cast a small shadow over Roger, thereby adding to the menacing look.

For a moment Roger thought that he was going to be grabbed but his movement forwards was only to pick up what was left of his brandy.

"How can you know it's a fake? I have a certificate of authenticity in the safe. Signed by an expert. This is a scam."

*You should know one when you see one.*

"It was only when the original was found in a warehouse in Italy that the issue came to light. The police believe that the reason your painting was stolen was to cover up the fact that it was a copy or as you say fake. It gives me no pleasure to say this but I think that you could be the victim of an expensive fraud."

*Fucking twenty-five million.*

Stets said nothing as he considered the situation. It was not an invitation for Roger to continue but he did so anyway.

"May I ask who you brought the painting from? I know that the police will be interested." Very interested.

"It's none of their fucking business nor yours."

"It's just that…"

"It's just that, I will not be treated as a mug. You disrespect me at your peril."

Both men moved their positions. Stets stood by the bronze puma and Roger turned towards the opposite of the room, steadily holding on to his brandy glass.

"You will obviously want to independently verify our findings with an expert…" *If you can find one alive.*

Roger engaged the exoskeleton suit via an upper body movement and walked slowly towards the painting that had caught his attention at the time of the first visit.

"Forgive me for being the messenger of doom but this painting, the Van Gough, *Chair and Window*, fake too, I fear." Roger was not looking at Stets as he broke the news but inspecting the canvas close up as though proffering his own judgement. *Braithwaite's parting words impacting as he knew they would.*

Roger turned a tad mechanically towards his host, who looked incandescent with rage.

"Don't tell me, you bought them from the same source."

This was too much for Stets. He threw his glass into the fire place causing chunks of crystal to dramatically rebound back on to the marble hearth.

"Fuck you, Robocop!" And with that he strode towards the door. He didn't look back but added with equal menace, "Make your own way home." Roger couldn't help but smile.

As he sat down on the sofa to relish his brandy, he heard the helicopter take off, very much without him. He would finish his drink and await the mini cab. His journey back would, he reflected, be less spectacular but he had enough excitement for one day.

# EPILOGUE

Although she had been his mistress for years, her nakedness still pleased him. Reidler stood admiring her from the doorway. Walking slowly forward, he reached out and stroked her long, dark hair, delicately. He barely dared to touch, so as not to damage the painted canvass with his exploration. He leaned forward to smell the oil painting as though to sample her fragrant aroma.

The Rubens had, by necessity, remained hidden throughout his period of ownership. He cared not that he couldn't display the masterpiece to a wider audience. It was his secret, his indulgence. He stepped away from the painting, never diverting his sight from the *Goddess's* eyes. He sighed with satisfaction before flicking the switch that turned out the low voltage light above the gilded frame. In turn, the oak panel that encased his illicit treasure closed automatically. He needed urgently to travel to London to meet with Pavlov Stets and thought that he would not be able to see his stolen, yet prized possession, a while yet. In fact, it was to be the last time he would see his mistress. As the bullet tore through his brain, the only disappointment for the assassin's paymaster was that the parting image from this world would have been such a beautiful one. The killer had been right to wait until the painting had been enclosed before carrying out the execution, for the oak panels that hid the *Goddess* were spattered in a red pigment, more Anish Kapoor than Ruben. The nuance was lost on the assassin but his paymaster would have enjoyed the transformation.

Reidler's assassination came without mercy or discussion. There were no negotiations, no attempt to seek repayment of the fraudulently obtained funds. After all, Stets had been humiliated and worse still, in public. The media had enjoyed discovering that, after all, the painting on show in Milan had been a reproduction. Stets had fallen foul of an expensive hoax, they said. For once, they implied, it was he who was the victim. Those with whom he aspired to mix as peers mocked him; behind his back, of course. For a man with huge pride and an even larger ego, punishment was always going to be summary. Had Stets been prepared to name his supplier then Reidler's reign would have been at an end. Stets was in no doubt that prison was not sufficient punishment. Revenge, for him, did not come with a release date attached.

The fact that immediately prior to his assassination, Reidler had been admiring, an original 'Goddess Jupiter' by Rubens, had been an unexpected bonus for Stets. It would compensate in part for the other forgery with which Reidler had duped him. He would sell the forged Van Gough's *Chair and Window* complete with its certificate of authenticity signed by the world's leading, albeit sadly deceased, expert, Braithwaite.

# POST SCRIPTS

The Bistro Vitani, just off Piazza del Duomo, was one of the most popular lunchtime venues in Milan. Today was no exception. As Pina and Roger entered into the foyer they were met with a hubbub of noise. The sound of social engagement. Most of it would be good-natured; catching up with friends and on gossip. Midweek there was more of a business feel. Men and women with jackets hung on the back of their chairs discussing projects, sales figures and potential recruitment. The feel was always the same, informal and vibrant. People came for the atmosphere but above all the food was highly rated. There was not a Michelin starred tasting menu insight. Pastas and raviolis of all variety. Fungi and forchetta, crispy fried courgettes, cheese grater's, giant black pepper pots, followed by tiramisu and strong espresso coffee.

Inspector Lottie or more accurately, *suspended* Inspector Lottie, had arrived early. He saw Pina and Roger enter. He couldn't help notice that they were holding hands. Roger was suited and booted and his robotic suit never failed to attract attention. Cutlery lowered and heads turned; No worry, Roger was used to it. Before the maître de had a chance to check their booking, Lottie had caught their eye, waving furiously from the far corner of the crowded venue.

He kissed Pina on the cheeks – *Hey I'm suspended* – and greeted his host, Roger, warmly.

"I hope you don't mind me starting without you," said Lottie as he raised his half empty glass.

"I'm glad you have and we will join you. A sparkling water, Pina?"

"Actually, I'll have a prosecco."

Roger raised his eyebrows in mock surprise that her teetotaller label had been removed but concluded that he as well had been drinking a little bit more of late. Lottie certainly had, as he contemplated his future without a police badge defining him.

\*

Portelli was nothing but diligent. Given that he only had few clients, he was able to dedicate himself to the task of trying to trace Anna's ancestors. Failure would mean a large windfall for the Italian Government. Inheritance tax was a complicated affair, much despised by wealthy Italians. However, if no beneficiary can be found, a deceased's estate defaulted to the state. Given that Portelli would receive a percentage of the estate's value come what may, it was professional pride, not greed that drove his quest.

An initial valuation of the Gauguin had been put at *no less* than \$50 million by Sotheby's. Given that such pieces rarely came up for auction he was told that this estimate was *likely to be conservative.* Portelli did not need a calculator to know that his 15% fee from the sale was worth having.

As a start point for his hunt, he had a name and a city; two cities, to be precise. He knew from the love letters that Anna was heading to Zurich from Vienna. That hardly narrowed matters down given that he didn't even know her date of birth. Would she not have married anyway with a resulting name change? Did she even make the journey successfully? Many Jews didn't. What if her plot was discovered? How did Andreas end up in Italy with the paintings? Did that reinforce the view that the scheme was foiled by the Nazis? Too many question without answers. As cruel as it sounded, Portelli concluded that it might be easier to unravel Anna's fate if she had ended up in a concentration camp. Portelli had read that records had been kept and that several Charities had retained and expanded their data base of detainees and Holocaust victims. He would start there.

Ten months later, Claudio Portelli arrived by taxi at a care home in Berg, a small town in Austria, close to the Slovakian border. It was some twenty miles from Bratislava airport where Portelli had flown into. He asked the taxi to wait. The building before him would have had a feel of grandeur in days gone by but looked tired and in need of refurbishment. That said, inside was clean and light gushed through the large sash windows. Portelli noticed the fresh flowers that adorned the reception area and was pleased to be greeted in a friendly manner. The staff were expecting his visit and he was lead into a side room facing out on to what appeared to be a vegetable garden. He was offered tea and chocolate biscuits and sat patiently reading an old copy of Vogue magazine.

The door opened and a member of staff in a bright blue uniform entered pushing a wheelchair. In it was an old lady, fast asleep. Her hair was thin and grey but well groomed. Her skin wrinkled but not dry. She wore a green tartan dress which rather clashed with the red blanket across her knees. This was *an* Anna Cohen. It was one of six *Anna Cohens* that Portelli had been able to narrow down from his research. They had all roughly fitted the bill by way of age, anywhere between seventeen and twenty five. Three had already died and the two others Portelli had visited were quickly excluded.

"Anna, Anna, wake up. This is Herr Portelli hear to see you. Remember, I told you he was coming." The nurse looked at Portelli and shook her head as if to indicate that she would not remember.

She then smiled at Anna and lifted a glass of water to her lips. Anna took a small sip. She was awake but hadn't yet observed Portelli's presence.

"I will be outside waiting Herr Portelli."

Portelli brought his chair a little closer to hers. She noticed him for the first time. She wasn't startled and Portelli thought that she even smiled at him.

"Anna, hello. How are you today? I am a friend of Andreas, Andreas Bartelli. Do you remember him?" He watched for a reaction – nothing; not a flicker of recognition.

*Another false trail…*

Portelli was patient and tried again.

"Andreas the artist. Your friend in Vienna." Still nothing. Anna closed her eyes. Portelli pulled out from his brief case a photograph of Andreas that he had salvaged from his possessions. It was unclear when and where it had been taken but it depicted him as an attractive young man, smiling and waving at the photographer

"Anna, sorry to disturb you..." he raised his voice in order to rouse her.

He was unsure as to the quality of her eyesight but held the photo up in front of her face, moving it slowly back and forth so as to aid focus. Anna opened her hand, gesturing to take the photograph from him. Portelli helped her grip it. She lifted the photo to within six inches of her face unaided. She struggled to hold it steady. As Portelli reached over to help, she pulled the portrait of Andreas to her lips and gently kissed it. She held on to the photo as her arm lost strength and her hand dropped to her lap once again. She closed her eyes once again but this time Portelli saw tears begin to run down her cheeks.

She was trying to speak but no sound came from her mouth. Taking the lead from the nurse, he raised the glass of water to her lips. She sipped slowly from it.

Portelli moved in even closer as she tried once again. He could just about discern her humming a Viennese waltz.

"Da da da da da
Da da da da dum

Da da da da da
Da da da da dum..."

He had found her.

*

Gauguin's Tahitian Princess fetched $78 million at auction in New York.

Having accounted to the auction house for their seller's premium, Portelli received $9,450,000 as payment for handling Andreas' estate.

He donated $1 million each to the charities that had helped him find Anna.

Inspector Lottie was reinstated following the investigation without loss of rank. He was warned that his unorthodox methods were likely to discredit him, Interpol and the Italian Police Force and would not be tolerated in future.

Luigi and Bella bought a larger house in the Tuscan hillside so that Bella's mother could come and live with them. As a consequence Luigi often regrets finding the paintings...

Pina's request for a year's sabbatical was granted. She is currently climbing Aconcagua in South America. Her boyfriend, Jimmy, is leading the expedition.

Carlos received a ten-year jail term.

Roger is currently investigating the suspicious loss in transit of a rare stuffed brown bear.